WEDDING DATE

MONICA MURPHY

Copyright © 2020 by Monica Murphy

All rights reserved.

No part of this book may be reproduced in any form or by any electronic or mechanical means, including information storage and retrieval systems, without written permission from the author, except for the use of brief quotations in a book review.

This book is a work of fiction. Names, characters, places, and incidents are used fictitiously. Any resemblance to actual persons, living or dead, events, or locales, is entirely coincidental.

Cover design: Hang Le
byhangle.com

Editor: Mackenzie Walton
Proofreader: Holly Malgieri

ONE

KELSEY

AS TIME GOES ON, and the dating scene becomes bleaker and bleaker, I made a secret vow with myself. None of my friends know this, though I have said it out loud a few times around them. Problem is, none of them take me seriously. They all just laugh and think I'm kidding.

I'm not.

Anyway, my vow is this:

I've sworn off men.

It sounds extreme, I know, and let's be real—this is a temporary situation. But come on. They're all *terrible*. And I know I'm painting with a wide brush by saying that, but it's true. The last few guys I've tried to go out with, the dates ended *spectacularly*—and not in a good way. A while ago, I convinced my friend Eleanor to get on that Rate A Date app with me so we could each find someone, and she meets the man of her dreams, who just so happens to be a pro athlete.

While I meet a total jerk who treated me like garbage and harassed me for weeks afterward.

Yeah. See? Terrible.

One good thing that came out of meeting the harassing jerk (his name is Paul, though that really doesn't matter) is that I have become friendly with his best friend, Theodore Crawford. Theo is sweet. Kind. He just got out of a serious relationship—engaged serious, which is *super-duper* serious—after he found out she cheated on him.

With his cousin.

He's in the anti-dating club as well. He's given up on women. He made that declaration to me a few weeks ago, when we went out for drinks together.

Yes, we're just friends. That's all I want from Theo, and that's all he wants from me, and it is positively liberating.

How did we meet up again after the disastrous double date I had with Paul and Theo and my friend Eleanor? Picture this:

I'm at a business mixer on a Wednesday evening at the Wilder Hotel in Pebble Beach, where I work. I'm already bored and wondering when I can leave when I hear someone say my name in this wondrous, questioning tone. I turn to find Theo approaching me, his big brown eyes drinking me in as if I were the best thing he's ever seen.

It was flattering, don't get me wrong. But considering I associate him with one of the worst first dates I've ever been on, at first I was reluctant to chat with Theo. Plus, I remember him being so incredibly sad. He'd only been separated from his ex-fiancée for a few months when I first met him, and he was still in a major funk.

But he was *so* fun that night at the business mixer. Talking nonstop and making me laugh. Telling me funny stories. Reminding me that if I was interested in investing money, he could help me.

I took him up on that offer and made an appointment with him. He took me to lunch. He convinced me to invest the five grand I had in savings, and I've seen some growth, which makes me happy. Since then, we've gone out for a few dinners, mostly for business-type stuff. We cross paths frequently at community events. I like Theo.

A lot.

But not enough to want to have a relationship with him. I have my guard up. A wall that is solid steel and no one can penetrate it. Like I mentioned, I've given up men, and while I know it's not a forever type of thing, I am making myself do this for the betterment of my soul. So I won't settle. I need to find a good man. One who'll take care of me. One who won't have a wandering eye. One who'll treat me as an equal. One who'll give me multiple orgasms.

I might have high standards, but shouldn't we all?

Theo understands me. He understands what I want right now, and all I want is friendship. Same with him. I don't think he's interested in me at all. He doesn't act like he is, and that's perfect.

Perfect.

We're meeting for lunch right now, as a matter of fact. He's coming to the hotel because he has a business meeting here at two. We're going to have a long lunch at one of the hotel restaurants, which has a patio outside with a gorgeous view of the beach. The weather is perfect for outdoor dining. The sun is shining, the water is a deep, dark blue and there's a slight breeze.

"Sorry I'm late," Theo calls in greeting.

I lift my head to find him making his way toward me, winding his tall, trim body through the tiny tables scattered on the brick patio. He's got a smile on his face and his brown eyes are warm and friendly as they meet mine.

He just instantly makes me feel comfortable, and that's rare.

Rising to my feet, I give him a quick hug. He briefly kisses my cheek. We settle in at our tiny table and he picks up the menu, though I already know what he's going to order. I always get a salad and he gets a cheeseburger. While we eat, I secretly salivate over the juicy burger he eats, and when he spots me making puppy-dog eyes at his food, he always cuts off part of it for me.

Theo is very generous. He also shares his fries.

"I have news," Theo says gravely after he sets the menu down.

I study his face. When I first met him, I thought he looked like the saddest version of Ross from *Friends* and Eleanor totally agreed with me. Now I don't get that vibe at all. He's got the dark hair and the dark eyes, but the glum expression has completely disappeared. He smiles a lot, and he has a nice smile with straight, white teeth. Those warm brown eyes that seem to dance every time he looks at me, and the thick dark hair that's a little too long on top, though he can carry it off. He's tall and fit and he wears impeccable suits that look expensive because they *are* expensive.

He's a successful investment manager at one of the local banks in Monterey. He makes a lot of money. He's not Alexander Wilder—my boss—level rich, but he does very well for himself.

"What's your news?" I ask when Theo hasn't volunteered any more information.

Uh oh. Unease settles over me, making me wary. He's giving me those old, sad vibes right now, which I haven't seen in a while.

Blowing out a harsh breath, he tells me, "I received an invitation this morning. To Jessica and Craig's wedding."

I blink at him for a moment. "Jessica? *The* Jessica?"

As in his former future wife.

He nods, his gaze flickering with an unfamiliar emotion. "Yes. That Jessica."

"They invited you to their wedding?" I'm so outraged on his behalf, my voice just rose about ten decibels.

"He's my cousin," Theo says with a shrug, seemingly unaffected. I wish I could be as cool as he's currently acting. "We're family."

"Don't forget Craig stole your fiancée. The woman you were going to marry," I remind him.

"Oh, trust me. I remember." His face is an emotionless mask, and my heart is heavy for him.

The server appears at our table and takes our order. Not only does Theo gets his cheeseburger with fries, he also orders a beer. Something he never does when he's in work mode.

"A beer, huh?" I ask once the server leaves.

"I need it to get through the rest of my day," he says. "I have to admit, seeing that invitation kind of rocked me."

I would assume so. "So you just received the invitation in the mail?"

"Jess sent it to my work address." I kind of hate how he calls her Jess, as if she's an old, intimate friend, which I suppose she is.

Thinking of her fills me with murderous images. I don't know what she looks like, but I imagine tearing her hair out at the roots and kicking her over a cliff, never to be seen again.

See? Murderous. I hate that she hurt Theo in such a cold, callous way.

"You're not going to go, are you?" I lean back in my chair, contemplating him. The breeze sweeps over us, ruffling his hair and sending it into his eyes, and he pushes it back in annoyance.

Look, I can admit that Theo is somewhat...attractive. Okay, fine, he's *really* attractive. He's definitely a catch for a certain woman. But that woman is not me. He's my friend.

Nothing more.

"I have to go to the wedding," he says, his voice deadly serious.

I balk at him. "Why? What does it matter if you show up or not? Everyone would understand why you don't. She was your fiancée. She practically left you at the altar."

"Not quite," he says with the faintest smile. "Our breakup wasn't that pitiful."

"You found them in bed together," I remind him. "Naked." I hesitate before I forge on. "That's pretty pitiful, don't you think?"

He winces. "Kelsey, you always have this...way of always keeping things extremely real between us."

I sit up straighter, my demeanor solemn. "Some say it's my best trait."

"Who says that?" He grins, and I can't help but laugh a little. "I'd say sometimes it's detrimental."

"I just don't want you to forget what they did to you," I say, unable to ignore how defensive I feel on his behalf.

As in, I want to defend him. Protect him. This is what friends do, am I right?

"I will never forget," he says, and I can tell from the serious way he's watching me, he means it. "Right now, though, I'd prefer not to dwell on the horrendous details of when my future marriage went up in flames."

Pressing my lips together, I nod once. "Sorry."

"Hey. It's all good," he says easily.

The server returns with our drinks. Theo gratefully reaches for the beer and takes a sip, leaving a thin line of foam on his upper lip. He licks it away quickly and I experience a weird dip in my stomach.

Yeah, no. I'm not ready for weird dips. I'm off men, remember? Especially ones I consider an actual friend.

"The main reason I wanted to meet for lunch with you is that I was hoping I could convince you to..." His voice drifts, and he glances down at the table for a moment before he lifts his head, his gaze meeting mine once more.

But he doesn't say anything.

I shake my head a little, giving him a confused look. "Convince me to what?"

"Be my date. For the wedding," he says softly, suddenly looking bashful.

My mouth drops open. "You want me to go with you to your ex-fiancée's wedding?"

"Yeah, I do. I definitely do." He nods eagerly.

"I don't know if that's a good idea," I start, trying to choose my words carefully, but he cuts me off.

"Honestly, Kels, what's the big deal? I need a date, we're friends, you're gorgeous, Jess will take one look at you and realize I made a major upgrade, and I'll look like I am on top of the world," he says, his words coming out all at once, like one long string of consciousness.

I'm guessing he's been thinking about this situation a lot. And he wants me in on it.

I'd love to help, but...

"I just worry about you," I admit, reaching out to rest my hand over his. "Have you seen her lately?"

He slowly shakes his head. "I was invited to a family get together recently, and when I found out they were going to be there, I didn't go."

"Right. Because you didn't feel ready to see her."

"Well, I feel ready to see her now." He flips his hand up

so now our fingers are interlaced, and he gives them a squeeze. "Come on, Kels. Go with me. Be my wedding date. We'll show everyone I'm completely over Jessica once and for all."

I don't know why, but the idea of going to Theo's ex-fiancée's wedding to his cousin fills me with dread. Like this is a bad idea.

Perhaps even the worst idea ever.

But have I mentioned how hard it is for me to resist Theo when he's looking at me like that with those big brown eyes? I'm suddenly filled with the overwhelming need to make him smile, make him happy, and so of course I say:

"Sure. All right. Let's go together."

TWO
THEO

THE RELIEF I feel at hearing her agree to go with me to Jessica's wedding nearly makes me sag in my chair. But I keep it together because I don't like showing signs of weakness. Especially in front of Kelsey. She always somehow encourages me to stay strong no matter what. Maybe because she's so strong too.

And stubborn.

And smart.

Did I mention beautiful?

The woman is a complete knockout. Long, shiny dark hair. High cheekbones, plump lips, brown eyes. Lush body with curves in all the right places. When I accompany her places, we get stares. Correction, *she* gets stares. Men watch her with their mouths hanging open and I fully expect to see drool falling from their lips. Women study her like she's a puzzle they want to figure out. Kelsey is absolutely stunning. To the point that if I don't watch out, I could find myself becoming attracted to her.

Okay, fuck it. I *am* attracted to her. You'd have to be dead not to be attracted to Kelsey. But I knew the moment I spent one-on-one time with her, no way could I ever have a chance. I shot my own self down, and once I got past that, I realized that we got along well. She makes me laugh. I make her laugh. We have great conversations. Sometimes they derail into arguments, but I wouldn't consider that a bad thing. We can state our opposing points and still respect each other in the end.

That's refreshing.

"When's the wedding?" Kelsey asks, knocking me out of my thoughts.

"In a month."

Her mouth pops open. "A month? And they only just sent out the invitations?"

"Jessica is not very...prompt."

Understatement. She's the queen of lateness, while I was—and still am—sickeningly on time. I'd hoped I could balance her out and make her if not on time, at least a little earlier to our commitments, but it never happened. She flat out didn't care.

About a lot of things, truthfully. Except herself.

"I hate it when people are late," Kelsey says, reaching over to grab her iced tea and take a sip. My gaze falls to the front of her button-up black shirt. It fits her loosely, but strains across her breasts.

Yeah, I'm checking her out. She doesn't even notice. I raise my gaze to her lips, how they're pursed around that straw. My entire being is screaming *ask her out on a real date!*

But my logical brain is telling me, *Don't do that. You'll ruin everything.*

So I stay far away from that subject.

"Me too," I tell her, grateful she's always on time, like

me. Sometimes she's early. Also like me. We have a lot in common.

"Are there other events?" Kelsey asks.

I frown. "What do you mean?"

"Wedding events. A lot of couples like to have showers together," she says.

My frown deepens. "I'm sure lots of couples love showering together, but what does that have to do with their wedding?"

Kelsey bursts out laughing. "Theo, you're freaking hilarious. Seriously, I'm talking about a bridal shower, but nowadays they have couple showers. You know, a party where everyone brings you a bunch of wedding gifts before the actual wedding, where guests are forced to bring more gifts."

I feel like an idiot. I know what they are, I just—my mind was in the gutter. "Right. A shower. I have no idea if they're going to have a couples shower."

"You should look into it. What if they invite you? Talk about awkward." She makes a face.

"Everything about this situation is awkward. You know this," I remind her.

The server shows up with our food, and I'm grateful for the interruption. I don't want to think about showers and gifts and what we need to bring or where I need to go. I don't want to go to this stupid wedding either, but my entire family basically said I'd look like the world's biggest pussy if I decide not to show.

Well, not my entire family. More like my brothers told me that.

I am the oldest of five. I have three younger brothers and a sister. Yes, my parents were busy in the early years of their marriage. Two of my brothers are fraternal twins and eternal pains in the ass. My sister hates all of us because we're very overprotective of her.

Okay, she doesn't hate us, that's extreme. But all of us are so overbearing, we scare off any prospective boyfriends she might have. This is why she never brings dates around us. Guess I can't blame her. As the oldest, I'm the responsible one. My other brothers love to give her endless shit. They do the same to me.

When your four brothers call you names and say that you can't bow out of going to your ex's wedding to your cousin, then you go. End of story.

"Let me guess," Kelsey says after a few minutes of silent eating. "Your brothers told you that you have to go to this wedding."

See? She knows me so well. "They're assholes."

"Clearly," she practically snorts. "But I also get why they're pushing you. Listen, Theo, I don't mind going. In fact, I'm dying to see this Jessica person who hurt you so badly. I'm also dying to see this jerk she left you for."

"Craig's not that bad—" I start, but she silences me with a look.

"He's horrible," she declares.

He's my cousin. I do tend to defend family members. Even when they do me wrong.

"But you need to come up with some sort of plan," she tells me, waving her fork in my direction.

I set my burger down, hoping what she's about to say doesn't ruin my appetite. "What do you mean, a plan?"

"You need to rub it in their faces how fucking fantastic your life is now that she's not in it." The giant smile on her face tells me she's excited by this idea. "We're going to strut into that wedding venue and show them just how great you're doing. You need to wear your best suit."

I nod. "Done."

"And you can't ever frown. Not once." She takes another sip from her iced tea, and I momentarily dream of her lips wrapped around something of mine. Fuck, I need to stop. "You frown a lot when you talk about Jessica."

"Wow, really? What a surprise." My sarcastic tone doesn't faze her.

"Let go of all that bitterness and act like the king you are," she says, sounding like my personal motivational speaker. "You're very successful at your job."

True. That's about the only thing that gives me real satisfaction these days. Some might call me a workaholic. Once upon a time, Jessica called me exactly that.

I always wondered if that was part of the reason she cheated on me. Maybe I wasn't fulfilling her needs. Those last few months leading up to the wedding, our sex life had taken a nosedive. She wasn't interested, and I was too tired to care. I figured stress from wedding planning was making her exhausted.

Turns out she was just getting plenty of dick from my cousin and didn't want mine anymore.

"And you need to act like you own that shit when you walk into that church or wherever they're getting married," she continues.

"You want to hear something funny?" When she nods, I continue, "They're getting married here. Out on the lawn." I wave a hand in the direction of the ocean.

Kelsey rolls her eyes. "Of course they are. Want me to sabotage the wedding? I could. Or maybe I could mess with the catering at the reception. I'm sure that's being held here too, right?"

"There will be no sabotaging or ruining food at the

wedding," I tell her, though I'm semi-grateful she offered. "I don't need to get revenge that way."

"Right." She nods. Smiles, though it's a vicious smile. Something you'd see on Maleficent's face right before she poisons someone. "The best way to get revenge on your ex is by showing how much you don't need or miss her."

Right after Jessica dumped me, that would've been impossible. And while my best friend Paul was doing his best to cheer me up by forcing me to go on a blind date with the very sweet Eleanor, that just didn't work. I wasn't in the right frame of mind. I was down in the dumps and in that moment, there was nowhere else I'd rather be.

Kelsey helped get me out of the dumps. I have plenty of friends. I spend a lot of time with my brothers. But having a woman friend whose no-nonsense attitude and gives great insight into how the female mind works is invaluable.

"Just like you were talking about," I tell her.

She nods. "Exactly. Too bad you haven't found yourself a woman yet. Like, an actual girlfriend."

"Right." I hand over a couple of fries and she greedily takes them.

"I suppose..." Her gaze grows thoughtful as she chews on the fries I gave her. "I could hang all over you and convince them that you're getting fucked—and well—every single night."

I nearly spit out the beer I just sipped. It takes everything for me to choke it down and I still end up coughing.

"What? Are you saying you don't want me to do that?" she asks with a little laugh.

I get over my coughing fit before I wheeze out, "Please tell me exactly what you're referring to."

If she's asking if I don't want to get fucked by her every single night, then she's dead wrong. But I can't take our relationship in that direction, so I keep my secret naked Kelsey fantasies to myself.

Sex will ruin everything between us. I can't risk it. I value her friendship too much.

"I'm referring to the idea of us showing up to this wedding and acting like a loving couple." That vicious little smile returns. "Wouldn't it be fantastic? Me draped all over your arm, my boobs pressed against your chest. You could kiss me out on the dancefloor during the reception. I'd allow you at least one. Even with tongue."

"This is probably not a good idea," I say cautiously, pushing all thoughts of wrapping my tongue around Kelsey's firmly into the darkest corner of my brain. Exactly where it wants to be, conjuring up all sorts of dark fantasies involving Kelsey. And me.

"Oh, come on, it won't be that bad. It could actually be kind of fun, right?" She leans over and socks my arm lightly, right before she reaches for my plate and grabs a couple more fries. "You can really stick it to her."

"Sure. Sounds great." My voice is less than enthusiastic and she knows it. Her shoulders deflate and she slowly shakes her head as she studies me.

"Don't act pathetic right now, Theo. Seriously. Be strong." She reaches out, and this time instead of stealing my food, she rests her hand on my arm, giving it a squeeze. "I know she did a number on you. And you were pretty down in the dumps for a long time."

Everyone in my family—even my brothers and father—let me be sad and angry for approximately one month after the break up. Once the expiration date hit, they told me I needed to get it together. No woman is worth that much misery and pain.

I couldn't disagree with them. Deep down, I knew they

were right. But that didn't erase the misery and pain Jessica inflicted on me. The utter humiliation. We sent out wedding invites, for God's sake. We lost our ass on deposits for the wedding and reception—mostly Jessica's family did, but I did too. My parents felt sorry for me, and I hated that. Then I had to explain to my hard-of-hearing, eighty-nine-year-old grandma what happened, and that sucked probably most of all.

Disappointing my family isn't high on my agenda. Looking like a complete loser isn't either.

So I toughened up and acted like nothing bothered me anymore. I was over her. Fuck that chick! She's a bitch.

I said that a lot to my brothers, because that's what they wanted to hear. I didn't really mean it, though. Jessica's not really a bitch. Coldhearted and unfeeling, yes. I can't be mad at her anymore.

In a month, she'll be family.

"You seemed better. I know you were better, but getting this invitation is not the reason to spiral down the toilet bowl of life, okay?" Kelsey squeezes my arm again, an encouraging smile on her face, and I can't help but smile back.

"Yeah, you're right. I won't spiral down the toilet bowl of life, whatever that means," I tell her.

She laughs. "Good, she doesn't deserve you thinking about her. You know she's not thinking about you, right?"

Ouch. Way to keep it real. "You're probably right."

"I am right. Trust me." She gestures toward my plate. "Ready to cut me off a piece of that burger?"

Sighing, I do as she asks, setting about a quarter of my burger onto the edge of her salad plate. I let her take over the conversation, watching her mouth move as she talks. As she eats. When Kelsey gets going, she never stops talking, which I initially found surprising. She has a bit of a mysterious way about her. She doesn't talk much about her family or her past. And trust me, I've asked. I'm a freaking open book, while she's sealed up tight.

Makes me wonder if she's hiding something.

THREE
KELSEY

"I NEED to find a gorgeous dress that will make every woman who sees me jealous," I announce to my friends.

We meet at Sweet Dreams Bakery and Café at least once a week for lunch. I drive in from Pebble Beach. Stella's family owns the place, and she works there. Caroline and Sarah both work nearby. So does Amelia. Eleanor used to work at a salon up the street, but she's moved to Las Vegas to be with her man.

If I fell in love with a professional football player like Eleanor did, I'd move anywhere he was too. Though I miss her. Terribly. We all do. She's the sunshine, optimistic queen. So is our friend Candice, but currently she's on vacation in the Bahamas with her husband, Charlie. The lucky B.

"Just look in your closet," Stella says, her voice dry as she contemplates me. "Pretty much everything you wear makes other women jealous."

I blow out an exasperated breath. Look, being born with this face has been both a curse and a blessing. I have no control over it. I got my looks from my mama. When she was my age, she was gorgeous. Stunning. And she knew it. She wielded her beauty like a weapon, and she was ruthless. She's been married five times. She's had endless boyfriends and fiancés throughout her life, right up until the very end. I have no idea who my father is, because she divorced him before I was even born. Or were they even married?

I have no clue, and I never was allowed to ask. Anytime I had a question about him, she shut me down. So I gave up.

When I was a little girl, she entered me in a bunch of beauty pageants—and I won most of them. I was well on my way to becoming the next JonBenet Ramsey, if you know what I'm saying. But then one day, it all stopped. Mom ran out of money. The guy she was married to at that time lost his ass in the stock market, and she divorced him.

While she went on the hunt for a new husband, I went through my ugly duckling stage. No more pageant wins for me. I was gangly and awkward. I desperately needed braces for my very crooked adult teeth. I had really long legs that I seemed to always trip over.

In other words, I was a mess. Mom would watch me with pity, always making comments under her breath. And it broke me. I wasn't her beautiful little doll anymore. I was ugly.

Oh, but then the braces came off. I learned how to style my hair—thank you, YouTube—and I started to develop. Next thing I knew, I was tall and curvy, I had perfect sized boobs according to my mother, and my face looked exactly like hers too. I thought she'd be happy.

Instead, she viewed me as competition.

"I need something that'll send someone over the edge," I say, earning curious looks from my friends.

"Explain yourself," Caroline says. "Who is this someone?"

"Theo asked me to be his date at a wedding," I tell them.

Sarah and Caroline exchange knowing looks. "Are you two finally going to date each other?" Sarah asks.

"No. Absolutely not," I say firmly. "We're just friends. If we take it to the next level, we'll ruin everything."

"You might not—" Caroline starts, but I shake my head, cutting her off.

"No. Friends. That's it."

"So why do you need a dress that'll send someone over the edge?" Stella asks, her gaze sharp. "I figured you were referring to Theo."

A chorus of "yeahs" accompany her statement.

"I'm not referring to Theo, I'm referring to…the bride." I bite my lower lip, knowing that I sound like a complete bitch. Who wants to upstage the bride on their wedding day?

Me, that's who.

"Whose wedding are you going to?"

"Doesn't it feel like there are a lot of weddings happening lately?" Amelia asks no one in particular. Everyone nods their answer, including me. "God, it's like a disease." Amelia had a nasty breakup with her ex, but has now found true love with a younger man who seems totally into her. It's actually really sweet.

"Theo was invited to his ex's wedding," I admit.

The protests immediately start. They all hate this Jessica person, thanks to me complaining about her. Eleanor complained about her too. She's the one who kept up contact with Theo first. After their disastrous first date—that I helped arranged via the Rate a Date app and Theo's best friend, the eternal jackass Paul—Eleanor met with Theo, and he eventually became her financial planner. He's also now Eleanor's boyfriend's financial planner, which is a huge deal. Mitch Anderson makes bank. He's worth a fortune.

So yeah, we all hate Jessica. She broke Theo's heart.

"I can't believe that bitch would invite him to her wedding, after she broke up with him like she did," Caroline says with absolute disgust.

"She's marrying Theo's cousin, so in theory, he deserves an invite," I say, wincing when they start protesting all over again.

"He shouldn't go!" Amelia says. "Who cares about that chick?"

"Theo feels like he has to go," I say. "Plus, his brothers told him he should."

They all know about Theo's family. Specifically the brothers, and how pushy they all are.

"He asked you to go with him then?" Stella asks.

I nod. "Of course, I said yes. I want to be there for him, and honestly? I'm really curious to see this Jessica. I want to know what all the fuss is about."

"I bet she's gorgeous." This is from Caroline, who has a bitter expression on her face.

Jealousy stabs me right in the heart, and I tell it to take a hike. Seriously, why would I be jealous of a gorgeous Jessica? Who cares what she looks like? She broke my friend's heart. Stomped all over it with sky-high stilettos.

I have no idea if she wears stilettos. I'm just assuming.

"It'll be difficult to outshine the bride at her own wedding," Stella says, ever the honest friend. "But out of any of us at this table, I have faith in you the most that you can do it."

I can't help but laugh, relief flooding me. Exactly what I needed to hear. "I'm going to give it an old-fashioned go."

"You can do it," Amelia says with a wicked smile. "What does Theo think about your plan?"

I go quiet for a moment, grateful when Sarah asks Amelia a question and shifts the focus off me having to answer.

What did Theo think of my plan? He seems reluctant. Like he doesn't want to walk into that wedding with his head held high and me on his arm. Theo is a very low-key person. He doesn't want to draw a lot of attention to himself, and he knows when he walks into that wedding?

All eyes will be on him.

The pressure of that alone must be enormous. I'm sure that's part of the reason he wants me to go with him. So I can carry some of that burden. But I draw attention too. It's the curse of my face. Sometimes I don't wear makeup, or I pull my hair back tight or even wear a hat so people won't notice me.

At this wedding, though? I want people to see me. I want them to believe Theo and I are dating, and yes, he is so over Jessica.

But can we pull it off?

"I have a question," I say, right in the middle of all of them talking.

Their gazes swivel to mine.

"What's up?" Stella asks.

"It's for Caroline and Sarah." Weird that two of the women out of our friend group participated in fake relationships. Like, who does that? Sounds straight out of a movie to me, but here I go...

Caroline and Sarah face me more fully, their brows raised in matching expressions.

"What's it like to pretend to be in a relationship with someone?"

"Oh, this ought to be interesting," Stella mutters.

"Are you thinking of doing that with Theo?" Caroline's eyebrows shoot up even higher.

"Well, it seemed to work for you and Alex. You guys are married now," I point out, before turning my attention onto Sarah. "And you're engaged to Jared. So phony relationships must be successful."

"Is that what you want from Theo? To *marry* him?" Sarah asks.

"*No!*" The word shoots out of me like a bullet, fast and hot. "Of course not. He's just my friend. But—I want us to look like a couple, you know? So everyone at the wedding thinks we're together."

"To prove to Jessica that Theo is over him," Caroline says.

I nod. "Yes. That. Exactly."

"Then you're going to have to act like a *real* couple," Sarah says. "Arm in arm. Loving glances. Flirtatious laughter. The works. And it can't seem awkward either. You need it to be believable."

"I can't believe we're having this conversation," I say, having a surreal moment.

"What about his family?" Caroline asks. "Doesn't he have like...twenty brothers?"

"It feels like it," I say with a laugh. "He has four brothers and a sister. His family is very close."

"Well, you need to break past that barrier first. You need to go have family dinner with them or whatever. Otherwise, you're the so-called girlfriend coming out of nowhere. They won't believe him. Or you," Caroline says.

Shit. I never thought of that, but of course Caroline is right. His brothers will call Theo out immediately if we suddenly show up and act like a couple. He pretty much tells them everything.

"I think we'll need to come up with a plan," I say, my mind already racing with all the things Theo and I need to do.

"That sounds like a start," Sarah says, her smile gentle. "I know you always say he's your friend, but are you sure you don't feel something...more for him?"

"I don't," I say vehemently. "I can't. Our friendship is perfect just as it is. We bring any sort of—romantic feelings into it, and everything's ruined."

"Everything?" Amelia asks. "So dramatic."

"And so true. I can't keep a boyfriend to save my life. Something always gets in the way." Like my face. Like other men being attracted to me and making whoever I'm with jealous. Or men who have certain expectations just because of the way I look. When I don't meet those expectations, they get angry.

"It sounds like you and Theo have so much potential, though," Amelia says, actually sounding like a romantic, which I know she's not. Well. Ever since she got together with her new boyfriend, she's softened up. Maybe she's a believer after all.

"Our potential is friendly. That's it. Sex complicates things."

"Sex complicates everything," Caroline says with a dreamy smile on her face. "But sometimes in the absolute best way."

"Maybe for you," I tell her. "But never for me. Sex ruins everything."

I need to remember that. In fact with Theo, I always do. Sex ruins it all. I've had a few friends with benefits. On occasion, I would hook up with this one guy I used to work with. The sex was good. There were no strings. He acted like he wanted nothing more from me, and I definitely felt the same.

But then he started texting me more. Followed me around at work. Making it really obvious that something was potentially going on between us. I didn't want to bring the so-called relationship into our workplace, so I told him to cool it.

He flipped out. Threw a fit. Made me uncomfortable. Then begged for my forgiveness. It was a mess. Luckily enough, he moved. Transferred out of our office and started working for Wilder Hotel Corp up in Seattle.

Him leaving was a huge relief. He was the final nail in my relationship coffin. He was the reason I swore off men.

And I'm sticking to that. No matter what happens.

FOUR
THEO

IT'S past ten and I'm lying in bed, scrolling through one of those dating apps—not Rate A Date, that one was for shit, at least for me—and checking out my matching prospects. There's some beautiful women out there. Beautiful, successful women with bright smiles and impressive careers, according to their profiles.

It's hard to tell, who's for real on these sites. Who I could be attracted to. I'm not even sure if I'm ready for casual dating yet.

I'm a long-timer. A life-termer, according to my jerk-ass brothers. Now that I've been single for a while, I'm wondering if I should get back out there. Start dating again.

None of these women appeal to me, though. I keep scrolling, my finger tapping at my phone screen again and again, the motion monotonous. Almost boring. Why am I doing this? It's almost like torture, scrolling past all these women, wondering what secrets they might be hiding behind their wide smiles and overblown profile descriptions.

I'm sure they're all perfectly nice, but I'm still a skeptic.

A doubter. I got played by Jessica, and it still hurts. I'm wary.

More than anything, I trust no one.

I secretly thought I would struggle with being single, but I've come to terms with it. After those first initial months of heartache and humiliation, I've slowly realized I enjoy being by myself. Growing up in a large household, I had no idea what that was like. Living alone. Having my own space.

Now I'm actually enjoying it. Not having to answer to anyone. Hogging the entire bed. Choosing my own movies/TV shows/documentaries to binge. Eating whatever the hell I want and not having my fiancée nag me on how I need less carbs and more proteins.

That's a very specific example. One I don't miss at all.

And if I want female company? I have Kelsey to hang out with. My friend. My beautiful, sexy friend.

I'm scowling. I can feel it. Kelsey is what my youngest brother calls a smoke show. She's unbelievably gorgeous. Sometimes I wonder what she's doing, hanging out with me all the time. She could get any man she wants. That face of hers could inspire poetry. Songs. Could make a man do something desperate, like cry at her front door, begging to be let in. Write her letters declaring his undying love.

Not only is she a beauty, she's also smart as fuck. Quick and funny and a good listener. She gives solid advice. She can drink beer and throw back shots like a champ. If I weren't so against dating women, I suppose I'd try to go for her.

Probably would chicken out after having the rather rude realization that I don't stand a chance with her. I'm not her type. I'm just—a guy. I have a successful job and make damn good money, but other than that, I'm pathetically average.

And my friend Kelsey is completely out of the stratosphere.

Exhaling loudly, I slide out of the dating app and decide to check out...

A porn site.

Shit, look. I'm a healthy male in my early thirties. If I want to partake in some porn, I'm allowed, right? I'm single. I'm not out messing around with an endless list of women. I actually haven't had sex in months. I need to relieve the tension somehow.

Sitting up a little, I scroll through the popular videos on one site, searching. I land on a brunette with cock-sucking lips and a face like Megan Fox in her earlier years. Not that she isn't hot now, but young Megan Fox reminds me of...

Kelsey.

I'm going to hell for this, but yeah. I'm about to jerk off to the porn star version of my friend.

I start the video and settle into my pillows. This woman is hot, spread out on a bed clad in a pair of virginal white panties and nothing else. Her legs are bent at the knee and she's nibbling on her index finger, her lush red lips parted, her gaze on the camera. You can see her bush beneath the panties, which I find surprising. Most porn stars I see are shaved bare.

I kind of like the bush. Makes it a little more mysterious.

Reaching inside my boxers, I rest my hand on my stirring dick, my eyes glued to my phone screen. She slips her hand beneath the front of her panties, her fingers slowly working beneath the fabric. One finger circles. You can tell what she's doing. Working that clit. I like to think it's actually happening, but I'm sure this chick feels nothing. It's all for show.

I push that thought to the side, annoyed I'd try to crap my own self out.

She arches her back, her eyes falling closed, her stroking fingers increasing their pace. You can't see anything since her panties are still on, but I turn up the volume because I'm a pervert and holy hell, *yes*. You can hear her.

She's wet.

I've got my hand gripped around the base of my growing erection, and the Kelsey porn star is writhing around on her bed when a man walks into the room, catching her masturbating. She's so engrossed with her own self, she doesn't even notice him. Only when he grabs hold of her hips and hauls her down to the edge of the bed does she supposedly even notice. A shocked gasp escapes her when he tugs her panties aside, shoves her hand away and proceeds to lick her up and down.

My ex hated oral. Giving and receiving. I never understood it. A blowjob feels *amazing*. I'm not a selfish bastard—I actually enjoy going down on a woman. But Jessica would always push away. Said it made her feel uncomfortable.

So we never did it. And I miss blowjobs like crazy.

My current favorite type of porn is when they go down on each other. Penetration works too, but right now, I'm all about oral sex. It's what gets me going. We all have our preferences, am I right? There's nothing better than a POV blowjob either.

In fact, I skip through a few minutes of the current video and get to that point. The Kelsey lookalike is now on her knees in front of the man, her tits swaying and her fingers gripping the base of this guy's dick. Her gaze never strays from the camera as she works her plump mouth over that cock.

I start to increase my pace, my gaze glued on her stretched wide lips, her licking tongue. I close my eyes. Imagine Kelsey doing exactly that to me. Her gaze on mine, her lips curled in a faint smile before she parts them and draws me inside.

A shudder works through me and I close my eyes. Lost in my mental porn reel.

This is wrong. I'm wrong for inserting Kelsey into my fantasy, but holy shit, I can only imagine the magic her mouth could work on my cock. A low groan escapes me. My hand is moving so fast, it's like a blur. My balls tighten up, and that telltale tingle starts at the base of my spine. Fuck, I'm close—

My phone rings. So loud, I drop the fucker.

Cracking open my eyes, I watch Kelsey's name flash across my screen. My hand is somehow still working my dick, never losing its rhythm, and then I'm coming. A stuttering groan falls from my lips as I jizz all over my fucking hand. My phone lies discarded on the bed, Kelsey's name still flashing, and without thought I reach over with my free hand and answer the call.

Wait a minute.

She's fucking FaceTiming me.

I leave the phone on my bed and somehow hurriedly shrug out of my boxers, cleaning my hand with them before I toss them onto the floor. I run my clean hand through my hair. Scrub it over my face. Pray to God I don't look like I just got caught masturbating.

"Uh, hello. Earth to Theo," she calls from the phone.

I glance down to see her pretty face filling my phone screen. Her dark hair is in a topknot on her head and she's makeup free. I see a headboard behind her and realize she's in bed too, wearing some sort of tank top with thin straps that show off her perfectly smooth shoulders.

I swallow hard, my gaze roaming all over that exposed skin.

Grabbing the phone, I hold it up in front of me, squinting at the image of myself. I don't look so bad. My face is flushed. I'm going to pretend everything is normal. "Hey, what's up?"

She never calls this late. Hope nothing's wrong.

Kelsey frowns. "You okay? Been working out?"

"Uh." I pause for a moment, blinking at her. "Yeah." How else am I supposed to answer? And I guess I did just give my dick a workout.

Her frown deepens. "This late? I know you've been focusing on your fitness lately, but I didn't realize you were this dedicated."

"What do you mean, I'm focused on my fitness?" Now I'm the one who's frowning.

"You've been working out more. You told me so yourself. If you're not stopping at the gym after work, you're jogging on the beach." Her eyes light up. "Hey, maybe we should run together tomorrow morning." On occasion, we've run on the beach together, though we've really never made a habit of it.

"You want to get together tomorrow? Is that why you FaceTimed me?" I ask her.

"Sort of. I didn't plan on running, but let's meet up. Or do you have an early meeting?" She frowns, her teeth catching her lower lip.

"I don't have to be at work until nine." Fridays are usually a catch-up day at the office for me. I rarely have appointments scheduled. I tend to make calls and concentrate on backed-up paperwork and cleaning out the endless emails in my inbox.

"Same here. Let's meet at Carmel Beach. Is that okay?"

"Sure." I pause for a moment, wondering about this call. It's not like her to FaceTime me, especially after ten o'clock at night. "What else did you want to talk about?"

"Uhh...nothing much." She sounds evasive.

Huh.

"Kels." I bring the phone up closer to my face. "Everything all right?"

She shrugs one smooth shoulder. "I've been thinking a lot about our date for Jessica's wedding."

Worry sizzles down my spine. "What about it?" Shit, if she backs out, I'm screwed. There's no one else I want to take to the wedding as my date. No one else I trust.

"I don't know. I'm kind of worried about how we'll look together. We're friends, you know? We act like friends."

"Okay." I say the word slowly. "So?"

"Well, if you want us to look like an actual couple, then we have to—*act* like one." She bites her lower lip again, this time with a wince.

"That shouldn't be too difficult, right?" What, I'll hold her hand? Pull a chair out for her? Big deal.

"Like, maybe we should act like we're *very* together, if you know what I mean." A single brow lifts.

"As in..."

This is one thing I've noticed about women: they think we're mind readers. Well, guess what, ladies? We're not. We're simple. We need things broken down and spelled out. We'll go along with what you want, for the most part. We just can't always figure out what you're trying to say.

She blows out an irritated breath. "You're being really obtuse, Theo."

Obtuse. Don't think I've been called that before. "Please explain."

"We'll need to act like a bona fide couple who can't keep their hands off each other," she says, rather primly I might add.

I think of porn star Kelsey. And real, talking to me right now Kelsey. My Kelsey is a lot prettier than porn star Kelsey. "Like a couple in love."

"More like a couple who are so hot for each other, they can barely stand it." She hesitates for a moment, an unsure look on her face. "Don't you think that's the approach we need to take?"

"I guess."

"You need to show Jessica that you've moved on from her. That you're now with a woman who wants to have sex with you whenever, wherever," Kelsey says.

"You know, she never liked it when I tried to go down on her." Well, shit. I guess tonight is true confession time.

Kelsey's frowning so hard her forehead is wrinkled. "Why in the world would she not like it?"

"I don't know. Said it made her feel uncomfortable. She didn't like giving me blowjobs either."

She just blinks at me. "That's insane. Isn't that what makes sex fun?"

"What, blowjobs? You like giving blowjobs?" I ask incredulously.

"I don't hate it."

I scrub a hand over my face, ignoring my stirring dick. "How did we get on this topic again?"

"I said we had to pretend like we're a couple who can't get enough. Blowjobs, whatever." She laughs.

"Right. Okay. We can do that," I say firmly, hoping I sound like I mean it.

"Of course we can," she practically scoffs. This woman loves a challenge. "Plus, won't your family call bullshit if this is the first time they've heard of me?"

"Oh, they know about you," I say.

Her face brightens. "Really? You've told them about me? Your brothers?"

I have. They all think she must be hideous if I'm not trying to hit that, and I quote. None of my brothers are believers in being friends with a woman. They think it's impossible. So she's either ugly or gives off ice-cold vibes.

Kelsey is neither. She's warm and sweet and smart. Easy to talk to. And very anti-dating right now. Same as I'm supposed to be.

"Yeah, I've mentioned you a time or two," I say casually, like no big deal. I probably talk about her too much. In fact, I know I do. My mother has asked more than once why I'm not dating this Kelsey person. Another direct quote.

"I think you should bring me around your family before the wedding," she says.

"Why?" I immediately start to sweat.

"Then it's more believable that we're together, Theo. Come on. You bring me to your parents' house for dinner or some other family event, and there I am. On your arm. By your side. Kissing your cheek. Running my fingers through your hair. Like we're together, you know?" She tilts her head. "It'll be more believable that way when we show up at the wedding."

"And you don't have a problem with this?"

"Nooo, I think it'll be fun. Come on, I trust you. You're not going to make any real moves on me," she says with a soft laugh.

See, that's the problem. Lately I don't mind the idea of making a real move on Kelsey. We're compatible in almost every single way. Why wouldn't we be compatible, sexually? I just jerked off to a porn Kelsey lookalike, for Christ's sake.

"My parents invited me over to their house Saturday afternoon. They're having a barbecue," I tell her.

"Really? What's the occasion?" Kelsey asks.

"There is none. They just—like to barbecue." At least a couple of times a month Mom is trying to get me to come over for a family meal. If it's during the weekday, I turn her down. I'm usually too busy with work and they always want to eat early while I'm always working late. But when it's the weekend, she's got me.

And she knows it.

"Are you inviting me as your date?" Kelsey asks, her tone teasing.

"I guess I am," I say with a smile. "Not sure what time, though. I'll text Mom in the morning and ask her. She wakes up at like five, so I'm sure I'll have all the details for you when we meet at the beach tomorrow."

"Okay, great! This should be fun." She laughs. "I can't wait."

"Yeah. Cool." I nod, feeling like a complete dumbass.

"Oh, and Theo?"

"Yeah?"

"I don't think it's gross at all when a man goes down on me. In fact, it's my favorite part of foreplay. I'm a fan of giving BJs too. Just so you know," she chirps, just before she ends the call.

Shit.

FIVE
KELSEY

I'M STANDING by a cypress tree not too far from the parking lot, stretching my calves, when I spot Theo walking toward me, his arm pointed behind him, keys clutched in his fingers as he hits the remote and locks his car. He's just far enough away that he can't tell I'm blatantly checking him out, and so I look my fill with an extra-critical eye.

Studying him as Theo the man versus Theo the comfortable friend.

I wasn't lying when I told him last night that I'd noticed he was working on his fitness. He's been working out more, and it shows. The gray T-shirt he's currently wearing stretches across his broad chest and shoulders in a rather appealing way. Just tight enough to show off his muscles. His legs are strong, his arms defined. Waist and hips trim. He looks good.

A lot better than he did when we first met. Back then, he was a little pale and the slightest bit doughy. Not fat. Not even chubby. Just—a guy who sat at a desk or on a couch all day and night. Someone who didn't get outside much and worked too much. He still works too much, but he also goes to the gym.

A lot.

Or he's always jogging along some beach. Like now.

"Hey," he calls to me when he draws nearer and we make eye contact. "Sorry I'm late. Traffic."

"It sucks," I agree, breathing deep when he stops directly in front of me. He smells good. Like citrus and wood. Sounds a little odd, but it works for him. "You ready?"

"I should stretch first." He starts doing exactly that, the hem of his T-shirt rising when he lifts his arms above his head. My gaze drops to that exposed sliver of skin. His flat stomach. His bellybutton, which is a perfect innie and has a line of dark hair arrowing straight down beneath the waistband of his shorts.

I tear my gaze away, telling myself it's just Theo. I shouldn't look at him like that.

But...

Maybe I should, considering I'm going to have to act like he's my boyfriend for a short period of time. Why I'm doing this for him, I'm not really sure, but since we've started talking and hanging out, he has always been there for me. He's a good guy. Nice. Dependable. Super smart. Responsible, with a good head on his shoulders. He also has a successful career. He would make someone a great boyfriend.

So why don't I want to snag him up?

I've been on a recent anti-man tear, so there's that. Theo feels like my partner in crime. He doesn't want to date anyone either. He treats me like a friend, not a potential fuck buddy. It's amazing how many men who I thought were my friends were actually just guys hoping I'd be their fuck buddy.

Frustrating.

Theo is the only man who actually *sees* me, who listens to what I say, and respects my wishes, always. I do the same for him. We're not interested in a romantic relationship. Specifically not with each other or with...anyone.

We're over it. Over love.

Or so I thought.

But it's been a few months. He's well over his ex, or so he claims. I'm starting to feel a little...antsy.

Okay, let's be real. I'm feeling horny.

I'm starting to wonder if I should climb back onto that saddle, and use Theo as my temporary horse.

Well. That conjures up all sorts of images.

"You okay?" Theo asks, his deep voice pulling me from my suddenly naughty thoughts.

I lift my gaze to his, shrugging one shoulder. No way can I tell him I just had the vivid mental image of climbing on top of him and riding him like the cowgirl I've secretly always wanted to be. "I'm great." I smile.

He tilts his head. "I think you're full of shit, but it's cool. I'll let it go."

This is another reason I like Theo so much. He calls me on my bullshit, but he doesn't expect me to explain myself either. I can be a little...extra sometimes. I know this. It's my worst trait. Theo allows me to act as extra as I want. Most of the time, he tells me I'm being completely ridiculous, but he doesn't make a big deal about it.

He just lets me be.

"Are you ready to start dating again?" I ask him out of the blue.

His head whips in my direction fast, his gaze meeting mine. "Are you?"

"I don't know." I shrug again. "I was just thinking about how I—don't hate men anymore."

Theo laughs, the pleasant sound sending shivers rippling across my skin. "Glad to hear it."

My voice is solemn. "I think you helped me with that."

"Me?" He rests his hand on his broad chest. "I'm honored. Come on, let's run."

He's not taking me seriously, I think as we start jogging across the soft sand. He probably thinks I'm being my usual ridiculous self, and he probably doesn't even believe me. If I were to tell him I'm having sexual fantasies about him? He'd probably laugh and tell me to buy a new vibrator.

I did. A few months ago. It doesn't cut it anymore. I want to feel a man's fingers touching me, not my own. I need that skin-on-skin sensation. I want a man to hold me close and run his fingers through my hair while I listen to his heart thump against my ear.

Oh my God, I think I want a fuck buddy.

I think I might want my fuck buddy to be...

Theo.

"Hurry up!" Theo yells, and I pick up speed, a grunt leaving me as I trudge through the sand.

Running on this beach is a complete bitch because of the sand. It's thick and our feet sink deeper the farther we go. I angle my body toward the water's edge, already needing the compacted sand that's down there. Screw this.

"Wimp," Theo says easily when he rejoins me to run by my side. "You usually go a lot longer in the deeper sand."

How can he talk so casually while I feel like I'm about to collapse? I'm totally winded. "I can't have conversation with you and run at the same time."

It took me twice as long as normal to say that. This is probably why he encouraged me to run right in the middle of my declaration. So we wouldn't be stuck in awkward conversation about dating or not. Which tells me he's not ready to get back out on the scene. And why not? He's a very attractive man. Smart and successful with a great career. Let's be real for a moment.

He is a fucking catch.

"Let's go to a bar tonight," I call to him as he runs ahead of me. "I want to help you pick up women."

Theo turns so he's running backwards, his expression nothing short of incredulous. "What the hell, Kels? I thought you wanted people to think we're a couple. Now you want to set me up in dark bars with total strangers? You're not making any sense."

I roll my eyes and increase my pace so I can keep up with him, hating that he's right. I'm totally not making sense. "You need to start dating again, Theo. Maybe we're spending too much time together."

"And maybe you're sending me mixed messages," he says. "You're being kind of weird, you know."

We run for a while, both of us silent. My mind is a whirl of information, all of it confusing. Theo's right. I did just suggest we needed to make it seem real between us. That's why he's taking me to his parents' house this weekend. So he can introduce me as his new girlfriend.

But he needs an actual girlfriend once this charade is over. Guess what? I need an actual boyfriend, too. I'm tired of being alone. I'm not what I would call lonely, thanks to my friends, including Theo. But I am lonely for romantic company. The kind that only a man could give to me. Plus, I really want to find a man who'll give me multiple orgasms at once.

That last one might be a myth, and I haven't come across one yet, but I'm not giving up on finding him. He's out there, and I look forward to the day he'll make me come three times in a row.

By the time we're back where we started, not too far from the parking lot at the end of Ocean Drive, I'm exhausted. My lungs burn. My calves ache. It's foggy and cold out here, yet I'm sweating. But damn it, I feel good too.

"Let's go to a bar tonight," I tell him again once I've rediscovered my voice.

Theo frowns. He's attractive even when he looks confused. It's almost as if he's become...more attractive lately. The dark hair and dark eyes. The olive skin. The muscles. Dude's got muscles for days. Who knew? "You mentioned that already. Why do you want to go to a bar?"

"I don't know." I shrug. "So I can practice being your girlfriend?"

The words fall from my lips like I have no control over them. He appears startled. *I* am startled. What am I trying to do here? I think about missing romantic contact with a man and now I'm basically asking Theo out on a date.

"If you want to do that, shouldn't I probably wine and dine you first?" He raises his brows. "I'm talking dinner," he continues at my confused look.

"Oh. Right." I laugh nervously, then clamp my lips shut. I sound like an idiot. "You want to go to dinner? Tonight?"

He rests his hands on his hips, his chest lifting with every accelerated breath he inhales. That run winded him too. "I'm tired of the bar scene. Let's have dinner instead. You like dinner, right?"

"I love dinner." Theo and I meet for lunch at least once a week. We see each other at various afternoon work-related mixers. A couple of cocktail parties, we've bumped into each other and usually spend the entirety of the event together. We had brunch once, but that was a rare moment.

We never, ever have dinner together. And I know why. Theo is always working through the dinner hour. He usually eats late—if he eats dinner at all. And when he does eat, it's usually a) at his desk, b) in his car as he drives home aka fast food, or c) some sort of frozen crap he heated up real quick in his microwave at nine-forty-five at night. I've told him time and again that it's not good for him to eat like that, but he always blows me off.

He's a man completely obsessed with his job. Which I suppose is a great trait for making money, but I worry that he neglects his health. And that's not good.

"Then let's go to dinner tonight," he says.

"Theo." I raise my brows. "Are you asking me on a date?"

I'm actually giddy at the prosect. And I never get giddy over dates. Or dinners with male friends. Not that I go out to dinner with male friends. I don't really have any.

Except for Theo.

"A date between *friends*," he says, his words deflating my giddy mood like a pinprick to a balloon. "And you're the one who asked first. So technically, *you* asked me out on this dinner date."

Fair enough. "Let's call it a mutual agreement."

"Okay." He scratches the back of his neck, his biceps bulging with the movement. My mouth goes dry, and it's not because I'm dying of thirst. "It's Friday, so I don't plan on working too late."

With Theo, that statement means nothing. He could work till ten. He could work till midnight. He doesn't know his limits. "It's Friday," I repeat. "Meaning everywhere we might want to go will be busy, especially if you work late."

"Then we'll have drinks first, just like you wanted." His smile turns sly. "Want to go to that French place Paul took you to when we went on our double blind date?"

"Absolutely not," I say firmly, not wanting any memories of his jerk best friend tainting the evening. "Let's pick somewhere different. Maybe here in Carmel?"

"Sure," he says easily. "You pick the place and text me what time you want to meet."

"Sounds good."

He glances at his Rolex. "Shit, I gotta go, or I'm going to be late. Text me."

He starts to leave and I watch him go, calling out his name.

"What?" He turns so he's walking backwards again. How does he do that? I'd stumble over something and hurt myself, I know it. I'm not the most coordinated person in the world.

"Promise me you won't forget about our date tonight," I say.

Theo frowns. "How could I ever forget *you?*"

His words touch my heart. I know for a fact he forgot about a couple of dates with his ex, thanks to him being completely consumed with work and losing track of time. It made Jessica angry.

So angry, she started cheating on Theo with his cousin. Not that I know the reason why she chose Theo's cousin, but hey. It's possible.

My expression turns serious. I can literally feel it make the switch. "Promise me."

His laughter dies. "I promise, Kels."

My gaze stays on him as he climbs into his sleek black BMW. He waves as he pulls out of the lot, and I watch as his car climbs up the hilly road until I can no longer see it. A sigh leaves me as I make my way toward my car. Emotions swirl within me, every one of them confusing. I don't know what I want. I don't know how I feel.

I guess I just need to go with it, and see where things take me.

SIX
THEO

I'M at my desk answering yet another email from last week when I hear my phone buzz, indicating a text message. I check to see who it's from.

Kelsey.

Let's go to Porta Bella. We can sit outside. I made reservations. 7:30. Don't forget!

Why is she so worried I might forget her?

Oh. I told her about those times I forgot about dates with Jessica. Work can take over my life if I don't watch it, and back then, I was so secure in my relationship with my fiancée, I figured I could do whatever the hell I wanted and she'd forgive me. Or she wouldn't care.

I was wrong. She cared. A lot. She ended up getting pissed. I'd neglected her for a while, she told me later. I didn't fulfill her needs.

My cousin did instead. Really nice, how he swooped in and stole her from me. At least she kept it in the family?

My phone buzzes again with another text from Kels.

???

Me: **I won't be late. See you at 7:30.**

She sends me back a row of kissy face emojis, and I wonder at them. Think back on her mood earlier when we met at the beach. She's kind of all over the place. Very contradictory. Maybe putting misplaced feelings on me?

What are those misplaced feelings exactly? Not exactly sure.

There's a knock on my door and then it pops open, my assistant Lyssa appearing. "Theo, there's someone here to see you."

I frown, trying to come up with an appointment I might've missed. "Who?"

"He says he's your cousin." She makes a little face. "Craig?"

Fucking great.

An irritated sigh escapes me and I run a hand through my hair, glaring at the mess that is my desk. "Tell him I'll be out in a few minutes."

"Will do." She quietly shuts the door while I mutter a few choice words under my breath.

Craig is the last person I want to deal with. The man who stole my fiancée. The man who fucked her behind my back for months while I was completely oblivious. He made me look like a chump. Like a complete dumbass. My own flesh and blood backstabbing me in the worst possible way.

Showing up at my workplace unannounced is so typical. The guy is a prick. We're the same age—we've always been competitive with each other. While in high school he was the jock and I was the nerd, I'm the one who's now got a successful job and am making lots of money while he's a beer delivery guy.

And there's nothing wrong with delivering beer. He makes decent money. He's worked there since he was twenty, and the delivery positions are coveted. He seems perfectly content with his career. But I know it burns his ass I make twice as much as he does—maybe more. Guess he got me back, though, by stealing Jessica right from under my nose.

The asshole.

Grabbing my phone, I open up the camera and quickly check myself out, baring my teeth to make sure I don't have anything in them. I'm wearing a suit, as per usual, though I shed the jacket a while ago. Also per usual. I decide to shrug the jacket back on and straighten my tie. Shove my phone into my front pocket of my pants and stand up straight, reminding myself he came to *my* workplace.

And I can kick his ass out if I need to.

I take a deep breath and exit my office to find Craig sitting in the waiting area near Lyssa's desk. He's slumped in the seat in his delivery uniform, scowling as he types furiously on his phone. I clear my throat to announce my arrival and his head jerks up, his scowl switching to a smile just like that.

"Cuz! It's so good to see you!" He hops to his feet and comes for me, smothering me in a hug. My body stiff, I reach around him and awkwardly pat his back, feeling like a robot.

Who the hell does he think he is? Coming in here like no big deal. We haven't talked in a year. Since before everything happened.

I pull away from him as quickly as possible, the smile on my face strained. "What's going on?" I try to keep my voice light. Casual. Like seeing him doesn't bother me.

But holy shit, does it bother me. Craig and I never resolved our issues. There was never any major confrontation between us. I didn't call him out on how he—*they*—deceived me, and he never asked for my forgiveness.

Him showing up at my office unannounced, acting as if we're cool with each other, is like his cheating with Jessica never happened.

"Not much. Been busy. Work's keeping me going. And then there's the wedding." His eyes flicker with some unknown emotion, but otherwise he acts like it's nothing. "How about you?"

"I'm good. Extremely busy." Heavy emphasis on *extremely*. "What can I do for you, Craig?"

"We haven't seen each other in a while and this is how you treat me?" Craig smiles, like it's all just one big joke.

I cross my arms, watching him, a single brow raising. This is some straight-up bullshit, if you ask me.

"Okay." Craig expels an exasperated breath. I'm tempted to punch him in his face, but I restrain myself. "I have, ah, a question for you."

"What is it?" I glance over my shoulder to see Lyssa watching us with obvious curiosity, her gaze dropping to her computer screen when I catch her. "Let's have this conversation in my office," I tell Craig.

He follows me inside and I shut the door behind him, leaning against it for a moment as Craig goes to the window that overlooks the Monterey Bay. "Pretty nice view you got here," he says.

"I like it." Most of the time, I don't even notice it.

Craig turns to face me as I make my way to my desk "You've really made yourself into something, haven't you?"

I shrug, feigning modesty. I'd love to rub it in his face that I'm pretty fucking successful, but there's something to be said for acting like it's no big deal too. "I do all right," I tell him.

"Yeah." Craig glances around once more, then down at himself, as if he just realized he's in his vaguely dirty uniform. Not that I'm judging him. "Jessica and I were glad to see you're coming to the wedding."

I nod. Don't say a word. The only reason I'm going is because my family is forcing me to. Not that I'm going to tell Craig that.

The silence stretches, and I wish he'd just get to the point.

"And that you're bringing a date." Craig smiles, his gaze hopeful. "You met someone, huh?"

"I did. She's amazing. Gorgeous. We've been together for quite a while now." Not a lie. Kelsey and I have been together that long—as friends.

"I'm so glad, man," Craig says softly. "Jessica and I—we never meant to hurt you."

"Right. Sure." My voice is clipped. "I don't doubt you two were very worried about me and my feelings."

"Hey, don't act like that. We felt like total shit after everything that happened. You know I love you like a brother," he says.

None of my brothers would've ever done me as dirty as this asshole, so that statement doesn't mean shit to me. "What exactly do you want, Craig?"

"Right. Uh, I've had a last minute bail out when it comes to my groomsmen. Literally. One of my friends—he just got sentenced and has to do some jail time." Craig frowns. "Lost his job and everything."

Sounds like Craig is hanging out with some high-quality people. "That's a shame."

"I know. Billy's had a rough time of it lately. But anyway, I now have a slot to fill and I was kind of hoping..."

His voice drifts and he smiles brightly. "That you could be my groomsman."

"Oh hell no." The words shoot out of my mouth automatically and without much thought.

His face falls. "Come on. We were always so close when we were kids."

"Were we, though? Really?" I ask, running my hand along my jaw as I contemplate him. He has to know the truth. I wouldn't call our relationship close. More like we had to spend time together because my father and his mother are siblings. *They* were close. Of course they wanted to raise their families together. We were together for every single holiday when I was a kid. Big family bashes reminded them of their own childhood, and yeah, I can't deny I have a lot of fond memories.

But most of them don't involve Craig. Forced by age and circumstance, that's the only reason we hung out together. Craig was always trying to one up me throughout our growing up years. I was the responsible one of my family. The oldest brother. Craig was an only child and completely spoiled.

"We totally were!" Craig exclaims, like my question is a no brainer. "I know you're probably not too—happy with me, but you have to know I didn't mean for it to happen."

"Uh huh."

"I swear! I had no idea who Jessica was when I met her." His expression turns contrite. "I met her on a site, you know?"

My entire body goes cold. "On a site."

Craig's eyes nearly bug out of his head at my flat tone. I'm guessing he just realized he stepped in it, the idiot. "Uh yeah. Not that it matters. I can't help it if we have the same taste in women."

He's trying to make light of this. Like it's a joke. As if him pulling the figurative rug from under my feet and sending me into freefall was just an oops moment. It wasn't. The breakup, the betrayal fucked with my head. Fucked with my life.

"I don't know if I can be your groomsman," I tell him truthfully. "Find someone else."

"My problem is there is no one else. I can't have one of your brothers. They'll give me endless shit," Craig says.

It would be their right to do so. He deserves endless shit.

"You're the only one I can count on. That Jessica can count on too. Come on, man. Just—give it some time to consider our request. Let me know by the end of the weekend, all right? I gotta go. It was nice seeing you. Text me."

I remain in place as Craig slips out of my office, the door closing quietly behind him. As if he was never there. My brain is swirling with too many emotions. All of them negative. Or utter disbelief. Why would he think I'd be open to being his groomsman? Like...fucking seriously? There's no way I can say yes.

No freaking way.

I LEAVE the office a full hour before I'm to meet Kelsey because I have a feeling traffic would be bad. And I'm right. By the time I turn onto Ocean Blvd., the road is completely clogged with cars. I turn onto a side street and make my way around it, finding parking only about a block around the corner from the restaurant.

Pays off to know how to get around congested traffic because you've lived in an area your entire life.

Carmel is where the elite hang out. The rich folks, or

the tourists. Kelsey works at Wilder Hotel—she's the assistant to Alexander Wilder, and the hotel's corporate offices are at the Pebble Beach location.

Alex travels the world, visiting the various hotels that are part of his luxury resort chain. Kelsey has traveled for him a few times, though not out of the country—yet. She has a feeling an opportunity will open up soon. She's ambitious. Dedicated. Hungry to grow her career, and I think her boss recognizes that.

All of Kelsey's friends hang out in and around Carmel as well. Most of them work in the area. Some of them even live close by. Stella Ricci's family owns a few restaurants, but not the one we're going to tonight.

I approach the quaint restaurant, detecting the faint murmurings of multiple conversations. The lights glowing on the outside patio, and the various giant pots full of fragrant, tumbling flowers. There's a table for two right at the front of the flagstone patio, a woman sitting with her back to me. Long, dark hair spills down her back in luxurious waves, and I know it anywhere.

It's Kelsey.

Stopping quietly just behind her, I press my hands against her eyes, covering them. "Guess who?"

"My favorite financial planner," she says, her voice teasing.

"Wrong."

"My favorite male friend."

I refuse to be swayed by the compliment. "Guess again."

"That rando who agreed to go to dinner with me tonight," she says.

"Bingo." I remove my hands from her face and round

the table, pulling the empty chair out and settling in. "You got a prime spot tonight."

"I'm trying to impress you." There's already a glass of wine on the table for me, and I reach for it, taking a few eager swallows. "Did it work?"

"You always impress me, Kels." It's the damn truth. I try not to stare at her, but holy shit, she looks amazing. There's a single candle on our table, its gentle light flickering across her beautiful face, making it glow, and I'm stunned for about the millionth time by her beauty.

"Aw, thank you." She smiles, reaching for her glass and taking a sip. "I ordered appetizers."

"So presumptuous."

"I know what you like." Her eyes sparkle as they meet mine across the table. "How was work?"

Craig's visit comes to mind, and I'm about to tell her what happened when our server appears beside our table.

"The appetizers you ordered, miss." The waiter is young. Attractive. And he's basically eye fucking my date.

"Thank you." Kelsey smiles sweetly. I swear sometimes she's completely unaware the spell she puts on men. Her beauty slays.

I glance at the table. See the giant tentacle lying across the plate, so large it flops over each side. "What the hell is this?"

"Grilled Spanish octopus, sir," the server tells me. "And a smoked salmon salad with goat cheese."

"I thought we could share the salad," Kelsey says cheerfully.

"And the octopus?" I raise my brows.

"I thought it would be fun, trying something different." She shrugs.

The server's still hovering, his eyes only for Kelsey. "I think we're good," I snap at him, wanting him gone.

He sends one last, longing glance at Kelsey before he leaves.

"You were so rude," she chastises, her eyes dancing.

I unroll my silverware from the cloth napkin sitting in front of me and grab my fork, reaching out to stab it into the salad that's right in front of her. "He was looking at you like you're a slab of octopus on a plate and he was starving."

She laughs, shaking her head as she unrolls her silverware as well. "The octopus is fun, am I right?"

"That's one way to describe it." I'm hungry, and the salad is delicious. So is the beautiful woman sitting across from me. Something must be in the air tonight, because just like the server, I can't stop eye-fucking Kelsey either. Her arms are exposed thanks to the sleeveless black shirt she's wearing. The shirt is sheer and covered with tiny white dots. Sheer as in I can see the black bra she's wearing beneath it, and the way her breasts strain against the fabric.

I take another gulp of wine, needing the alcohol to fortify me.

After both of us devour the salad—it was pretty good, plus we got competitive, our forks banging against each other as we strived for that last bite—we decide to tackle the octopus. It's actually pretty damn delicious, and we're laughing as we cut into the tentacle, both of us lamenting the death of the octopus.

"Normally I don't eat this sort of thing," Kelsey says, resting her fork on the edge of the plate.

"Me either. I like seafood, though." Thank God, considering there's so much of it where we live and it's always fresh.

"Same." She takes another drink of her wine. "You never did tell me how your day went."

"Have I got a story for you." I fill her in on Craig's surprise visit to my office. How casual he acted, like it was no big deal that he showed up like he did. And then I hit her with the big bombshell at the end—him asking me to be a groomsman.

Kelsey's brown eyes go wide and her glossy lips part. "He did not."

I nod. "He sure as hell did. Can you believe it?"

"No." She shakes her head, her expression darkening. "He has a lot of nerve."

I love that she looks ticked on my behalf. "I know. He's a dick."

"He so is," she says vehemently. "That's why you should agree to do it."

It's my turn for my mouth to drop open. "What the hell? Did you just say I should be a groomsman?"

I'm spelling it out, just to make sure.

"Yes. You totally should." Her expression turns haughty. Damn, she's pretty. "Show them you've got class, Theo."

"Maybe I don't want to." I let my fork drop so it clangs against the plate and I cross my arms. I feel like I'm five.

She bursts out laughing. "Of course you don't want to. But you *should* agree to do it anyway. Show them both you're mature, and you've got a handle on your emotions. Don't let them rattle you."

I consider what she says for all of about five seconds. "Yeah. Not gonna do it."

"Oh come on." She rolls her eyes. "Show those fuckers you're over her."

I say nothing. Just take a swig of my wine. Have another bite of octopus.

"You *are* over her, right?" Kelsey asks, her expression curious.

My gaze meets her, and I see the faint worry there. Does she think I still have feelings for Jessica? I suppose I do. But none of those feelings involve getting back together with her, or wanting her back. Or even missing her.

"Of course I am. Fuck her. Fuck him too, if I'm being real right now." I shake my head. Wipe my lips with my napkin. "I hate that he can just come into my office and disrupt my day like he did."

"Uh huh. I'm sure you do," Kelsey says carefully. "That's why it would be smart if you *did* agree to be a part of the wedding. That way you could disrupt their special day in your way, you know what I mean? At least for a little while. You'll be in all the wedding photos, for God's sake."

"That's true. Would she really want me as a reminder for their rest of their days? Making an appearance in their wedding photos?" I let the disgust—and the effects from the wine—wash over me. "I wouldn't want that sort of reminder personally. That's why I can't do it."

"Oh Theo." Kelsey smiles, this devious little curl of lips that is evil and sexy, all at once. "Yes, you absolutely can."

SEVEN
KELSEY

THEO FROWNS, completely perplexed by my words, no doubt. "What are you talking about?"

"Be a part of their wedding and let's put on a real show for them," I say, my entire body warm and loose from the wine I've been drinking. I might be a little buzzed and currently studying the man across from me with alcohol-clouded eyes.

He is so stupidly good-looking in that suit. When did that happen? I've never denied Theo is attractive, but lately I'm tempted to fan myself every time I get around him, he's so hot.

His hair is a little mussed, as if he's been running his fingers through it in frustration—a habit I can't help but notice. He's sporting five o'clock shadow on his cheeks and firm jaw. What would that stubble feel like, rubbing against my face if he kissed me? My inner thighs?

My entire body goes up in flames at that last thought.

Reaching for my wineglass, I take another gulp, sad when I finish it off. "We need more wine," I say absently. Theo's not even listening to me.

"What do you mean by putting on a real show?" He is adorably confused.

"Well…I was thinking something like buying the sexiest dress I can get away with wearing to a wedding and show up in it. I'll hang all over you the entire time. Once the reception starts, I will never leave your side. We can dance the night away and I'll let you touch my ass. I'll also let you kiss me," I explain, drunk on the idea of being with Theo like I'm his girlfriend.

His eyes flicker with interest at my words, but otherwise his expression stays the same. Polite. Attentive. "You'll really let me *kiss* you?"

I roll my eyes. "Is that the only part you zeroed in on? I figured you'd like the part about me wearing the sexiest dress I can get away with at a wedding."

"How sexy are we talking?"

"How formal is this wedding?"

"I'm guessing fairly formal. Ours was supposed to be," he says with all the nonchalance of referencing yet another boring day.

I don't know how he does it. I don't know how he's able to control himself around his cousin and not tear him apart with his bare hands. Craig stole his fiancée. And now the asshole has the nerve to ask Theo to be one of his groomsmen?

Is the dude completely clueless? Or is he purposely trying to drive Theo insane?

Realizing Theo is waiting for me to continue, I scramble to come up with something to say. "I'll find a dress with a drastic neckline or a super-short skirt," I tell him, wondering if I could possibly find both.

"A drastic neckline?"

"To show off my tits, Theo," I tell him, pleased when his cheeks turn the faintest red at my saying the word *tits*.

Too cute.

"They're my greatest asset," I remind him with a laugh.

"Nah, that's your face," he says quickly

My laughter dies and my chest grows warm. "What?"

"Your face." He waves a hand in my general direction. "You're fucking beautiful, Kels. Hasn't anyone ever told you that? Of course they have. I'm sure there's an endless list of men who've told you you're beautiful."

Fine, yes, but their compliments never felt as good as the one that Theo just delivered. I can barely contain the smile that stretches across my face and I duck my head, staring at my hands curled in my lap as I try to gather my emotions.

He thinks I'm fucking beautiful. I honestly believed he never noticed, and I was okay with that.

I'm okay with him noticing too.

"My family won't believe that we're together," he says.

I lift my head at his statement. "What do you mean?"

"You're too gorgeous. Out of my league. Jessica might not believe it either," he says morosely, reminding me of the Theo I first met. The one who was consistently down and out, who believed he had zero game and thought all women were out to get him.

I liked that Theo too. His bitterness fueled my bitterness toward the opposite sex, and we were bitter together. Like partners in crime.

"I am not out of your league. Look at you." Now I'm the one waving at him. "In your fancy suit, drinking expensive wine—"

"That you ordered." He smiles.

I grin. "Right. But you pulled up in your gorgeous BMW—"

"You like my car?" He sounds surprised.

"Stop interrupting me," I tell him coolly. "Yes. I like your car. You have a lot of things going for you. And I'm just...me. Just doing my thing. Why wouldn't I go for you?"

"You really mean that?"

"Yes." I nod. "I do."

We stare at each other, the candle flickering, laughter sounding from the table behind me. I would totally go for a guy like Theo if I hadn't sworn off men. He's so kind. So real. He's got his shit together, and after the endless string of dates and semi-boyfriends I've dealt with over the last few years, that's refreshing.

Theo clears his throat. Glances longingly at his empty wineglass, as if he hopes it would magically refill too. "Well. I—"

"Are you two ready to order dinner?"

I startle, jerking my head up to find the server smiling at me, his gaze smoldering. He's rather flirtatious. "Oh, I forgot..." I glance over at the menu sitting discarded beside me.

"Grab us another bottle of wine and we'll be ready to order when you come back," Theo tells him, his voice bossy. Demanding.

Wow, that was kind of hot.

The server shoots him an annoyed glance as he says, "Of course. I'll be right back."

The moment he's gone, Theo lets out an irritated...

Growl?

"What's wrong?" I ask him, reaching for the menu and cracking it open.

"He's flirting with you," he gripes. "Or did you not notice?"

"I guess so." I'm surprised Theo did. And he sounds almost...

Jealous?

What in the world is going on here?

"Asshole," he mutters as he grabs his menu and jerks it open, like he wants to rip it in half. "What are you going to get to eat?"

"I'm not sure." I lift the menu up a little, peeking over the edge so I can study him. Theo appears surly and discontent. He's scowling as he reads the menu, his hair falling over his forehead, almost into his eyes. He swipes at the thick strands distractedly, his upper lip curling the slightest bit and my lips part.

Maybe I've had too much wine, but Theo's—doing something for me tonight. Sexually. I haven't had sex with someone in a while. Too long, really. I know he's going through the same thing. I'm guessing we're both full of repressed urges that are bubbling closer and closer to the surface.

The server returns a few minutes later with more wine. He refills each of our glasses and then takes our orders. Theo asks for pan-seared scallops. I order garlic chicken. The server tries to engage me in light conversation, but I offer up one-word answers until he finally takes the hint and leaves.

"That guy won't let up," Theo says, still sounding a little growly. "What a dick."

"I'm not interested in him," I tell Theo, reaching across the table to rest my hand over his.

Theo's gaze lifts, meeting mine, and now he's the one who's smoldering. We look into each other's eyes for a too long to be thinking friendly thoughts moment. "I think I'm drunk," he finally says, slipping his hand out from beneath mine.

Blame it on the alcohol. That's a good excuse. Though he's probably right. I'm just—putting feelings onto Theo that have no business being there.

Right. Of course. That's it.

AS THE EVENING CONTINUES, we make a few mistakes.

First, we drink too much.

Second, we laugh. A lot. Plus, a man who makes me laugh? One of my absolute weaknesses.

Third, we don't eat enough bread. I've always heard that bread soaks up alcohol quickly, but Theo is exhibiting excellent control when it comes to food tonight and I've been avoiding carbs lately so...

Yeah. Here we are, arguing about leaving a tip for our server. Theo wants to give him five bucks.

"That's not enough," I tell him, letting my irritation shine through. "Just because he flirted with me..."

"Fine. I'll leave him five dollars and you leave him your phone number. That should be more than enough tip for him," Theo says grimly.

What in the world?

"I'm not giving him my number." Now I'm kind of pissed. "Why would I do that?"

"He's totally into you. I'm surprised he's not sporting a boner every time he gets near our table," he bites out.

"Please." I wave a hand. "I'm not interested."

"You're extra nice to him," he throws at me like a jealous boyfriend.

"It's called being polite, jackass." I grip the edge of the table, glaring at Theo. "There is a difference, you know. Or are you going to be like all those other guys?"

Well. Those were fighting words I just tossed at him.

"What the hell are you talking about? What other guys?"

"Don't play dumb. You know what I mean," I say.

I watch as he scratches out a more than generous tip for our server onto the receipt and signs his name with a flourish, dropping the pen onto the table. He grabs his credit card and slips it into his slim black wallet before opening up the jacket he just shrugged back on and tucking the wallet into the pocket within.

"I don't know what you mean, Kelsey. Spell it out for me," he says, leaning back in his chair.

Ooh, I'm angry. I don't even know why. Wait, I know why. I don't like what he said. What his words implied. "Men I've been with in the past always believe I'm flirting with every man I talk to when I'm only being nice. Cordial. It's annoying. I haven't once flirted with the server tonight, Theo, but you accused me of doing exactly that. And it's not fair."

Grabbing my purse from the ground, I rise to my feet, tossing my napkin onto the table. "Thanks for dinner. I owe you."

With that, I turn around and exit the restaurant's patio.

Within seconds I hear Theo call my name. I ignore him, picking up the pace as I head for where I parked my car. It's completely dark outside, and there aren't very many streetlights that line the roads, so I'm squinting as I hurriedly walk, hoping that I'm going in the right direction.

Did I mention that I'm still fairly buzzed? And there's no way I should be driving home. I live too far. In a small, shitty studio apartment in Monterey. I don't like talking about my place to anyone. Not even my friends. It's the worst.

More than anything, that awful apartment depresses me.

"Kelsey!"

I turn right onto the next street, knowing without a doubt I'm going in the wrong direction. But I don't care. Forget the car. My mission is to get away from Theo. Maybe I should call an Uber. I can get home and have someone drive me to pick up my car tomorrow.

Though it might get marked by the meter police. And if it sits long enough, especially on a Saturday, it'll probably get towed.

Whipping out my phone, I realize that's a chance I'm willing to take.

I bring up the Uber app when I feel fingers curl around the crook of my elbow, stopping me. I whirl around to find Theo standing close. Too close. He's breathing hard too, like he'd just been running after me.

"There you are," he says between heavy breaths.

I try to tug my arm out of his hold but his grip is too tight. "What do you want?"

"Why'd you leave so fast?"

"I'm mad, Theo, okay? Don't you get it?"

He frowns, his dark eyes full of worry. His hold on me gentles, and oh God, he slowly slides his fingers up my arm, a scattering of goose bumps following in their wake. "I'm sorry. I'm a little drunk. I'm mad too. At that stupid server. And you."

"Why are you mad at *me*? I'm here with *you* tonight," I remind him.

Theo snorts. I don't think I've ever heard him do that before. "As my friend."

"What's wrong with that? That's what we are, right?"

Right?

The word echoes in my head as we continue staring at each other. My breath start to accelerate too, and it's amazing, how his hand on my arm somehow steers me closer to him. I don't know how he did that. I don't know what's happening right now either.

He dips his head down.

I tilt my head back.

Our gazes are locked. My breath lodges in my throat when I see how he watches me.

Like he...

Wants me.

EIGHT
THEO

YEAH, no. Can't do it. Can't kiss Kelsey and ruin everything. Our friendship. The easy camaraderie we share.

It was fun tonight, eating dinner with her, drinking and talking and laughing. The stupid server had to keep staring at her for too long and it set me on edge. Worse? I was jealous. Jealous of a guy who doesn't even know Kelsey, who obviously thought she was sexy as fuck and couldn't stop looking at her. Can I blame him? No. Was I being ridiculous? Yes. She's here with me. She came to dinner with me.

And then I had to go and ruin everything.

I let go of her and take a step back, needing the distance. She takes a gulping breath. Exhales with a shudder. My gaze drops to her chest.

Stop it!

I lift my traitorous gaze to hers—her eyes are glazed.

"We're in bad shape."

She blinks at me. "What do you mean?"

"You're drunk." I point at her. "I'm drunk." I tap my thumb against my chest. "We can't drive."

"This is why God made Uber," she says with a finality

that must sound logical to her, but nope. Not working for me.

"No Uber." I shake my head. "I can't leave my car here all night."

"Pick it up in the morning." She starts tapping on her phone, and I swipe it right out of her hand. "Hey!"

"Let's go sober up somewhere." I glance around, my gaze snagging on intersecting street up ahead. Just around the corner is Sweet Dreams. "We can get coffee."

"Sweet Dreams is closed."

"Damn it."

"Theo, there is nowhere to sober up." She glances around, her expression brightening when she faces me. As if something suddenly hit her. "Wait a minute! I know where we can go. Stella's apartment."

"Uh, will Stella be there?"

"No, she lives in her nonna's house now. No one lives in the apartment above Sweet Dreams, though most of the furniture is still there. I hear her brothers use the apartment sometimes, so it's pretty much fully stocked." She makes a gimme motion with her hand. "Hand over the phone so I can text her."

I reluctantly hand it over. She starts typing, and I watch her, momentarily entranced. Damn it, she's beautiful. Why didn't I kiss her again?

"Okay, yes." She's nodding and typing at the same time. I can hear the whoosh of a text being sent and received, again and again. "Stella said we can crash out at her apartment."

"You have a key?"

"She hides one. I know where it's at. Come on." Kelsey grabs my hand and we start walking toward the very street I was just staring at.

Within minutes we're at Sweet Dreams. Stella's old apartment sits above the bakery/café, and we go around the back of the building, heading up the narrow stairway that leads to the apartment. There's a tiny black mailbox hanging on the wall beside the door, and Kelsey reaches behind it, withdrawing a key dangling from a little chain.

"Ta da," she announces, waving the key in front of my face.

"That doesn't seem very safe," I say, watching as she sticks the key into the deadbolt and unlocks it. "Leaving the key behind the mailbox."

"No one has found it so far," she sing-songs, wagging her butt back and forth as she turns the handle and opens the door. "Come in."

I follow her into the apartment, blinking against the bright overhead light when she turns it on. The apartment is tiny. Sparsely furnished. There's a couch, end table and a small coffee table in the living room, along with a flatscreen TV hanging on the wall. Kelsey goes to the lamp sitting on the end table and switches it on.

"Turn off that light." She points at the fixture on the ceiling and I do as she says, grateful the harsh light is gone. "How about we watch a movie?"

"Or we could go to bed," I suggest.

Her eyes flare for the briefest moment. Like she believes I'm suggesting we go...have sex. And that she's...interested.

Say what?

"I didn't mean, like, go to bed and get naked." I chuckle nervously, banishing the image of a naked Kelsey from my brain. "I meant, uh, that we should go to sleep. You can take the bed. I'll sleep on the couch. Or isn't there another bedroom?"

"Theodore."

I meet her gaze, feeling like an idiot. A feeling I've never experienced with Kelsey before. "Yeah?"

"It's like...nine o'clock on a Friday night. We're not going to sleep yet." She plops onto the couch and pats the empty space right next to her. "We're going to watch a movie."

Keeping my gaze on her, I shrug out of my suit jacket and drape it over the back of the couch. Loosen my tie, then yank it off. Undo the buttons at my wrists and roll up my sleeves. Kelsey turns on the TV, then proceeds to log into her Netflix account, but I can tell she's also watching me.

Huh.

"Come on. Help me pick something out." She sounds impatient and I go to her, settling beside her but not too close.

Close enough to feel her warmth. To smell her perfume. When she turns to look at me, her hair brushes against my arm and I want to groan.

What the hell are we doing? What the hell am I *thinking?*

"I'm sorry about our argument earlier. And how I stormed off," she says, her voice small. "I became—irrationally angry."

"I'm sorry too. I was a jealous asshole," I say, meaning every word.

She slowly shakes her head. "I don't know what you have to be jealous about. I wasn't even paying attention to that guy."

I refuse to get into it. Is this what it would be like, becoming involved with Kelsey? Would I be jealous of every guy who looked at her with undisguised interest? Would I become a possessive asshole ready to fight every jerk who dared look her way?

Nah. I'm just—wary. On the defensive, thanks to Jessica cheating on me. With my cousin.

I need to stop thinking about her. And Craig. Who cares? I don't care.

We scroll through the Netflix menu until we finally settle on some new creepy movie with true horror vibes. I hate scary movies, but Kelsey seemed dead set on it, so I don't argue. Instead, I sprawl my legs wide, throwing my left arm along the back of the couch. If I wanted to, I could reach out and tug on the ends of Kelsey's hair. Run my fingers through it. See if it's as silky-soft as it looks…

She's sitting on the edge of the couch and glances over her shoulder, smiling at me. "Don't you look comfortable."

I shrug one shoulder. Trying to act like this is no big deal.

Really? Her nearness is driving me out of my mind. We've spent plenty of time together, but always in public. At restaurants. Conferences. Cocktail parties. That sort of thing. We've never been at each other's house. Or rode together in a car. We've kept our interactions fairly neutral.

There is nothing neutral about this location. It feels like a hookup pad. There's a bedroom in this place. Pretty sure there's maybe two? And yeah, if there are two bedrooms, we could each sleep in our own bed and act like this night is no big deal. Just two friends sleeping off a drunken evening. Get up early and head on to our respective homes and pretend it never happened.

Or we could share a bed, get naked and get down to business.

I'm thinking I prefer option two.

"Want a snack?" Kelsey asks, her sweet voice pulling me from my dirty thoughts.

"A snack?" I'm frowning. "I thought no one lived here."

"What do you mean?"

"If no one lives here, then there shouldn't be any food, right?" I send her a pointed look.

"I texted Stella and asked if she left any snacks behind." Kelsey pauses the movie she literally just started and leaps to her feet, looking very pleased with herself. "She said we have a few options."

She dashes into the tiny kitchen and I can hear her rummaging around. The tear of a plastic wrapper. A microwave door opening and closing, then the distinct beeping as she hits buttons and the microwave hums to life.

The scent hits me right before it starts to pop.

Popcorn.

"You want a Coke?" she calls.

"Sure."

She fills a couple of glasses with ice and cracks open two cans of Coke, and I can hear the glugging sound of the soda as she pours them into our cups. Every little sound is heightened in the otherwise quiet of the apartment. I don't even hear any traffic pass by on the road outside. It's like we're the only two people in the world, about to indulge in shitty microwave popcorn and Cokes—I haven't drunk soda in almost a year, but screw it—watching a scary movie so I can have nightmares later tonight.

It's worth it, though. To spend the rest of the evening with Kelsey. Snuggled up with her on the couch. Sharing a bowl of popcorn with her.

"You need some help?" I ask as I stand and stretch my arms above my head, a little groan leaving me when I feel the ache and strain in my muscles. I'm tired. It was a busy week. I always look forward to the weekend, yet I find myself still working. For once, maybe I should ignore my laptop and my inbox and just—relax.

"Please," she says when I'm already in the kitchen. "Grab the drinks. I'll get the popcorn."

We return to the couch, the drinks on the narrow coffee table in front of us. Kelsey settles even closer beside me, the bowl full of popcorn resting in her lap. I reach for a handful at the same time she does, our fingers sliding against each other in the warm popcorn, and everything in my body goes on high alert.

Who knew popcorn could be considered erotic?

Yeah. I'm drunker than I thought.

"Sorry." She removes her hand from the popcorn and grabs the remote, pressing play on the movie. "I can't believe we're hungry after eating all that food at dinner."

"Popcorn is my favorite," I admit, grabbing a handful and shoving it in my mouth.

"It's mine too!" She turns to look at me with wide eyes. "I *love* it. Kettle corn is my utter weakness."

"Yeah. Same. I live for that shit they make fresh at festivals."

"Right? It's hot and sugary, yet salty too?" A low murmur of approval escapes her. "Delicious."

My mouth is dry from that sexy noise she just made, and I cough, nearly choking on the popcorn I'm still eating. "So." *Cough cough.* "Delicious."

Again, I'm an idiot. What is this woman doing to me? Why am I suddenly having these feelings?

There's nothing sudden about these feelings, jackass. You've just been suppressing them. You've been attracted to Kelsey for a while. For months. You have a favorite porn star who looks like her, for God's sake. Face your fucking feelings for once and tell her.

Nope. Can't do that.

We watch the movie in silence, the only sound

munching popcorn or one of us sipping our Cokes. I'm trying to concentrate on the storyline, but I can't. Kelsey is too damn distracting. The way her brows lower when a scene from the movie becomes tense, her full lips pursed. The little squeal she makes when a knife arcs through the air, landing right in a gasping woman's chest.

I cover my eyes a little too late when that happens. Scary movies freak me out. When I was ten, a friend of mine invited me over to spend the night. He was a horror movie lover. He learned to appreciate them thanks to his parents, who also had a strange fascination with them. We all settled in to watch a movie called *The Fog*.

That shit scarred me for life. Vengeful sea ghosts out to right the wrongs brought against them one hundred years later by slaughtering as many people as possible during the course of one night? No thanks. Ten-year-old me was freaking the hell out.

My friend thought it was hilarious. I tried to play it off. Until I woke up screaming at two in the morning and my friend's mom had to call my mom, who came and picked me up.

I keep telling myself this shit isn't real, but I lose my appetite. No more popcorn for me. I try to think of other things. Like the beauty that is Kelsey. But my beauty is also totally into this movie, and she's enjoying every single minute of it too.

The little sadist.

Slice goes the knife as the killer stabs the shit out of some innocent dude, the blade wielded a little too close to that guy's junk to make me comfortable. Unable to help myself, I slap my hands over my eyes, praying the gruesome scene is almost over soon.

Kelsey starts laughing, and I know I've been caught.

"You're covering your eyes like a little kid," she says gleefully.

I spread two fingers wide so I can look at her. "This shit is scary."

"Oh, come on. It's hilarious. She just sliced off that guy's penis." Kelsey laughs some more, her eyes dancing.

I'm too focused on the fact that she said the word *penis*. And how she found it funny that he got it sliced off. I don't care if it's a movie, she seems way too happy to have witnessed that.

"You still hating on men?" I ask her, letting my hands drop.

The movie is forgotten. "What do you mean?"

"Is that why you're loving this movie? It seems like our killer is hell bent on making everyone suffer." I'm only just now coming to this conclusion.

Kelsey shrugs. "I don't hate *you*."

It's the way she says it. The vulnerable tone of her voice. The soft look on her face. The glow in her eyes. We stare at each other a moment too long, the guy who just got carved up screaming in agony still and I do something completely out of character.

I rest my hand on her knee. Briefly.

Curve my fingers around so they're sliding up her inner thigh. Slowly.

My gaze never strays from hers, and regret smacks me in the chest for only a moment.

She doesn't stop me. She doesn't say no. She doesn't push my hand away from her.

Holy.

Shit.

NINE
KELSEY

ONE SECOND I'm laughing about the movie, way too into the scene where she slices off that pathetic dude's dick, and the next...

The next...

Theo's touching my knee. My thigh. His fingers are firm. He knows what he's doing. His touch is—not friendly. Not friendly at all.

It's...sexual.

My entire body goes on instant alert. Heat blooms in my chest. In other body parts too. My mouth goes dry and I tilt my head down, watching as his hand creeps up, getting closer and closer to where I start to throb.

Throb for him.

Oh my God.

What is even happening right now? I could blame the alcohol, but I don't think that's the problem. I'm definitely more sober than I was at the restaurant. Maybe we've been building up to this moment for months and I never even realized it.

Honestly? I tended to keep him at arm's length. Just like

I do with everyone else in my life, with the exception of the friends I've made in the last year, thanks to Caroline. Who knew that moment she spotted me in the bar at Tuscany restaurant after I got stood up by my date and invited me to have dinner with her friends would change my life forever?

Change it for the better.

They're the only ones who know the closest version to the real me. And even then, they don't see everything. Because I don't let them. Being vulnerable isn't smart. My mother hammered that home way too many times to count. She had a wall up throughout her entire life—and so do I.

Don't get too close, the tiny voice in my head whispers. *They might find out your secrets.*

What's scary? Theo has the potential to bust all my walls down. Every single one of them. And I bet he doesn't even realize it.

He currently says nothing, and neither am I. I wait in breathless agony as those fingers smooth back down to my knee. He's a tease.

I like it.

Without hesitation, he reaches for me. I go to him. His arm snakes around my waist and pulls me in closer. I rest my hands on his hot, hard chest, my gaze locking on the spot where his collar lies open. I want to press my mouth right there, on his bare, warm skin. I want to feel his pulse throb beneath my lips. I want to hear him groan. I want to feel his hands in my hair.

I have no idea what's come over me, but when I lift my gaze to his, I see the same deep need reflected in his eyes. He's thinking the same thing. He wants the same thing.

I want him. He wants me.

What's stopping us?

Logic, the word whispers through my brain.

Friendship.

Both of those words should make me hesitate, but I don't.

Curling my fingers into his shirt, I pull him in closer, his face hovering above mine, his lips right—there. I zero all my focus in on his mouth. His full lower lip. It's sexy.

I'm tempted to bite it.

Our breathing accelerates and his head dips. His mouth grazes mine. It's a question.

Do you want this? Should we do this?

Leaning in, I press my mouth to his in answer.

Yes. Yes.

Can he feel my internal begging? Because I am. Begging, that is. I can sense his hesitation, and I wonder if it's that moral high ground he so carefully cultivates. He wants the public to see a certain version of him, just like I do. The man has been in denial for months. He's not in pain. He doesn't care if his fiancée cheated on him with a blood relative. No big deal, right?

It's a huge deal to Theo. He hurts. He bleeds. He's mortal. Throwing himself into his career to forget all that pain is only half his story.

I want to know the rest of the story. I want to discover the rest of the man.

His lips are soft, and the moment they touch mine with true purpose, tingles sweep over my skin, making me shiver. Even as I long for more, I also know this probably shouldn't happen, I think as he kisses me again. His big hand slides up my back, until his fingers are in my hair, tugging on the ends. A moan escapes me at that first pinch of delicious pain, and he does it again.

I decide to provoke him by sinking my teeth into his plump lower lip. Not too hard at first. Just enough to sting.

He growls and deepens the kiss, his tongue sliding into my mouth. I circle my tongue around his eagerly, a sigh escaping me when he retreats, his kiss chaste once more.

Fuck chaste. I want more.

Climbing on top of him comes naturally. I straddle his lean hips. Wrap my arms around his neck. Thrust my fingers into the thick, soft hair at his nape so I can tug his head back and kiss him like I mean it. He kisses me back like he means it too. As if he's always meant it and has restrained himself for far too long.

I can feel all that restraint pulsating at the surface, and I want him to unleash it all over me.

Hands start to wander and I press my chest into his palms whenever I can. Still no words are spoken. It's probably better we do this in silence. Words will just mess everything up, and I can't risk it.

Though I do whimper when his lips find my neck. I love it when someone kisses me there. It's one of my more sensitive spots. His lips are damp. Hot. I'm shivering as he continues kissing my throat, his hand sliding beneath the hem of my shirt, making connection with the bare skin of my waist. His fingertips are rough. His lips find my ear. So do his teeth. I tilt my head to the side, giving him better access, and he takes it.

My hands go to the front of his shirt and I start undoing the buttons with trembling fingers. I've never seen him without his shirt off, and I'm eager. Sloppy. Shaky. It takes me longer than it should to undo all those stupid buttons, and he doesn't once reach out to help me, the bastard. When they're finally undone and his shirt hangs off him, I pull away, my gaze dropping to the glory that is his bare chest.

It's wide and muscular, but not too overdone. Dark,

curling hair covers the spot between his pecs, spreading over his pecs too. A dark trail leads down to his navel and past, arrowing below his pants.

My mouth waters at the thought of following that path.

I've always had a fairly casual attitude toward sex. I lost my virginity at the age of fifteen with no regrets, and have had regular sex ever since. I wouldn't call myself sex crazed, but I do enjoy it. And I've had sex with a variety of men. Does this make me a…slut? I don't refer to myself that way. Of course I don't. I just have more of an attitude like a man. They get to do whatever they want, whoever they want, and no one gives them any shit for it.

Women who act the same way? Forget it. We're too loose. We spread our legs too easily. It's freaking insulting.

Most of the time, I have sex because I want to feel something. Lose myself for a few minutes. Get out of my headspace.

Right now, though, for some reason, all I can do is think. Think about Theo. Worry about the consequences of what we're doing. How it will change everything. Or it can change nothing, considering I'm pretty damn good at pretending certain things never happened.

That's the way I need to handle this. Enjoy the moment and then act like it never, ever occurred in the first place.

A shrill scream fills the room, both of us jerking aware.

It's the movie. I don't even look at the TV to see what's happening. Instead, I rest my hand on the center of his chest, where I can feel his heart thumping beneath my palm. His skin is so hot, and his muscles tense up from my touch. Does he not want this?

I chance a glance at his face to see the turbulence in his dark eyes as he studies me, the determined set of his jaw. Oh, he wants this. Just as much as I do.

Once our gazes lock, it's on. He shrugs out his shirt. I kiss him all over his chest. His hands tug impatiently at my blouse and I help him help me out of it. He groans at first sight of me in just my bra and rains kisses on my plumped-up cleavage, his hands cupping me, his lips a teasing, too-light caress.

I want more.

He unhooks the bra like a man with infinite experience and I shrug out of the delicate lace. The moment he wraps his lips around my nipple, I clutch him to my chest, my eyes sliding closed at the rhythmic pull of his mouth. His lower half is lodged between my thighs and I wrap my legs around him, clinging to him. Wishing we were already naked.

And then suddenly we are. Clothes are hastily discarded. Mouths searching skin. Hands. His fingers slip between my legs to find me drenched for him, and when he keeps stroking me there, I immediately draw closer to the edge. So close, I'm about to tumble right over in only a matter of seconds.

He's gone. Leaving me on the couch a gasping, shaking mess. He grabs his pants from the floor and withdraws his wallet. Digs a condom out. Tears the wrapper off and holds the ring in front of his erection.

I watch in complete fascination as he sheathes himself. He's big. Long. Thick. Impressive. And it takes a lot to impress me. I've seen plenty of dicks to know when I've got a high quality one in front of me.

Theo's is a good one. Top grade.

Still no words are spoken. The air is filled with panting breaths, harsh inhales, shaky exhales. The movie is still going, and I assume it's heading toward the climax. The music ramps up, becomes intense. Louder.

Theo handles me as if he's done so for years. He grips

my hips and adjusts my body, one hand moving between my thighs to spread them wider. He's poised above me with a knee on the couch, his cock in his hand as he draws the head through my soaked folds. A hissing sound escapes me at first contact and I toss my head back, my eyes sliding closed as he torments me with both his fingers and his erection.

When he slides inside, I sigh with relief. I need this. More than I ever have. Once he's fully settled, he pauses, and I squirm against him. He pulses deep within me, I can feel him and I squeeze my inner walls, wrenching a groan from his throat.

"Fuck." His gravelly voice does something to me. This is a version of Theo I've never heard or seen before. As I've spent more time with him, I've grown to like him. Maybe even become...attracted to him.

Okay, yes. Why am I bothering to deny it when he's literally inside my body right now? I'm very attracted to Theo. And being with this gruff, sexual version of him is...

Hot.

I can't deny it.

He starts to move. Slowly pulling out before pushing back in. I keep my eyes closed, enjoying the smooth glide of his cock moving inside me. I lift my hips, keeping rhythm with him. It's easy. There's no awkwardness here. We move together, picking up the pace at the same time, our skin soon growing slick with sweat. His hands bracket my hips, stilling me completely, and he starts to pound inside me. His fingers bite into my skin. His thrusts are hard. Brutal. As if he's taking all of his aggression out on me.

I let him. It's hot. My stomach clenches. My clit throbs. I'm so close. My entire body tenses, and I gasp once. Twice. Three times.

Theo finds my clit, circling it with his finger again and again.

"Oh. Shit." I choke the words out, the intensity of it all making my brain go fuzzy. I lick my dry lips and he kisses me, swallowing my moan, his tongue tangling with mine.

I'm coming. His mouth, his finger, his cock. It's all too much. I shudder and shake, a keening cry I've never heard before leaving me when he doesn't let up.

He just keeps stroking. Keeps pounding. One hand still gripping my hip, his fingers cutting into my skin. His other hand is between our bodies, fingers playing with my clit. Destroying me. It's almost too much, and I writhe beneath him, desperate to get away.

Desperate for him to keep touching me like that.

"Fucking hell." The guttural groan he makes has me right back where I started only moments ago. Teetering on the edge, ready to...come again.

He's fucking me so hard, his balls slap against my ass with every thrust. Blindly I reach out, my fingers making contact with his chest, and I slide them down, touching his stomach, tracing the hair that leads from his belly to his cock. It's soft and damp and when my fingers make connection with the base of his erection, I hear a sharp intake of breath.

"Touch yourself," he commands, and I do it.

His hand falls away and I stroke my clit, my fingertips brushing against him every time he shifts closer. With my free hand I cup my breast. Toy with my nipple. Crack open my eyes to find him watching me with utter fascination.

"You're so fucking hot," he whispers when his eyes meet mine, and I smile. Increase my pace. I'm going to come again. I know it. And while I'm helping myself out, he also has plenty to do with this, which makes him my multiorgasmic-dream-come-true man.

"Are you going to come?" he asks.

I nod. "Again," I whisper.

He smiles, looking very pleased with himself. He is a mess. Nothing like the usual, straightlaced man I know. He's sweaty and naked and open and raw. I glance down to watch his cock move within my body, sliding in and out, and I sink my teeth into my lower lip, clenching my inner walls around him, gripping him tight.

"I'm gonna come too," he admits. "Hold on."

I don't get why he told me to hold on until I do. His movements become completely out of control, grunting every time he pushes inside me. I give up on stroking myself and just hang on for the ride, overwhelmed by his movements, how he takes complete command over me and I let him do it. This entire experience tonight has been so unlike any I've ever experienced...

A shuddery groan escapes him as he stills above me, and I open my eyes once more to watch as he falls apart. And he does so with complete abandon. His quaking body is a beautiful sight and he pushes inside me so deep, I feel the spasms take me over too.

Two orgasms created by one cock, I didn't think that was possible.

I think I'm in heaven.

TEN
KELSEY

WE STILL ON **for the BBQ at my parents' house?**

I stare at the text from my newest sexual partner and good friend, wondering how I should respond. Hating how unsure this all makes me feel.

What happened last night between us was one of the hottest experiences of my life. Which is absolutely mind blowing, considering who I had sex with. Sweet, unassuming Theo. My friend. The guy I had no real sexual feelings toward until last night. Who knew he was such a savage? He fucked me like he didn't care about my feelings, and honestly?

So hot.

After it happened, once our heart rates calmed and our breath settled, he hurriedly pulled his clothes back on and said he had to leave. I nodded in understanding, grabbing the thin throw blanket that was draped across the back of the couch and wrapping myself up in it so I wasn't the only naked one in the room. He offered me a kind smile, said "see you tomorrow" like no big thing, and slipped out through the front door.

That was it. No, *thanks for the fuck*, or even *I had a good time*. Nothing.

We had sex, he made me come twice, and then he left.

Way too easy, right? I know for a fact he's an emotional guy. He cares—sometimes too much. He can do long-term relationships, which means he knows how to catch feelings. Most women think that's a fabulous trait in a man.

Me? Not so much.

But I was mildly offended by his behavior last night when he left so abruptly. He acted like a total player. As if I were some random one-night stand. Now he's texting me about going to dinner at his parents' house, for God's sake, like nothing ever happened between us. Something I suggested we do to make us look like a legitimate couple.

Yeah. That's right. This was my idea.

Deciding I should answer him, I type out a response.

Yes. What time?

He responds quickly, like he was anxiously waiting for me.

Theo: **They want us there at two. I can come pick you up, say around 1:30?**

Me: **Give me directions and I'll meet you there.**

Theo: **Won't that defeat the purpose of us looking like a couple?**

He's so right, damn it. And won't we look like a couple now? We've seen each other naked. He's been inside me. He made me come with his fingers.

My body goes hot at the memories. Stupid body. I need to take some advice from our girl, our *queen* Taylor Swift, and fast.

I need to calm down.

Me: **Okay. You're right. But let me meet you somewhere.**

I glance around my shitty apartment, frowning. Stella's apartment that no one lives in is better than this hellhole, but it's all I can afford, considering my credit card debt, car payment and the outrageous rent. It's old, the building is decrepit and my neighbors aren't of the highest quality. Old Mrs. Fillmore who lives next door to me is a complete sweetheart, though, and I like to keep watch over her, just like she keeps an eye out on me. She's the only saving grace at this place.

Theo: **Why don't you want me to come to your apartment?**

Damn it, he's too smart. No other guy would ever care. Most of them would be grateful I don't want them to see my home. They're all afraid staying over is a sign of commitment. Or they worry about walking through my front door and seeing one too many cats, or that everything's decorated pink and frilly.

Men. They're ridiculous.

Me: **I live really out of the way.**

This is sort of the truth.

Theo: **I don't mind making the drive. I've told you that before.**

He's so thoughtful. So nice. Of course he doesn't mind. This is the man, after all, who fucked me so well, I worried I might pass out at one point. Seriously, my vision went hazy and I sort of forgot myself. Having sex with Theo was like an out of body experience.

Who knew?

Me: **I'll just meet you in the Safeway parking lot.**

We've done this before. He knows exactly what parking lot I'm talking about.

Theo: **You're really frustrating sometimes.**

Me: **Really, Theo? You weren't complaining last night.**

Oh shit. I just went there.

Theo: **Neither were you.**

Ha. He went there too. I don't fight the smile that spreads across my face. You're damn right I wasn't complaining. Two orgasms in a matter of minutes will do that to a girl.

Me: **??**

He hates it when I respond like that, and I respond like that a lot.

Theo: **Fine. 1:30 at the Safeway parking lot.**

Me: **See you then!!!**

I send a couple of kissy face emojis as per usual. He sends me a red angry face emoji in response, and I can't help but laugh.

At least he's acting normal. Like what happened last was no big deal.

Of course, we haven't laid eyes on each other yet.

"I SHOULD WARN YOU. My family can be...kind of overwhelming," Theo says as I climb into his slick BMW and shut the door. His car payment is probably as much as my rent. Worse, he probably owns the car free and clear, which makes me feel like an incompetent loser. I'm saving a little bit of money and trying to get my shit together. He's been helping me with that, Mr. Financial Planner Extraordinaire, but Theo's responsibleness makes me feel totally behind sometimes. Most of the time. As if I'm lacking, which I sort of am.

But hey. I'm still young. He's like in his thirties. He went to college and obtained a fancy degree, where I've been working my entire adult life, trying to get ahead. Of course he's got his shit together. I'll catch up.

Eventually.

"What do you mean, they're overwhelming?" I ask.

"They're a little crazy." He winces. "I'm the calm one."

"Huh. Well, I'm not scared. I know all about crazy families," I tell him, which is the truth. I could tell stories for hours about the things certain family members have done. None of them good. Most of them illegal.

He sends me a piercing gaze, one hand draped over the steering wheel, the other wrapped around the car's gearshift. He's wearing a black polo shirt and jeans, and there is nothing sexual about his outfit whatsoever, yet I can't help but think how sexy he looks.

Maybe it's the way the shirt fabric stretches taut across his firm chest. Or how tight the denim clings to his thick thighs.

I have a thing for thick thighs. Say that three times fast.

"Really?" He sounds curious. Probably because I never mention my family to him ever, and he's tried to ask. I just always divert the conversation. "You'll have to share those stories with me sometime."

"Sure," I say lightly, though I'm really saying *never going to happen*.

It's none of his business.

We make casual conversation the entire drive, and I'm lulled into what I can only assume is a false sense of security. We never once bring up last night. Or what happened between us. How I could still smell him on my skin when I first woke up this morning, or how sore I am between my thighs. I really took a pounding.

And I'm not complaining.

The drive to Theo's parents' house is long, and they live on one of those winding country roads that takes us deep into Carmel Valley. They seem to go on forever, and I'm sure it would be a more pleasant drive if I wasn't so nervous about meeting his parents. But I am. Nervous. My palms are sweating, which is ridiculous. This means nothing.

But I want them to like me.

When we finally pull up to the closed iron gate, I sit up and take notice. It's green and lush everywhere the eye can see. And there are so many grand oak trees, I can't help but wonder how long they've been on this earth. Probably hundreds of years.

"This is amazing," I breathe once we pull through the gate and we're heading down the endless driveway.

"My parents own sixty-five acres," Theo says, sending me a quick glance. "I grew up out here."

"It's so beautiful." We drive past a pond surrounded by trees that has the cutest little wooden dock. There are ducks floating along the surface of the water, and it all looks so peaceful and serene, I can actually feel my entire body relaxing.

I hadn't realized I was so tense in the first place.

"My parents don't ever want to leave. They love it out here," Theo explains.

"I would too if I were them," I say, my gaze locking on the two beautiful horses grazing in a field. "You have horses?"

"My sister used to ride when she was a little girl, but after a while, she got tired of it. Mom never tired of it, though. I think she got those horses more for herself." The fondness in his voice is obvious. Theo loves his mother, which is endearing. He always speaks highly of her, and truly, that is the sweetest thing alive. I've not had many long-term relationships, but every single guy I've dated had mom issues. Which makes sense, because I have mom issues too.

Theo loves his family. He's close with all of them. They take care of each other, and that is such a foreign concept to me, I'm not sure how I'm going to feel when I meet them. Are they all going to be sugary sweet? Extremely polite? I want them to like me, but I don't want them to try too hard. Cloying, over-the-top behavior is the worst.

"Stop worrying," Theo murmurs, reaching out to settle one of those large, surprisingly talented hands on my knee and giving it a gentle squeeze. I'm wearing a dress today, and his hand on my bare leg sears me straight through. "They're going to love you."

He releases his hold on me and I immediately miss it. I send him a quick glance, but he's concentrating on the road ahead, allowing me to look my fill. He didn't shave today, so the stubble lining his firm jaw gives him a rakish air. I devoured historical romances in my very early twenties, when I was looking for pure fantasy material. The emotionless, uptight duke with the proper manners and cold heart who's secretly a freak in the sheets? I loved that.

Also figured it was absolute bullshit.

But that description aptly applies to Theo. Looking at him, he's rather unassuming. Regular guy who works hard. Appears to come from a wealthy family. Very responsible. Attractive, but not outrageously so.

Though he's been stirring something inside me a little

more than usual, I must admit. And the sex thing...that was really surprising. We were positively combustible.

"Are you worried?" he asks after I haven't said anything for too long.

"Kind of. I don't meet parents very often," I admit.

"I know. You've mentioned that before." He glances over at me, only to find I'm already watching him. His expression softens, and I wonder if I look as nervous as I feel. "My parents are very approachable people."

"Like you?" He's the most approachable person I know, besides my group of best friends.

"Like me." He nods. "I also look a lot like my dad."

"Then he must be extremely attractive," I tease, though I'm being serious. "A complete DILF."

"A DILF?" I'm about to explain when realization dawns. "Ah, shit. I don't want you thinking about my dad like *that*."

I laugh. I can't help it. "Don't worry, I'm not into older men."

"Thank God," he mutters.

"Though you are a little older than me," I point out.

He sends me another look, one I can't decipher. "Not by much."

"You're thirty five?"

He rolls his eyes. "Thirty-three."

"I'm only twenty-seven."

"Six years isn't much," he says.

"But you're an older man. Something I can always hold over your head." I'm teasing, and he smiles.

"Being older means I have more experience."

"I'll say," I mutter, and he chuckles. The sound sends a warm sensation stirring in my stomach.

We pull into the circular drive, and Theo cuts the

engine. I stare up at the house, grateful it isn't as intimidating as I thought it might be. Though it's still gorgeous. It's a ranch house, with slate rock steps that lead to the window paned double doors.

One of those doors opens and a trim older woman steps outside, her arm raising in a wave as she eagerly starts down the steps toward the car.

I turn to face Theo once again, panic zipping through my veins. "Oh God, she's coming right for us."

He laughs. "She's my mom. She's happy to see me."

My mind is racing with all sorts of things to say, but it's like the words are lodged in my throat. Theo's gaze lifts, zeroing in on a spot just past my shoulder. He's watching his mom approach the car, I know it.

And then he does the craziest thing.

He leans down and kisses me.

His gentle mouth on mine immediately settles my racing thoughts, my pumping blood. I return the kiss, my lips parting easily for the quick swipe of his tongue and he takes advantage, sliding his fingers into my hair.

He pulls away at the same time the passenger door swings open and his mother practically drags me out of the car. "Oh my God, you're gorgeous!"

She hauls me into her arms and gives me a bone-crushing hug. I stand there helplessly, blinking at her when she grips my shoulders and holds me at arm's length so she can really examine me.

"Mom," Theo groans, climbing out of the car and slamming the door. "Stop. You're scaring her."

It's true. She's a little terrifying. And for such a small woman, she's incredibly strong.

"Theodore, you never told me your Kelsey was so beautiful." The words are said warmly. Reverently. Mom always told me my beauty's a curse. She accused me of drawing the wrong kind of attention from men, even though it isn't my fault. I can't help the way I look.

Funny thing is, I look exactly like her.

"Hey guess what, Mom? My Kelsey is beautiful." He stops directly beside me and reaches out, prying his mother's fingers from my shoulder that's closest to him. "Let her go. Introduce yourself. You're freaking her out."

"Oh! Sorry. My name is Patricia," his mother says, sticking her hand out for me to shake. "But you can call me Patti."

"It's nice to meet you," I tell her, realizing quick the hand out was a ruse.

She grabs hold of mine and pulls me in for yet another hug. "It's wonderful to meet you."

"Mom." His tone is a warning and she lets me go, smiling at me in apology. "Where's Dad?"

"Out back, messing with the barbecue." Patti's smile is still for me. It's like she can't stop looking at me. "My husband is obsessed with his new barbecue. The kids got it for him for his birthday from Costco, and he tries to cook everything on it."

"Even pizza," Theo adds.

His mother laughs, and it's a pretty sound. Pleasant. Friendly. I like her. She makes me feel comfortable, and I appreciate that. "The pizza wasn't bad."

"If you say so." Theo grabs hold of my hand like it's the most natural thing in the world, and smiles at me. "Let's go inside. I want to show Kelsey around the house."

"Wonderful." His mother watches us, and I can tell she's pleased. I have no idea what that's really like, pleasing a mother. The mother of a man I'm supposedly seeing. Most of them were never pleased to see me.

Did I mention I went through a bad girl phase? Of course I did. After my mom died when I was nineteen, I was on my own with no guidance. No help. No supervision. I was working three part-time jobs and trying to make ends meet, always craving attention, whether it was good or bad. I slept with one of my supervisors on the side to try to get a promotion. Gave him blowjobs while on the clock and everything.

Never did get that promotion, but he sure benefited from the arrangement.

Listen, I'm no angel. Truthfully, I'm ashamed of my past. Of the things I've done. But I can't make what I've done disappear. Once I got the job at Wilder, I changed my behavior. No more screwing the boss. Oh, I occasionally messed around with someone I worked with, but it was never serious.

That's me. The never-serious girl. Until I started to realize I deserve better than that. I *can* be a serious type of girl. I think. I want to try. But I need to find a man who loves me for me, not because of my face or my body. That's all surface stuff.

But I only seem to meet men who can't see beyond the surface. They're dazzled by my face. They don't care to actually get to know me. They just want to be seen with me. Show me off to their friends, like Paul did with Theo when we all went on that double date together. When Theo was set up with Eleanor.

I really miss her. Can't blame her for moving in with her hot, NFL-playing boyfriend, though. I'd do the same thing. Mitch worships the ground she walks on.

What's that like? I have no clue.

It's weird, how Theo never mentioned my looks to his mother. I mean, I know we're just friends. And he didn't think of me like that. But still. Men always mention my looks first. My face. It's what I've always led with.

Until now.

We enter the house, Theo's hand still firmly locked with mine, and I come to a stop in the entry, taking it all in. The floor is terra cotta tile, a plush multicolored rug covering the majority of it. Multiple family photos line the wall directly in front of us, all of them featuring happy faces smiling wide for the camera. I move closer so I can examine the photos, my gaze locked on a very young, very adorable Theo standing next to an older version of himself—I assume it's his father—both of them grinning.

"My dad," Theo explains when I turn to him. "I was fourteen in that pic. Right around eighth grade graduation, I think."

He's tall and painfully thin, but I can see the warm, familiar sparkle in Theo's eyes. I glance at the photo, then at the live Theo in front of me, smiling. "You were cute."

"I was shy and a complete introvert," he says, shaking his head with a chuckle. "Too scared to talk to girls."

The summer before high school I was reckless. Desperately wishing I was older. Wearing too much makeup. I'm sure I would've terrified Theo if we'd known each other, if we were closer in age. "You were adorable."

"If you're into nerds." He brings our linked hands closer to his mouth and drops a kiss on my knuckles, his gaze never leaving mine. I'm oddly touched. Strangely breathless.

But then I glance to my left to find his mother watching us with adoring eyes, and I know he did it for her.

My heart sinks.

He leads me through the sprawling house, his mother trailing after us and making the occasional comment. The tour is quick, the house beautiful yet well lived in, and eventually we make our way through the large kitchen and out the back door to the yard, where the rest of the family is congregating.

His father is at the giant barbecue with his back to us, one of Theo's brothers standing beside him as they both stare at the sizzling meat on the grill. Another guy is sitting at a picnic table across from a woman who appears to be in her early twenties, and I can only assume they're Theo's brother and sister. The man clutches a sweating beer bottle as he argues with the woman, who has an indignant expression on her pretty face.

Just another family Saturday, I suppose.

"Hey, you made it." Theo's father shuts the lid on the barbecue and makes his way toward us, a warm smile on his face, his gaze on me. "You must be Kelsey."

I let go of Theo's hand and step forward. "Nice to meet you."

His dad pulls me into a quick hug, not nearly as long or as bone crushing as Patti's. "Sorry, we're huggers," he says once he releases me. "Theo's told us a lot about you."

"Dad." Theo sounds vaguely accusatory.

"Oh Jim, don't embarrass him," Patti says as she plants herself firmly by her husband's side. "It's just been...rough these last few months. For Theo. We're just so happy he brought you here to meet us," she tells me, her voice lowering, like we're keeping a big secret. Right in front of him.

"Right," I say with a nod. She's referring to the breakup with Jessica.

"And then there's the wedding." Patti shakes her head, oblivious to the death stares both her husband and oldest son are currently sending her. "Can you believe Craig asked him to be a groomsman? The nerve of that boy. He was always such a bold one. Even when he was young."

"Mom," Theo says sharply. "We don't need to talk about that right now."

"No, I suppose we don't," Patti says, still oblivious. She turns her attention to me. "I'm just grateful he's met you, Kelsey. You've helped him get out of his slump."

I glance over at Theo, who looks like he wants to die. "We've been there for each other," I say truthfully.

"Theo mentioned you two started out as friends first," Patti says. "Isn't that the best way to fall in love? With your friend?"

Fall in love? Yeah. I don't think so. But I paste on a bright smile and nod, making my way over to Theo so I can stand beside him once more. "It's the best."

Theo slings his arm around my shoulders, his gaze on someone else. "Hey."

His brother approaches, the one who was standing by the barbecue only a moment ago, and good Lord, I think he might be more physically attractive than Theo. Hazel eyes, dark, wavy hair that's a little bit overgrown, and he walks with swagger. My absolute crack not even a few years ago. "Is that your girlfriend, bro? She's way too fucking hot for you."

"Jesus, Mason. Watch your mouth." Jim slaps the back of his son's head. "There are ladies present."

"Sorry." He doesn't sound sorry at all. His gaze is only for me, and it's currently eating me up with it. "This is really your girl, T?"

Theo's arm tightens around my shoulders. "Kelsey, this is my obnoxious younger brother, Mason."

"His charming younger brother." Mason doesn't even hesitate—just reaches out and grabs my hand, pulling me out of Theo's arms and in for a hug. He smells good. He's muscular, but I feel nothing. Not even a glimmer of attraction. "Nice to meet you, K."

"He shortens everyone's name," Theo says irritably.

Everyone's talking at once, voices rising as if they're all trying to be heard over one another, and Theo tugs on my hand, pulling me away from the group. "Let me show you around outside," he says.

We walk through the backyard, past the picnic table that now stands empty. "Who was your sister sitting with? One of your brothers?" I ask, glancing around.

"Yeah. She was with Max. Don't know where they went, though." Theo sounds distracted. Maybe even a little...angry? Frustrated? I don't know why. He said his family is big and loud and obnoxious, and they've already sort of proven to be exactly that, and not all of them are here yet.

Not that I mind. It's kind of fun, to see them all in action. His parents seem really sweet. His mom is overprotective, but I can tell she means well. His brother is a cocky asshole, but I've always been drawn to cocky assholes, so we'll probably get along fine.

"How many brothers do you have again?" I ask, practically running to keep up with his long strides.

"Three," he says distractedly. "There's five of us total."

I realize we're heading toward another building that sits in the near distance. It looks like a smaller version of the main house. He walks right up to the front door and opens it, striding inside, our hands still linked.

"Ali?" he calls, but there's no answer.

I'm frowning. Pretty sure he's calling his sister. But why?

"Looks like no one's here," he says, stopping abruptly in the short hallway.

I turn to face him fully. "Are you o—"

He grabs hold of my face and kisses me, cutting off my words. The kiss is long and deep and with plenty of tongue, and at first all I can do is just stand there and take it, I'm so shocked. His lips soften, become coaxing, and I find myself falling under his spell. Returning the kiss as if I'm starved for him.

And I am. Starved for him. It's just as good between us as last night. Maybe even more so, here in this small, empty house I'm assuming his sister lives in. In the middle of the afternoon with bright sunlight pouring through the windows and out in the open where anyone could catch us. Not that they would care.

We're supposed to be together, after all.

Theo breaks the kiss first, and I blink my eyes open to find him watching me. His damp, swollen lips are parted, and there's this...feral gleam in his eyes. Like he's on the hunt and he's scented me. Ready to move in for the kill.

A shiver streaks down my spine and my heart rate speeds up.

He streaks his thumb across my lips back and forth, his touch, his gaze hypnotizing me. "Your mouth drives me fucking crazy."

I blink up at him again, shocked by his confession. I didn't think any part of me drove him crazy. "Really?"

"Yes, really," he practically growls, kissing me again. He somehow walks me backward until my butt hits the wall, and then he's pressing me against it, his body close to mine, his hands dropping to curl around the back of my thighs and hauling me up. I go with it, wrapping my legs around his waist, shocked by his strength. Aroused by it.

Damn, Theo is strong.

I wore a dress because I wanted to make my best first

impression on his parents, and at this moment I definitely don't regret my decision. He slips one of his hands beneath the skirt, his fingers skimming the inside of my thigh. Grazing the front of my panties. I gasp into his mouth and he pulls away, his eyes never leaving mine as he strokes me there. Deliberately slow.

A complete tease.

"You're wet," he murmurs.

My eyes fall closed when his fingers sneak just beneath the thin fabric, making contact with my sensitive flesh. I press my lips together to repress the moan that wants to escape.

"And hot."

A whimper leaves me when he presses his thumb against my clit. What is he doing? Why is he touching me like this? Like he can't control himself and has to have me in the middle of the afternoon? Theo's always in control.

Always.

His mouth finds mine again, and I kiss him with all the enthusiasm I can muster, which is a lot. His fingers keep time with every stroke of his tongue, until I'm a panting, moaning mess, so close to coming I feel like I'm teetering on the edge of the earth, ready to plummet into an endless sky. I thrust my hips against his seeking fingers, needing more friction when...

A door creaks open. The front door.

Oh. Fucking. Shit.

Theo retreats from my mouth, his fingers remaining beneath my panties, his entire body going still as he glances toward the front of the house. I'm panting, my chest rising and falling frantically with each ragged breath, and he sends me a meaningful glance, one that says *be quiet*.

I keep my lips tight, but it's no use. Theo circles his

thumb around my clit, and another whimper escapes me. He presses his body to mine to keep me in place against the wall, clamping his other hand over my mouth.

Oh fuck. That's hot.

We stare at each other, my entire body trembling as we wait in breathless anticipation to get caught. No one says a word. Until...

"Theo?" a sweet voice asks. "Are you in here?"

I watch Theo tense up even more, his gaze cutting to mine. His expression is dark. Sexy. He strokes me again, sliding one finger inside my core, and a helpless noise leaves me, muffled by the press of his hand.

I glance down, catching sight of the impressive erection beneath his jeans, and I clench my inner walls around his finger, wishing it were his cock. His eyes darken even more, his gaze returning to mine as he inserts another finger inside me and starts move them in and out.

In and out. Again and again.

Oh. *God.* He's touching me like this on purpose. Knowing his sister is looking for him, for both of us while he finger fucks me. We're just on the other side of the tiny kitchen. It wouldn't take long for her to round the corner and find us. Talk about embarrassing. Talk about making a horrible first impression.

But she never comes searching for us. Instead, we hear the unmistakable click of the door shutting, and once she's gone, I figure Theo would remove his hand from my mouth.

He doesn't.

"You're close, aren't you?" he whispers harshly, his fingers starting to move in earnest. "Do you want to come?"

I nod wordlessly, my lids wavering when his finger hits a particularly sensitive spot. God, that feels so good.

"Can you breathe?"

Another nod. His fingers loosen around my face but remain in place, and I can't help but think how freakin' hot he is. How forceful he's being, how assured. I had no idea Theo could act like this.

He keeps stroking, his pace increasing, his thumb drawing tighter circles around my clit. It takes nothing to make me come. The situation alone had me halfway there, and an agonized cry falls from my lips when the orgasm slams into me. I'm a trembling mess, crying out against his hand and he drops it, replacing it with his mouth as he kisses me.

Devours me.

"You're so beautiful when you come," he murmurs against my lips once the shuddering has subsided. "I could watch you do that again and again."

I slowly open my eyes when he pulls away, frowning in confusion. Still in shock over his actions, how he had complete and utter command over me and my body. I don't know what we're doing, or why we're doing it. But I don't know how to ask. I'm almost afraid I'll break the spell if I do.

So I remain quiet instead.

ELEVEN
THEO

I'M STILL NOT sure what's come over me. Or why I attacked Kelsey like that.

Oh, fuck it. I know exactly why. I hated the way Mason looked at Kelsey. Like a potential conquest. As if he could snap her up, no problem. I'm sure he wonders why a woman like her is with a guy like me.

Can't think about the fact that she's not necessarily *with* me, though I definitely had her last night. Hottest night of my life. I did things to Kelsey I didn't know I was capable of.

Same with just now. Who the hell am I, slamming her against the wall and fingering her with my sister only a few feet away? Pressing my hand against Kelsey's mouth as I made her come with a few strokes of my fingers.

I'm feeling no remorse, though. No guilt either. I don't apologize. Why should I? I think Kelsey liked it.

A lot.

Slowly I loosen my hold on her, my hands resting lightly on her waist as her feet land on the floor. Only then I let her go. She lifts her head, offering me a shaky smile as she runs her fingers through her hair, and I take a step back, giving her some space.

I steel myself, ready for her to ask what the hell is wrong with me, or why did I do that, but she says nothing. Neither do I. Reaching down, I readjust my cock, wincing as I do so. I'm hard as a rock. Would give anything to sink inside her tight, wet heat and fuck her senseless, but we need to go out to the backyard before my family launches a search party.

Knowing them, they totally would.

"You hungry?" I ask.

Kelsey throws back her head and laughs, as if my question surprises her. "I'm starving," she admits.

"Me too," I say with a grin. "I have no idea what my father is cooking, but I'm sure it's delicious."

"Let's go then," she says.

"Let me wash my hands first," I tell her, making a stop in the kitchen and washing the smell of her off my fingers.

She doesn't seem the least bit embarrassed, and I'm grateful. She doesn't act full of regret either, which is a positive sign. What we're doing is probably dangerous. We're entering forbidden territory in regards to our friendship. Fucking on the low most likely isn't the move. Something will happen and eventually, our friendship will be ruined. That'll suck.

But it's too late. There's no turning back now.

We exit the house, me grabbing her hand and stopping her before she gets too far. She turns to me in question, her brows lowered, her mouth formed in a sexy little pout, and I want to kiss her.

Badly.

"You okay?" I ask, my voice low.

She nods, those sexy lips curling into a faint smile. Seeing it is like a punch to the solar plexus. She's a gorgeous woman. A woman I made come only a few minutes ago, and take my word for it, that is some powerful shit. "I'm great."

"You sure?" Jesus, I sound like old, insecure Theo right now. I need to knock it off.

"Yes." She takes a step forward, her hand going to the front of my jeans, her fingers curling around my erection. "How about you?"

A choked sound leaves me when she gives my dick a firm stroke. "Could be better."

Her knowing smile blows about a billion brain cells. "Maybe I could help you with that. Later."

I raise my brows. "Is that a promise?"

She gives a throaty laugh. "If you're lucky."

We pull away from each other when we hear more laughter, and realize my family is closer than we realized. I let Kelsey walk ahead of me, my gaze locked on her swishing hips, her perfect ass. That dress will be my undoing. It's red with little white flowers scattered all over it, and it shows off her long, sexy legs. Accentuates the dip of her waist, the curve of her hips. She is truly the most gorgeous woman I've ever been with. Totally out of my league. Maybe that's why it was so easy to be her friend, when I realized that was all she wanted from me. I could forget about her beauty because I figured I never had a shot.

Now, I not only had a shot, I've taken a few. Took one after becoming a quietly enraged, jealous asshole. Over my brother, of all people.

This woman is turning me inside out. I don't know if I like it.

Once we get closer to the back patio where my family is gathered, I catch up to Kelsey, grabbing hold of her hand so we can look like a united front. Ali spots us first, her expression full of surprise.

"There you two are!" she says, a little frown wrinkling her forehead. "Where did you go?"

"We took a little walk," I say vaguely.

"Your property is truly beautiful," Kelsey says to my mother, who's standing next to Ali. "I love it here."

"Hopefully Theo will bring you around more often," Mom says, shooting me a challenging look. I roll my eyes at her.

What is it about parents that make us revert to sullen teenagers?

I introduce Kelsey to my sister, and to Max, who both greet her politely, but not too over the top like the rest of them. They're a little more restrained, like me.

Both Mason and Max are standing with Dad, both of them checking out whatever's cooking on the barbecue. "Where's Cam?" I ask, referring to my other brother, Camden. He's the one closest in age to me, the one I fought with constantly when we were young. The one I'm closest to now.

"He said he'll try to make it, but no guarantees. Had to work today," Mom says, shaking her head. "I produced workaholic sons, I'm afraid," she tells Kelsey.

"It takes a lot of coaxing from me to get Theo to leave his office at a decent time," she tells my mother, sending me a warm look. Like we're a loving couple who can't get enough of each other.

Not so sure about the loving part, but I definitely can't get enough of her since last night.

"Oh Theo. Here you have this gorgeous girl who wants you to spend time with her, and you're always in your office?" Mom tsks and shakes her head. "Shame on you."

"Hey, I've gotten a lot better." *Since Jessica.*

The words hang in the air, unspoken but nevertheless

true. That was Jessica's biggest complaint. I never made time for her. Craig has all the time in the world for her, I guess. That's why she left me for him.

That and our sex life dried up. We rarely did it, and when we did, it was fairly standard. Missionary. Boring. Hell, most of the time we didn't even take all of our clothes off.

Maybe that's why I'm unleashing on Kelsey now. It's been so long, I'm like a deprived prisoner who's finally broken free.

"Food's almost ready," Mom calls as she makes her way toward the kitchen door. "Ali, will you come and help me, please? And Kelsey?"

The panicked look Kelsey has on her face fills me with concern, and I lean over, dropping a kiss on her cheek. "Don't be scared. They won't bite," I whisper in her ear.

She blinks at me, a tremulous smile on her lips. "You're really good at this pretending stuff," she says, giving my hand a hard squeeze before she releases it and joins my mother.

Once the women have entered the house, I go over to the barbecue to talk to my dad and brothers. Of course Mason has something to say.

"What the hell, T? Where did you find that gorgeous woman? She is way above you on the food chain, you know." He starts laugh.

Dad smacks his shoulder and sends him a scathing look. Max shakes his head in disgust. They're twins, Mason and Max, but they are also complete polar opposites of each other. Meaning most of the time, Max thinks his twin is an absolute asshole. Yet they balance each other out. They would do anything for each other. And all of us.

"Be nice," Dad says with a scowl. "I'm just glad your brother found someone after Jessica."

"We were afraid she fucked with your head permanently," Mason says, his tone grave. "Getting ditched right before the wedding has to be a major blow."

Leave it to my douchebag brother to remind me of that. "It sucked, yeah. But Kelsey has been a good distraction."

"I'll say," Mason says right before he cracks up.

"You need to shut the hell up," Max grumbles. "Leave him alone."

Mason stops laughing. They may be opposites, but Mason is always seeking Max's approval, which he rarely gets. "I'm just joking."

"It's a sensitive subject," Dad says, making me sound like a baby. "Getting dumped practically at the altar will do that to a person."

"Dad, what the hell." He's not making things any better. "It wasn't at the altar."

"Close enough," Mason says. "And I heard Craig asked you to be one of his groomsmen? Is that true?"

Gossip travels fast in our family.

"Yeah," I admit, not wanting to have this conversation.

"And you told him to go fuck himself, am I right?" Mason's brows shoot up.

"I told him I'd—think about it."

They all gape at me like I've straight lost my mind. Max is the first one to recover. "You're going to *think* about it? What's there to think about?"

"Your answer should've been 'hey, shove it up your ass, Craig'." Mason shakes his head, his expression full of disgust.

"You also should've kicked him out of your office." This comes from Dad.

They all three make a valid point. I appreciate how defensive they are of me. I also miss Cam. He'd probably be on my side with this.

I know he would be.

"Where is Cam anyway?" I ask. "Mom mentioned he's working."

"That's what he told us," Dad says, cracking open the barbecue lid to check yet again on his sizzling steaks. "Hope your girlfriend isn't a vegetarian."

"She's not," I tell him.

"Thank God. These steaks are going to be a masterpiece," Dad says reverently, making the rest of us crack up.

"What is Cam doing that's so important he skips a family get-together?" I ask, ignoring the disappointment I feel at my brother not being here. I wanted him to meet Kelsey. He wouldn't turn it into a bro moment. He would've been polite and asked her questions. Would've maybe dug some information out of her, possibly more than I ever could.

That's one thing I don't get about Kelsey. She's warm and fun and sweet and funny. A little sarcastic at times, but never cruel. But she's got a wall erected so high, I can't climb it. She never mentions her family. Ever. I have no idea where she grew up. Hell, I don't know where she lives currently, since she doesn't let me come over.

She's a mystery. One I've been wanting to figure out. Now even more so.

"He's got some sort of meeting in San Francisco this weekend," Dad says, grabbing his tongs and flipping the steaks over yet again. He turns the barbecue off before he shuts the lid. "Didn't say what it was about, though."

I turn to Max and Mason. "Did he mention anything to you?"

They both shake their heads, wearing equally confused expressions. The twins are fraternal, and you can definitely tell them apart. But their gestures, and the way they move and speak, are very similar. It's obvious they're twins.

My three brothers run a barbecue food truck together, and while I've invested in it as well, I'm the background guy, running the financials. They get their love of barbecue from my father. Cam started it up first with a couple of college buddies at the time, but his friends found different careers after graduating, while Cam wanted to keep running the truck. He recruited the twins to help him about five years ago, and now they have a pretty popular business. He's talked of expanding, and I agree it's the right move.

So what the hell is he doing, meeting with someone and not telling us about it?

"I wondered why he wasn't here, showing you how to do this." I wave my hand at the barbecue.

Dad thrusts a giant fork at me, a grim look on his face. "Those are fighting words, son."

We all laugh, the four of us turning when we hear the door open and the three women come back outside, each of them holding a giant plate of food.

"Mom's trying to fatten us up," Mason says with a sigh.

"No way." I pat my flat stomach. "I've been working out constantly. Eating right." Most of the time. Those burger lunches aren't so good for me. "I refuse to let her tempt me."

"Trying to look good for your new girl?" Mason teases.

I started working out for myself. I was feeling like shit after the breakup, all depressed and *woe is me*. Stood on the bathroom scale Jessica left behind after she took all her stuff, and got the shock of my life.

I was the heaviest I'd ever been.

I threw out all the junk food, from pantry to fridge, and

started going to the gym again. I wasn't fat, but I was soft. Pudgy. I hated it.

I hated myself.

Now I feel on top of my game. With everything.

Except for Kelsey. She fills me with a shit ton of doubt. I have no idea where our relationship stands.

Or what we're going to do about it when the wedding is over. Pretend we never did any of this and go back to our old ways? I'll stand by and eventually watch her date some loser while I remember how good the sex was between us?

That sounds pathetic.

But hey. It's all fun and games until someone gets hurt.

TWELVE
KELSEY

"OH MY GOSH, I can't eat another bite," I say with a groan as I lean back in my chair, as if creating distance between me and my plate will make me stop.

"There's still dessert," Patti chirps, and the entire table groans.

"We all don't have your metabolism, Mom," Ali says, making Patti frown. "She can eat whatever she wants and it never seems to affect her," Ali tells me.

"That's not true," Patti says.

Ali rolls her eyes and giggles. "It's so true. And so frustrating. I look at that chocolate cake sitting on the kitchen counter and gain five pounds."

"Oh no, chocolate cake is my weakness," I say with a little moan.

Theo's brothers stare at me with open mouths. Theo clears his throat. "Good to know," he says, his gaze all for me.

My cheeks go hot. Did I sound sexual with that moan? I was only thinking of food. Chocolate cake really is a weakness of mine.

Men. They make everything about their dicks, I swear.

"Perverts," Ali mutters, making me burst out laughing.

We chatted continuously throughout the meal. Theo's little sister—she's only twenty-one and quietly confessed to me she just dropped out of college—is very talkative, which I appreciate, since that means I didn't have to reveal much, while she's an open book. Every question I asked, she gave a long answer, and I let her talk. It was perfect.

Every once in a while, Theo would shoot me a look, as if he was trying to figure me out, and I just smiled. Let him think I'm a mystery—let his entire family think so. Actually, let's hope none of them notice that I'm not talking. That's preferable.

"Hey, serious question right now," Patti says, her attention turning to Theo. And me. "Are you two going to the wedding?"

"What wedding?" Theo asks innocently.

Mason and Max both crack up while their mother takes her napkin, wads it up into a ball and throws it at Theo, making direct contact with his cheek.

"You know what wedding I'm talking about. Your cousin's," she says.

"And Jessica's?" Theo raises a brow, his expression downright defiant.

I rest my hand on his thigh, trying to tell him he should stop acting like this and just answer the question. The situation is awkward enough.

"Yes," Patti says on a sigh. "And Jessica's."

"Are *you* going?" Theo asks pointedly, his gaze surveying the table.

"We were invited," Max says.

"Every single one of you?" Theo seems surprised.

"We're family," Mason reminds him. "We grew up together. So yeah. All of us were invited."

"And we're all going," Ali adds, her expression vaguely guilty. "Though it was wrong, what Craig did to you."

I can feel the muscles in Theo's thigh grow rigid. Clearly, this isn't a comfortable topic of conversation, and they know it.

"We're going too." Theo glances in my direction, his hand reaching for mine, which is still resting on his thigh. "I need to RSVP."

The table goes silent. In the distance, I hear one of the horses neigh. A breeze blows through the trees, making the leaves gently rattle. It's a peaceful, sunny Saturday late afternoon, yet you could probably cut the rising tension at this table with a knife.

Such a cliché, but it's true.

"Did Craig really ask you to be a groomsman?" Ali asks.

"Alice," Patti snaps, and I startle. That's the angriest I've heard her sound, and while shocking, it still wasn't even that bad.

"It's okay," Theo says gently, squeezing my hand. Is he talking to me or his sister and mom? I'm not sure. "Yes, Ali, Craig asked me to be one of his groomsmen. He showed up at my office out of nowhere Friday afternoon and asked me to be a replacement."

"A replacement?" Patti asks with a frown.

"I guess one of his friends got sentenced to jail time?" Theo shrugs.

Patti gasps, resting her hand on her chest. "Craig did hang around a dark crowd when he was younger."

"The nerve of that guy, asking you to stand beside him while he marries your ex," Max mutters, shaking his head.

"He's got balls," Mason adds.

Ali titters nervously. Both Patti and Jim send their kids looks that are meant to silence them, but I don't know how effective they are. Everyone in this family has strong opinions, and they're not afraid to voice them.

"Whatever. He's ridiculous, always has been. But don't worry about it. I'll just—turn him down and we'll attend the wedding. No big deal," Theo says, linking his fingers with mine. His touch is an assurance, and I glance down, watching his long fingers curl around mine, wondering if this is all fake. The way he looks at me, how he touches me.

Of course it is. This was our plan all along. The sex thing? That was repressed need exploding all over each other—quite literally. We both haven't had sex in so long, it was bound to happen. No big deal.

We'll go back to normal once this evening is over. We might mess around one more time, possibly even the day of the wedding, but that's it.

Maybe? I don't know. Everything that's happened between us is so confusing.

The wedding might be so stressful, though, that Theo won't be into it. Into me. I can't imagine what he's dealing with, or how he feels about everything. He's told me some of his worries and concerns, but we don't dwell on Jessica and what she did because it hurts him.

Maybe those feelings are still repressed too. Maybe...

He's still in love with her and this marriage is slowly killing him.

"I don't think Theo should turn him down," I say, surprised by my own declaration.

So is the rest of the table. They're all staring at me as if I dropped a bomb in the middle of dinner. Which I sort of did.

"What do you mean?" Patti asks carefully.

"Yeah." I glance over to find Theo contemplating me. "What exactly do you mean, Kels?"

He knows what I mean, but I guess he's going to make me explain myself in front of his family. Maybe so he can get their opinion? I can tell they're all very close. And they genuinely love each other. Seeing them almost makes me wish I came from a bigger family.

I release his hand and start talking. And gesturing. A habit of mine when I'm nervous. "Craig sounds—clueless. Like he has no idea how badly his betrayal hurt his cousin and his family. Maybe if Theo agrees to being one of his groomsmen, it's a way for all three of them to come to terms with what happened."

"Come to terms with Craig screwing his fiancée behind Theo's back? Why is that even necessary?" Mason asks, sounding like a defensive little brother. This warms my heart, especially since I thought he was a complete douche when I first met him.

"It can also show Jessica that Theo is completely over her," I point out, my gaze meeting Theo's. I want to drive home that point. I want him over Jessica. Once and for all. "What guy would agree to something like that if he was still in love with her?"

Right?

They all start murmuring. Theo studies me as if I've grown two heads, and worry immediately fills me.

"Maybe I shouldn't have said that," I confess, my voice low and just for him.

He smiles, though it's strained. "You keep pushing for me to be in their wedding."

Pushing? I'm almost offended by his word choice, but I choose to ignore it. Instead, I lift my chin, going for indignant. "I think it's the right move."

"I don't know." His voice is full of doubt. "It might not be."

"But it could be." Reaching out, I gently nudge his hand where it rests on the table. "Come on. Just do it. Let's show Jessica you're completely over her."

He nods. Looks away. And again, I'm filled with worry.

My suspicions might be correct. He could still be madly in love with her. I suppose I can't blame him. He was with her for years. He was going to marry her. That's a major declaration of love, and I have no idea what that feels like. To be so in love with someone, you can imagine spending the rest of your life together. I usually can't see beyond next week with a guy. Well, I can with Theo. As his friend. His secret hookup.

"It's not a bad idea." This comes from Max.

Theo turns his attention onto his little brother. "What do you mean?"

"Being a groomsman. Showing Jessica you're over her. She's a complete bitch for what she did to you."

"Maxwell," Patti breathes, but Max only rolls his eyes.

"Mom, it's true and you know it. I'm sure you think Jessica is a total bitch for cheating on your son," Max says irritably.

"Of course I'm disgusted by her behavior, and Craig's especially. I just don't call them names out loud," Patti says with a little sniff.

Jim reaches out and gives her shoulder a squeeze. "It's okay, sweetheart. We're all defensive of Theo, and we're allowed to insult Jessica on occasion. And Craig as well. I still can't believe what he did to my son. I held a real grudge against him there for a while, but I *think* I'm over it. Not so sure about Theo, though."

I almost want to laugh, but damn, it's true. Jessica

deserves their hatred. Despite being a relative, so does Craig. Truthfully, maybe they should be madder at him. Yet these people are nice enough to go to the wedding anyway because they're family of the groom.

"I say go for it. You should agree to be a groomsman," Max continues. "It'll probably drive her crazy that you're in her wedding. Go ahead and torture her on her special day. She deserves more. It's the least you can do."

Thank you, Max, for agreeing with me, I think with a small smile.

Conversation switches to a different subject, but Jessica and Craig's upcoming wedding is forefront in my mind for the rest of the time we're there. We all help clear the table and bring everything into the kitchen. Patti serves chocolate cake and vanilla ice cream and I beg off, knowing that'll all go straight to my thighs. Theo spoon-feeds me a couple of bites, though, which is a small, sexy moment we share.

Wild. Who knew I'd share sexy moments with Theo?

We leave soon after dessert, Theo and I both claiming that we're tired when they all protest. The skeptical looks his entire family sends our way makes me think they don't believe us, which is fine. Maybe we look like we want to escape so we can have a little private time on a Saturday night.

Perfect.

Once we're in his car, headed back into town, Theo finally says something about...us. "I think they bought it."

"Are you referring to your family?"

He nods.

"Buying us being in a relationship?"

He nods again.

"Great. That was our plan," I say, sending him a meaningful look.

Not that he's actually looking at me. He's concentrating on the road. "My mom cornered me when you went to the bathroom."

Unease slips down my spine. "Oh?" My voice is chill. *I am chill.*

Not really. Inside, I'm quaking. I don't know if I want to hear what his mom had to say about me.

"She likes you." He hesitates for a moment. "A lot."

"I like her too," I admit, savoring the relief that floods me. I'm not the woman who meets mothers. I usually don't make it that far in a relationship.

"I feel like shit because I'm lying to her," Theo says.

His words make me feel like shit too. Like we're lying to each other. I know I can't be in a relationship with Theo. Eventually I'll break his heart. And he's had it broken one too many times already, and in the most spectacular way. I refuse to do that to him. I care about him too much.

As a friend, though. Just as a friend.

"You want to come back to my place?" he asks after a long minutes of uncomfortable silence.

Yes. The word is on the tip of my tongue, but I pause. Maybe it's a bad idea. Okay, there's no maybe involved. It's a really bad idea. I can't hook up with Theo again. Sex might get tangled up in real emotions, and we'll end up hurting each other.

We are a disaster waiting to happen.

"I get it if you don't want to. Or can't." He flashes me a friendly, normal Theo smile, and it eases my worry a bit. "You've given me enough of your time today, coming to my parents' house like you just did."

"I didn't mind, Theo," I tell him softly. "I had fun. Your family is nice."

He makes a dismissive noise. "They can be a pain in the ass."

"Not really." I shake my head. "I liked them a lot, even Mason."

Theo laughs.

"And your mom is so sweet. So is your sister. I wish I could've met Cam, though."

"I wish he'd been there too. Maybe we could get together with him for dinner one night this week." Theo presses his lips together, like he realized too late he shouldn't have made that offer. And I suppose he shouldn't have. We really don't need to make more plans together with his family until the day of the wedding, right?

"That sounds nice," I finally say.

"Yeah." He sounds distracted. I am too. I don't think I should go back to his place, though I've never been there. It'll be very...lonely if I go back to my shitty apartment by myself. But it'll be a mistake if I go home with Theo. We know what's going to happen if I do.

My body runs hot at the thought.

We're quiet for the rest of the drive, until Theo finally pulls into the Safeway parking lot and pulls into the empty slot next to my parked car. "Thank you for coming with me," he says as he shifts the car into park.

My heart feels hollow. I hate thinking of him still being in love with Jessica. She doesn't deserve him. I don't either, really. He's too good for me. Too smart, too successful, too...

Sexy. Like, he's perfect in bed. But maybe that was a fluke. Theo doesn't seem like the type to go totally alpha on a woman. He's so calm usually. The mild-mannered, financial-planning nerd who looks good in a suit.

"I had a good time, Theo. Really." I glance over at him

to find he's already watching me. We stare at each other, the air slowly starting to crackle between us, and it seems natural to me when I reach for him.

Only to find he's reaching for me too.

THIRTEEN
THEO

I FELT LIKE A DICK EARLIER, asking her to come back to my place. Of course she doesn't want to. What happened last night, what happened earlier in my parents' guesthouse when we almost got caught by Ali, none of that should've ever happened in the first place. It was a mistake. Kelsey and I are friends only. That's it.

So why does it feel so right, pulling Kelsey into my arms? Yeah, it's sort of awkward kissing her over the center console in my car, but fuck it.

I want her.

I rest my hand on her cheek, slide my fingers into her thick, soft hair. Everything about her is a turn on. The taste of her lips. The little murmuring sounds she makes. Her silky hair clinging to my fingers. Her scent fills my head, making me want more, and when she settles her hand on my chest, dead center so she can feel my thumping heart, a clawing desperation ravages at the pit of my stomach.

No way do I want to let this woman leave tonight. I need to convince her to come home with me.

But how?

"Jesus, Kels." I groan when I pull away from her, hating that's the first thing I say to her after kissing her like I need her to fucking live.

She smiles, her eyes darkening even more than usual. This girl will be the death of me if I don't watch it. "Do I still make you fucking crazy?"

I nod furiously, overcome. Unable to speak.

Kelsey reaches for the front of her dress, undoing the tiny buttons that line the front of her bodice. My breathing accelerates as she reveals more and more skin. Her cream-colored bra made of lace.

See through lace.

Her dark nipples poke against the fabric, hard and tempting, and I lick my lips. Lift my gaze to hers. "Come home with me."

My voice is terse. A command. Those dark eyes flare with heat, and she reaches inside the front of her dress, her fingers drifting across her nipple, back and forth as she catches her lower lip with her teeth for a teasing moment before she releases it. "You're not going to touch me?"

I frown. Is she playing some sort of game? She wiggles in the passenger seat, her skirt riding up her slender thighs, and without warning, she whips the dress up and over her head, leaving her sitting there in just her panties and bra.

Fuck.

"Theo?" Her voice rings with innocence, but it's a lie. There is nothing innocent about this woman sitting beside me right now. She's a temptress, trying to drive me out of my mind. A fantasy come to life.

"I'll touch you when we go back to my apartment," I tell her, a ragged breath leaving me when she draws her index finger around her tight little pink nipple.

"I want you to touch me now," she demands, her voice throaty. Sexy as fuck.

Glancing around, I see an older woman approaching with her grocery cart full of bags. If she looks to her left, she'll spot us. She'll see Kelsey sitting in my car in only her underwear and she'll think we're a bunch of perverts.

Fuck that.

Throwing the car into drive, I peel out of the parking spot, the older woman glaring at me as I pull out in front of her. Kelsey throws her head back and laughs, reaching behind her to unhook her bra and toss it into the backseat of my car.

"What the hell?" We come to a stop at a red light, and I stare at her, my gaze switching between her mischievous face and her perfect tits. Those hard nipples. My mouth waters.

I want to suck them.

But I don't. I'm in the fucking car, for Christ's sake, trying to keep a cool head so I can drive home at a decent speed and not draw any attention.

"You don't like me taking off my clothes?" She laughs again, and I wonder what I'm witnessing right now. Where did this side come from? I know sex with Kelsey is like nothing I've ever experienced before, but this is a whole new scenario for me.

"I like you taking off your clothes." I gesture around us. "But it's a Saturday night in the middle of a busy intersection, and you're just sitting there in your panties and nothing else. Anyone could see you."

She sinks her teeth into her lower lip again, her eyes big as she watches me. "You want me to take them off?"

Holy Jesus on a stick.

The light turns green and I press on the gas, the car

lurching forward as we speed through the intersection. I'm trying my best to focus on the road ahead of me, the many cars around us, but all I can see in my peripheral is Kelsey sliding her fingers beneath the front of her panties.

She moans.

What the hell is she doing? I glance over at her quickly to catch that, yep. She's touching herself. I can literally hear how wet she is.

My dick jerks against my jeans.

A sigh escapes her and she lifts her legs, propping her feet against the car's dash. Her thighs are spread and she continues touching herself, her eyes falling closed.

How am I supposed to drive when she's looking like that?

Unable to take it, I somehow find the sense to hit the blinker and turn right onto a residential street, pulling over to the curb in front of a random house, throwing the car in park. Her eyes open to watch me, and she's breathing loudly, her fingers busy. I undo my seatbelt, then reach over and undo hers before I slip my fingers under her panties, pushing her hand away.

"Oh God," she says, throwing her head back and closing her eyes once more. I don't understand what's going on, or why she flipped that internal switch and decided to go into full on temptress mode, but I can't control myself.

I want to make her come with my fingers. Now. And when I get her home, I want to make her come with my mouth. Then I want to fuck her into oblivion and make her come yet again.

"Faster," she whispers, and I increase my speed, concentrating on her clit, loving how she automatically spreads her legs wider for me. Her scent fills the confines of the car, musky and sweet, and I lean in, kissing her as I continue stroking her pussy.

I run my mouth down her elegant neck, across her chest, pulling a nipple into my mouth and sucking hard. Swear to God she gets wetter, and I pull away from her, watching my hand busily work her into a frenzy.

"Tear them off," she demands between panting breaths.

I frown.

"My panties." She opens her eyes, her turbulent gaze meeting mine. "Tear them off of me."

I do as she says, twisting my hand around the thin fabric and pulling hard. They cut into her skin, she gasps when the band pinches her skin, and then the lacy cotton snaps, coming apart in my hand. I toss the panties aside, my gaze locked on her glistening pussy, my wet fingers.

"I'm coming," she says, just as her entire body starts to shake. "Oh God, Theoooo…"

I don't even know what to say. I can only watch, fascinated by her writhing body. The way her tits shake, her left nipple still damp from my mouth. The last time I fingered a girl in my car, I was still in high school.

What's happening now takes it to an entirely different level.

By the time the shuddering subsides and I've removed my hand from her body, she's a sated, sleepy beauty. Her lids are at half-mast as she smiles at me, reaching out to run her fingers through my hair, just above my ear.

"You're amazing," she murmurs.

"You're fucking wild," I tell her straight out.

She laughs. "What do you mean?"

"Why did you just do that?"

"You didn't like it?" Little Miss Innocent is back, and she's so full of shit.

"I have a naked woman in my car. I loved it," I say, shaking my head. "We were surrounded by people in the parking lot. On the road."

"Isn't that what made it more fun?" She arches a brow.

I don't want to admit it, but yeah. Of course she just made the evening a hell of a lot more fun.

"I didn't want to wait to get back to your place. I just—want to do it now. With you. In your car." She sits up, trying to look prim and proper, though she's still naked. "You can drive me back to Safeway now."

"What? No, come back to my apartment—"

There's a blur of movement. Naked skin and swaying breasts, and then she's climbing on top of me, her tits in my face and her wet pussy on top of my denim-covered dick. She wraps her arms around my neck, buries her fingers in my hair and starts kissing me.

It's heated in an instant, the temperature ratcheting up, our hot breath filling the car. She reaches for the front of my jeans, nimble fingers undoing the snap and zipper before she eagerly pulls my erection out.

"You have a beautiful cock," she whispers, and I want to laugh. I also want to puff my chest out and tell her *you're damn right*.

I do none of that. Instead I seek out the button on the side of my seat and push it back, giving us more room.

We're going to fuck. Right here, right now. She's not letting up.

"I have condoms in the center console," I tell her as she starts to stroke me.

"Aren't you prepared." Kelsey smooths her thumb around the head, gathering precome and using it to lubricate her hand. She strokes me in earnest, her pace increasing, my breaths turning ragged and just like that, I'm right on the edge. Ready to blow my wad.

Literally.

I scramble for a condom from the center console and somehow manage to slip it on my dick. She rears up, gripping the base of my cock as she lowers her body on top of it. She's completely naked and I'm still clothed, and we're parked in front of an unfamiliar house on an unfamiliar street. I don't even know where we are.

Kelsey slowly starts to move. Rising up, until I'm almost all the way out, before she plunges down again. Her pussy feels unreal. Hot and tight and so wet. She squeezes those inner walls around me like it's something she practices, and holy hell, the sensation is amazing.

She's amazing.

Wild.

Completely out of control.

Trying to drive me out of my mind.

I don't get it. I can't think too much about it. I just let myself go, and sink into the pleasure.

"Touch me," she murmurs, and I reach for her breasts, squeezing them in my palms. Lean forward and lick one, then the other. "My clit."

I let go of her right breast and stroke her, groaning when I feel the slow drag of her pussy on my dick. This is hot. This is unbelievable. I feel like I'm starring in my own personal porn video. There's something illicit about doing it in an unfamiliar neighborhood on a Saturday night, where anyone could catch us.

Like the fucking cops.

Jesus, what the hell is wrong with me? With us?

Right on cue, a car turns onto the street, its lights flashing across Kelsey's naked body as she rides me, offering me a quick glimpse before she's shrouded in darkness once more. Her nipples are plump and swollen. Her normally pale skin is flushed rosy red. Her eyes fathomless, her lips damp.

I think I'm fucking Snow White.

"Could you come right now?" she suddenly asks, reaching down, past my hips, her fingers searching for and finding the control buttons. She sends the seat back, until we're practically horizontal and she's hovering above me.

Our bodies are still connected. I glance down, watching in complete fascination as my cock disappears inside of her, only to reappear seconds later.

"Could you?" she asks again, and I lift my gaze to find her watching me.

I nod frantically. "Fuck yeah."

Her smile is slow. Almost evil. Her hips twist, and she rests her arms on my shoulders as she moves her body. Up. Down. Fast. Faster. I match her pace, my hips lifting. Thrusting deep. Fucking her just as hard as she fucking me.

I'm close. Oh fuck, it's going to happen. I'm going to come. Oh. Shit. Right...

She pulls off of me and wraps her hand around my dick once more, jacking me so fast, I come all over her fingers. Shooting long strings of come on her breasts. She bends her head, darts her tongue out to lick at the semen dribbling all over my dick, and a downright pitiful cry falls from my lips as I watch her.

"What are you doing to me?" I ask her once my breaths have calmed and she finds some napkins in the compartment box to clean us both up.

That evil smile reappears. "Luring you into my spell."

Hell yeah she did. I didn't fuck Snow White.

I just fucked Maleficent.

FOURTEEN
KELSEY

"KELSEY? Could we talk for a few minutes in my office, please?"

I glance up from my laptop to find my boss, Alexander Wilder, standing in front of my desk, a neutral expression on his classically handsome face. I can figure people out. It's a trait of mine that I'm proud of. But Alex Wilder? He has the same expression whether he's happy, sad. Mad or glad.

It's frustrating.

I've given him no reason to be pissed or disappointed in me, unless he somehow found out about my Saturday evening tryst I had with Theo, and why would he bring that up at work? He wouldn't. He's not inappropriate. Alex is an upstanding boss who treats everyone who works for him with complete respect.

A complete turnaround from any other guy I've worked under since I was sixteen. They all wanted to get in my pants. The women who were my bosses? Hated my pretty face and judged me on sight.

Not Alex. Never Alex. If he weren't married to my friend Caroline, I might have a massive crush on him. But even before I knew Caroline, I didn't have those kind of thoughts about Alex. More like I had scary respect for him.

He's a little intimidating sometimes.

A non-existent crush on my boss makes me think of Theo. The man I do have a minor crush on. I still can't explain what came over me Saturday night. I wasn't drunk. Well, not on liquor.

I think I was drunk on pheromones. Theo's in particular. Being in that car with him, his scent surrounding me, I was intoxicated. Horny as hell. He wanted me to come back to his place, and I thought it was so sweet, so cute, but I didn't want sweet and cute.

I wanted sexy. Raw, take-your-satisfaction fucking. That's what I got. Once we were finished, I made him drive me back to my car and I went home. Fell right asleep too. Like a little toddler worn out after a busy day.

Theo hasn't texted me since. I haven't texted him either. What can I say? *Thanks for indulging me?* I could've got us into some trouble, I'm sure. But I didn't.

And it was worth it.

"Sure. Of course," I finally say when I realize Alex is waiting for my answer. I shut my laptop and rise to my feet, brushing off the front of my black pants before I round the desk and follow him to his office.

He waits for me at the door and I walk past him, surprised when he pulls the door shut. This must be a private conversation. Most of the time when I talk to him in here, we make idle chitchat and that door is always open. He even takes important business calls with the door wide open.

"I have nothing to hide," he told me once, right when I first started working for him. "Unless I absolutely do not want to be disturbed, my door will always be open."

I thought that was so progressive of him. Maybe even a little reckless.

He settles behind his desk and I sit in one of the comfortable chairs in front of it, poised on the edge of the seat, hating the nerves that suddenly sweep over me. What if I'm being fired—

"You look scared out of your mind, Kelsey," he says dryly. "Don't worry. I'm not letting you go."

I breathe a sigh of relief and slump in my chair. "Thank God. You frightened me."

He chuckles and rests his hands on top of his desk, twisting his platinum wedding ring around and around his finger. I love that Caroline is my friend. His wife is one of my favorite people. And her friends took me in so easily, making me a part of their group as if I always belonged.

I've never really felt like I belonged with anyone.

Ever.

"I have a proposal for you," he starts, his gaze meeting mine. "Even though I'm probably a fool for making this offer."

I frown. "Why are you a fool?"

"I'm a fool if you take me up on it and leave me." He exhales loudly and grabs a pen, pointing it at me. "You're an incredible asset to Wilder Corp."

I blink at him. "Thank you."

"And while I want to keep you here forever here at our office, I know you have the potential to climb the corporate ladder, and the only way you can do that is if you take an executive position within Wilder." He hesitates for only a moment. "Somewhere else."

"Like where?" Oh, wow. This could be—exciting.

"There are two positions that just opened up. One in Las Vegas."

I think of my friend Eleanor. I would interview for that position without hesitation.

"And one in London."

Wait a minute. "London as in England?"

He laughs. "Yes. London, England. The UK. Ever been there?"

I shake my head. "I don't even have a passport."

"It's a gorgeous city. And we have a gorgeous hotel there."

"I've seen photos." It's beautiful, located not too far from Buckingham Palace, in Trafalgar Square.

"It's been recently renovated, and we've been at max capacity ever since. Wilder London needs an assistant manager for the location. I think you'd be an excellent candidate for the job," Alex says.

My mind is spinning with the possibilities. "What about the Vegas location?"

"Same position. Neither of them have been posted yet. Both employees gave their notice first thing this morning. I'm sorry to lose them in those positions, but they're both remaining with the company in a different capacity." He sends me a look, one I can't quite decipher. "When I received the emails letting me know, I immediately thought of you."

"I'm flattered." I rest my hand against my chest, hoping I can calm my racing heart.

"You deserve it. You're a hard worker, Kelsey." He flips open a file I didn't even notice was sitting in front of him. "But you have no college experience, which is usually a requirement for an executive position."

My heart starts to sink. Why'd he get my hopes up if that's the case? "I've had to work multiple jobs since I lost my mom. I never got a chance to go to college."

"I know." He sends me a sympathetic look. I told him a little bit about my life during our initial interview. A brief summary. He doesn't bring it up, which I prefer. He knows how to keep things strictly business, unlike other bosses I've had in the past. "As I just mentioned, we require a bachelor's degree for executive positions, especially here at the corporate office. *Or* we require experience within the chain. This is why I'm telling you about these positions. I wanted to see if you're interested in interviewing for either of them."

"I'm interested," I tell him eagerly, making him chuckle.

"Good. I'd hoped you would be. If you want to stay with Wilder, it would be a smart move to take a position at one of our hotels. A management position would be a big responsibility," he says.

"I know," I say, fighting the nerves that suddenly want to take over me.

"One I think you're capable of, or else I wouldn't make this suggestion." He smiles faintly. "You can work at one of the hotels for a year or two. Maybe a couple of them, and then eventually, if you want, you can come back here and work for me."

I could leave here. Try something new, live somewhere new. "When are the interviews supposed to happen?"

"Soon. We'll want to fill both positions ASAP so training can start." He tilts his head. "So you *are* interested, correct?"

"Definitely," I say, my voice firm.

"In which hotel?"

"Both of them."

He laughs. "That's what I was hoping. Well then, I'll let Celeste know you'd like to interview and she can start putting everything together for you."

"Will I have to go to Vegas and London for the interview?" Shit, I can't. I don't have a passport.

"We can video chat or Zoom or whatever. But I would recommend you start the application for your passport today." He rises to his feet and I do too, in a daze as he reaches out to shake my hand. "I'm glad to hear you're interested, Kelsey. I know you're going to make a great manager someday."

"I appreciate the compliment, but I don't have the job yet," I tell him.

He winks. "I have all the faith in you."

"WELL, Kelsey, looks like you've finally turned into one of us," Stella says as she settles into the chair next to mine.

We're at Tuscany, the restaurant Stella's older brothers own in downtown Carmel, at one of the bigger tables in the back. I got here at five-fifteen and immediately ordered a bottle of wine.

"What do you mean?" I ask as I pour Stella a glass.

"You're calling emergency meetings like the rest of us. It must be something serious." She glances around the empty table, her fingers curled around her glass. "Am I the first to arrive?"

"Considering you work pretty much across the street, yes." I'm practically bouncing in my seat, I'm so eager to tell her about my new job prospects. But I'd rather wait until everyone else arrives and I can explain everything all at once.

"Who else is coming?"

"Sarah, Caroline, Amelia and Candice." I miss Eleanor

so much. I wish she were here. I'm tempted to FaceTime her right before I tell everyone my news.

Though maybe they won't be as excited for me as I am for myself. I don't know, I still feel a little unsure about my friendship with this group of women. And I know that's my own insecurities shining through, since they've never given me any reason to doubt them. It's more like I doubt myself.

"The whole gang, huh? This must be big." Stella's eyes go wide. "Please tell me you've finally started banging sweet, sexy Theo on the side."

I was taking a drink at the exact moment she says *banging sweet, sexy Theo* and I nearly do a spit take. Instead, I choke on my wine and start coughing. Stella watches me patiently, reaching out and patting me on the back until the coughing finally subsides.

"I'm guessing it's true," Stella says.

I don't want to lie to her, so I try to divert instead. "He's just a friend."

"A very bangable friend. Seriously, he's getting hotter as every day passes. I saw him jogging on the beach yesterday. In shorts. That's it." Stella waves her hand at her face as if she needs to cool off. "Had to act like it was no big deal since I was with Carter, but you know. Your 'friend' is smokin'."

I think of his naked chest. His naked everything. His rather impressive penis. I cannot reveal my secret to Stella, no matter how tempting. No way. "He's been working out a lot," I say nonchalantly.

"And it shows. Seriously, Kelsey, why *wouldn't* you bang him? You two spend enough time together as it is. It only makes sense you two will eventually end up together. I was surprised you weren't with him yesterday," Stella says.

I'm surprised too. We like to go for runs together, especially on the beach. "Where did you see him?" I keep my tone as neutral as possible.

"At Carmel Beach. Carter and I were taking a walk yesterday afternoon and we recognized him. Had to yell at him to get his attention since his AirPods were in his ears, but we chatted for a while." Stella inherited her grandmother's gorgeous little house that sits right by that beach, while her grandmother moved into a condo. Now her nonna has a better social life than all of us put together.

"Oh. Nice." I take a big gulp of wine, dying to ask what they talked about. But it's none of my business.

"He mentioned you."

I go completely still. "What did he say?"

"That you two are bangin'." Stella grins.

My mouth drops open. "He did not."

Now Stella starts laughing. "You're right. He didn't. But the guilty look on your face just gave you away. I need all the dirty details."

My face goes hot. Holy shit, I'm blushing. And I don't blush over anything. "You tricked me."

"I sure as hell did." Stella looks very pleased with herself. "Come on, K. You can't keep all that inside of you. You need to confess your darkest secret."

I glance around, ready to spot one of our friends approaching the table, but no one's here yet. Not even Caroline or Sarah, and they both work nearby. "Fine." I scoot my chair closer to Stella's and lower my voice. "We might've—fooled around."

"Fucking finally!" Stella exclaims.

I rest my hand on her arm. "I don't want anyone else to find out, though."

Stella's expression turns bewildered. "Why not? We are the perfect friend group to help you out with this. Everyone has advice to offer. We've all gone through some crazy starts to our most recent relationships, trust me."

"Right. I know." I nod, contemplating what Stella said. Why am I so scared to tell them the truth? Am I afraid they'll judge me? These ladies are the most non-judgey people I know. They'll probably high-five me for finally having sex with Theo. And they wouldn't make me feel guilty for not wanting to take our relationship further either. They'd support me no matter what.

But I'm not big on opening myself up to anyone. Certainly not my family. Never really to any of my friends. The men in my life? Nope. I keep that as casual as possible. So having this group of friends I hang out with regularly, along with Theo...

Is completely out of my norm.

"Think about it." Stella pats my arm in a motherly gesture. "Once the girls get here and the wine is flowing and we're all fat and happy and full of carbs, drop your Theo bomb and ask for advice, if you want. We will all have something to say."

That's what I'm afraid of.

"And it will all be positive," Stella adds, as if she's had a glimpse into my doubtful mind.

I smile at her. "Okay. I'll think about it."

"Good. But in the meantime, if you want to share any sexual details about Theo in the sack, I'm all ears," Stella says with a laugh.

"We never actually made it to a bed," I say, trying to suppress my smile.

Stella's laughter dies, though her eyes still gleam. "Do tell."

So I do. I share most of the details, though not all. It feels good to get it out, to confess to someone what Theo and I have done. What I still want to do with him, despite knowing it's a huge mistake.

"But is it?" Stella asks when I finish my story.

I frown. "Is it what?"

"A mistake. You and Theo. Why can't you be in a relationship," Stella explains.

I shrug. "I don't know." Because he's still in love with Jessica? God, I can't say those words out loud. Then it makes my worry—and his potential feelings—all too real.

"He probably doesn't see me like that," I say when Stella still hasn't said anything. I look around the restaurant yet again. Where are our friends? I need them to save me from this conversation.

"Please." Stella scoffs. "He fingered you in his parents' guesthouse like he has no control around you. He definitely sees you like that."

I am not one to get embarrassed over my sexual experiences, but when Stella puts it like that, it's a little mortifying.

"It would be a mistake if we became involved," I continue.

"For who? Not you guys. You seem totally into each other."

I send her a mean look. "You make it very hard for me to justify my not wanting to be with him."

"Because I think it's a mistake. You two make total sense together."

"I don't do serious."

"Well, now you do. Look." She reaches out and settles her hand on my forearm, her touch light. Calming, even. "I used to be you, so I have no room to judge. I slept around. I experimented with drugs. I was a wild child, rebelling against my parents in every way possible. I didn't believe in relationships, even though my parents have been married forever and I come from a loving family. I thought that was all a bunch of bullshit."

I nod solemnly, taking in her words. "It *is* a bunch of bullshit."

"Right." She smiles. "But then Carter came back into my life. He rocked my world. Not only sexually, but just...in general. I realized I didn't want to lose him. And now I'm with a man who loves me for me, who respects me, and who makes me laugh. We're going to get married, I just know it."

I'm happy for her. That sounds blissful.

And impossible.

"You deserve love and happiness, even though you think you don't." She leans forward, her gaze never straying from mine. "I see you, Kelsey. I know what you're thinking, and you're wrong. About all of it."

I smile and give her a hug, because she's so kind to say that. But really?

I don't believe her.

At all.

FIFTEEN
THEO

I SHOW up at the restaurant fifteen minutes late, which pisses me off to no end, but I can't control the shitty traffic around downtown Carmel. It doesn't matter what time of year or day it is, this place is always packed with cars and parking is impossible to find. I hate it.

Of course, I could've left the office a little earlier, but I got caught up in work, as usual, and it took my sister texting me if I was going to make it to dinner tonight to remind me that I needed to get a move on.

She sent me that text because she knows my habits . Good thing she did, too.

Tonight's meeting wasn't originally on my schedule. Cam called me earlier, asking if I was busy and if I would meet with him for dinner so we could discuss a few things. He was vague when I asked him what he wanted to talk about, and then mentioned that Ali would also be there.

Kind of odd, but I agreed.

I enter Tuscany and approach the hostess stand, glancing around the interior of the restaurant to see if I can spot either Cam or Ali, but they're nowhere to be found.

"Can I help you?" asks the pretty blonde hostess with an eager smile.

"I'm meeting someone here. The reservation should be under Crawford, I think. For three?" My gaze snags on the long table at the very back of the restaurant, where a group of women are sitting. There's one woman in particular who looks familiar, but all I can see is the back of her head.

She reminds me of Kelsey.

But I'm probably just hoping it's her, because since Saturday night, it's like I can feel her everywhere. I can't get what happened in my car out of my mind. The woman owns her sexuality like no one else I've ever been with, and it is seriously the hottest thing alive. She goes after what she wants, and she takes it.

Makes me feel like I can do the same thing. Like I did in my parents' guesthouse, which had also been pretty hot.

We haven't spoken since Saturday night, when I drove her back to the Safeway parking lot in a sexual daze, my thoughts scattered, my entire body buzzing. I'd just come all over her hand not ten minutes prior and already I was thinking about how I would get her naked again. She slipped her dress back on during the drive, and by the time I pulled up next to her car, ready to make my pitch on convincing her to stay the night with me, she was already exiting the vehicle, thanking me for a fun time and flashing her bare ass when she swung around and her skirt flew up. She slammed the passenger door, hopped into her own vehicle and waved at me.

Then took off.

I sat there for a couple more minutes, still in a daze. Stunned she would ditch me so easily after what happened. She left her panties crumpled on the floorboard. Her bra on my backseat. I kept them both. Does that make me a complete perv?

Probably, but I don't give a shit.

No texts from Kelsey. No phone calls. Not even a FaceTime. I suppose I could call or text her, but every time I try, I get nervous and don't know what to say, so I give up. Maybe she feels the same way. It's weird, that I haven't seen her at all, and I'm starting to wonder if what we shared over the weekend ever actually happened.

Maybe it was all in my head.

I went for a jog on the beach Sunday afternoon to ease the tension. There's only so much jacking off a man can do in a shower or in a bed, and I couldn't even manage to get through two minutes of one of my favorite porn star's clips before I shut it off with a groan.

Now that I've had real live Kelsey, a porn star Kelsey lookalike doesn't cut it.

While out running, I bumped into Stella Ricci and her boyfriend, Carter Abbott. We talked for a while, and Stella asked about Kelsey, which I thought was a little odd. But I blew it off and made casual conversation with both of them, secretly wondering if they could somehow figure out that Kelsey and I have now had sex. Am I giving off some kind of vibe? Do all of Kelsey's friends know that we've taken our friendship to the next level? Or am I her dirty little secret?

I don't know what's worse.

"Yes, they're already here," the hostess says, and I jerk my gaze back to her, noting her frown. I wonder if she had to repeat herself. I was pretty lost in my thoughts just now. "Shall I show you to the table?"

"Please."

I follow after the woman, searching for my brother and sister. I spot them at a table tucked into the back left corner of the restaurant, on the complete opposite side of the room from that large table of attractive women.

Pretty sure that table is full of Kelsey's friends—and Kelsey.

"There you are," Ali says with a smile when she spots me. She rises to her feet and I go to her, kissing her cheek before I settle in beside her, Camden sitting before us.

I grimace at my brother once the hostess leaves us alone. "Sorry I'm late."

"Traffic?" Ali asks.

"As usual." I flip open the menu.

"Stayed a little too long at the office?" Cam asks knowingly.

I send him a quick look. "Always."

They both laugh. Our server appears quickly, taking my drink order. Cam orders a few appetizers as well, and once our server's gone, he leans across the table, his gaze intense. "I have a proposition for both of you."

Nothing like getting right to it. Though beating around the bush has never been my brother's style.

Ali and I glance at each other before I warily ask, "What is it?"

"Why aren't Mason and Max here?" Ali asks.

"They already know about my proposition, and they're fully on board." He leans back in his seat and rubs his hands together eagerly, a little smile curling his lips. "I'm sure your immediate answer is going to be no, but hear me out first, okay?"

"No," I tell him, making him laugh.

"The reason I didn't go to Mom and Dad's this weekend is because I was in San Francisco, making an offer on a business. The owners flew in from Vermont, which is where they live now, so we could discuss everything. They had some valid concerns, and I shared my plans with them, which they approved of. They took my offer. The property is mine. Ours, if you want in on it." Cam leans back in his chair with a pleased grin.

"You're being too vague," I tell him. "And what exactly did you purchase? A fleet of food trucks?"

"Even better. I bought..." He chuckles and shakes his head. "A farm."

"Wait a minute, a *farm?*" Ali's frowning. "Why in the world would you do that?"

I'm quiet, my mind searching, thinking of old businesses in the area. It hits me fast. Pretty sure I know exactly which farm he's talking about. "The old Carmel Valley Farm?"

Cam nods, pleased. "That's the one. You're now looking at the new owner. Well, Mason and Max are a part of this too. This is why I'm meeting with you two tonight. I wanted to see if you'd like to be owners as well."

"I don't have any money. Not investor-sized money," Ali says. "I don't even have a college degree."

Much to our parents' disgust and disappointment. They were upset when Ali dropped out of college last spring, before the semester was even over. She claimed she needed the break. From what I've heard, she spends most of her days holed up in the guesthouse, watching Netflix or constantly on her phone.

"You don't need one to work at the farm, little lady." Cam smiles. "You've got all the experience I need—you can be the farm's social media manager."

Ali's eyes sparkle with interest and she sits up straighter. "That sounds interesting. Tell me more."

"It'll be the usual. Posting on various social media accounts, specifically Instagram and Facebook."

"TikTok is where it's at currently," Ali says with a nod

as she grabs her phone and starts scrolling. "I'll start searching farm life now."

"I knew you'd be good at it," Cam says, making Ali smile. Poor girl hasn't felt good about much since she returned home. "And we could work up a contract where you buy into the business in increments. I want us all to be part owners. It'll be our family farm. Carrying on our legacy."

"The thing is, though...we're not farmers," I remind my brother.

"We grew up on a ranch," Cam points out.

"Yeah, but it's not an actual real, working one. Dad isn't Kevin Costner playing John Dutton in *Yellowstone*." I do love that TV show, though.

"Which is too fucking bad. The Dutton family is badass," Cam says with a laugh.

The Carmel Valley Farm has been around since I can remember. When we were little, it was a place families took their children to year-round. You could pick fresh vegetables. There was an apple orchard where they'd give you a bucket, and off you'd go. In the fall they offered hayrides and a pumpkin patch. I remember they even sold Christmas trees at one point, though the Sullivan Family Tree Farm eventually ended that.

In my early teens, business seemed to fall off, and fewer and fewer people took their families there. After I graduated high school, the recession hit and took the farm out of business once and for all. It's been sitting empty ever since.

And it looks it, too. Some of the buildings aren't in the best shape, and the land is completely overgrown. The apple orchard hasn't been tended to in years, and looks downright wild. It's kind of a mess.

"This is going to be a huge project," I tell Cam.

He nods, his expression turning serious. Finally. "I know."

"So where do I come into this?" I ask warily, smiling up at the server when she appears at our table with my drink and the appetizers.

We all remain quiet as she sets everything on the table. Once she's gone, Camden starts back up again. "Silent investor, as you always are. You're a busy guy, I get it. But I was hoping you'd like to invest into the new family business and help us grow."

"What about the food truck?"

"We're going to serve barbecue at the barn. Max and Mason will still run the food truck and the takeout shack we'll eventually open up," Cam says. "We'll start out serving food at the barn during the weekends, Friday through Sunday." Excitement lights up Cam's eyes and he's wearing that million-dollar smile once more. The one that convinces everyone his farfetched ideas are the best they've ever heard. "We're planning on having a couple of shops on site. There will be an ice cream store, plus a store featuring merchandise, handmade goods, stuff like that. We're going to have a pumpkin patch just like the old days, along with some goats and cows. Chickens. It'll be like a real farm."

"This sounds like a lot of work. You're not playing at having a farm. You're going to be running an *actual* farm," I say, reaching across the table to grab a homemade mozzarella stick and dunking it in the marinara sauce before I cram it into my mouth. Holy shit, that's delicious.

"And you sound skeptical." Cam is still grinning. "I get it. I'm taking on a huge project, and I don't know fuck all about farming." He sends a sympathetic look in Ali's direction. "Sorry."

She waves her hand. "Please. You guys curse in front of me all the time."

Poor Ali. She's not wrong.

"It's a huge undertaking, and I don't know how you're going to do it all." I believe in my brother. Cam is smart and determined. Whatever he sets his mind to, he gets it done.

But a farm? With shops and animals and growing fruits and vegetables? He'll have to hire a large staff. He'll need someone to run that staff—and the farm. He knows about barbecue thanks to the food truck and growing up watching our father. The rest of it, he doesn't know shit.

"I'm not going to do it all," Cam says, grabbing a mozzarella stick for himself. "I'm going to hire plenty of staff."

"Including someone to manage the farm?"

"There are couples all over this country who live on-site and will help manage a farm, plus there are a ton of teenagers in the area I can hire to work the store and the ice cream shop. Whatever. I've been researching this for *months*, Theo. I know what I'm doing," Cam says, sounding vaguely offended.

"If you've been researching this for months, why didn't you mention it to me sooner?" I ask.

"Because I knew you'd react like this." Cam drops his half-eaten mozzarella stick onto his plate. "I have a plan in place. Mason and Max are on board. I told Mom and Dad all about it yesterday, and they support me."

"I support you," Ali says, making Cam smile.

"Everyone does." Cam frowns. "Except for you."

"I never said I don't support you," I tell him. "And what about Sullivan's Tree Farm? Aren't they basically doing the same thing? Why would you want to compete with that?"

"They're seasonal. We'll have the farm open year

round, and we really won't focus on Christmas as much as they do. Trees are their thing, and I'll let them have trees. Everything else is fair game." Cam sits back in his chair and smirks, looking very pleased with himself.

This is just—a lot. A huge endeavor. Are you sure you want to take this on?"

"I'm so sure, I've already made the offer and it's been accepted. I'm doing this," Cam says firmly. "Want to see my business plan?"

There is nothing I love more than reading someone's business plan—no fucking joke. "I do."

"I brought it with me. I'll give it to you after dinner. You can read it over later tonight and let me know what you think tomorrow."

"Can't wait." I smile, wanting my brother to know that even though I have doubt, I do support him. He's a smart guy. Ambitious. He goes after what he wants, even if the idea sounds farfetched. Like starting up a food truck. I thought it was ridiculous when he first came up with it, and my brothers now have a successful business. Instead of expanding into more food trucks, which is the natural progression, Cam goes out and buys a freakin' barn.

Not the typical path I would take, but I have to give it to him. He's got good ideas, and he knows how to execute them.

We make small talk until our dinner arrives, and halfway through the meal, Ali suddenly makes an observation. "I think your girlfriend is here."

She directs this statement at me.

My fork drops with a clatter onto the edge of the plate, and my gaze immediately goes to the table of women across the room. That's where I see Kelsey standing by the table, her hand on Stella Ricci's shoulder—who is still seated—before she walks away.

I watch her, completely fascinated. She's dressed in black, her long hair tumbling down past her shoulders in luxurious waves, and more than one man turns his head to watch her as she passes by their tables. She disappears into a short hallway that I know leads to the bathrooms, and without thought I rise to my feet, ready to chase after her.

"Did you not realize she's here?" Ali asks.

"No," I tell her distractedly, leaving the table and making my way through the restaurant toward that hallway. I'm lying, but I didn't want to explain myself.

"Theo! What are you doing here?"

I glance over my shoulder to see Stella turned around in her chair, watching me with surprise in her eyes. I offer a little wave but otherwise say nothing. She flashes me a knowing smirk and turns to face the table once more.

Huh.

I can't let that smirk bother me. I'm a determined man, eager to find his woman. Of course, when I stop in front of the bathroom doors, Kelsey is nowhere to be found. Because she's in the women's restroom.

So I wait.

I lean my shoulder against the wall and check my phone. I have a few notifications, but nothing crucial. She's in there so long, I'm scrolling through my inbox when the door finally swings open and there she is.

She stops short when she sees me, her eyes wide, and her freshly glossed lips pop open. "Theo."

"Kelsey." I shove my phone into my front pocket and stand up straight. "Hey."

"What are you doing here?" She doesn't sound happy to see me.

What the fuck?

"Having dinner with my brother and sister." I pause, gauging her reaction. It's not any better than it was a minute ago. "What are *you* doing here?"

"Meeting up with friends." She shrugs, her expression impassive.

"Yeah, I saw Stella."

Her eyes widen a little bit. "Just now?"

I nod. "She saw me first. Said hi."

"Oh."

That's it. Just that little *oh*. Wonder what she means by that.

Maybe I'm overthinking this entire conversation.

"Ali noticed you and mentioned to me that you were here," I tell her. "So I had to come find you."

"Right." Kelsey crosses her arms. "You'd look like a bad boyfriend if you didn't."

I don't know why, but what she just said makes me feel like shit.

"I haven't talked to you at all since Saturday." I take a step closer to her, catching a hint of her delectable scent. Instantly my body reacts, wanting more of it.

Wanting more of her.

"I've been busy." Another shrug. Her entire demeanor is completely closed off, yet I approach her anyway.

"Too busy to text?"

"You could've texted me."

"True." I stop just before her and reach out, tucking a strand of silky hair behind her ear. "I've missed you."

She rolls her eyes.

"It's true. You usually text me every single day, Kels. Without fail. Until last weekend. I wonder why?" I trace the curve of her cheek with my index finger until she dodges out of my touch.

My hand falls, and I fight the disappointment that wants to take over me.

"I've been doing a lot of thinking," she starts before clamping her lips closed. Someone walks by us, a woman who enters the bathroom. Kelsey waits until the door shuts. "And I'm wondering if our plan is a little—messed up."

I frown. "What plan?"

"The wedding plan." She averts her gaze, like she can't look at me.

"You mean you being my date?" She nods. "And us pretending we're together?"

Kelsey nods again.

Though really, are we pretending anymore? We're friends who've now become lovers. Dangerous, I'm sure. Dangerous in the fact that we can't go back to being just friends. And while I mourn the loss of that friendship, I'm also excited to see where we go next.

Is she, though?

Doesn't seem like it.

"Yes. I don't know if this is a good idea." She waves a hand in between us.

"What exactly are you referring to?" I arch a brow. What is up with everyone being so damn vague tonight?

"This." Another hand wave. "Us."

"Really." I glance around, realizing no one else is near, save for the woman in the bathroom. There's a door just behind where Kelsey is standing, with one of those standard red exit signs lit above it. "We're not going to make a decision like this in front of the bathrooms at Tuscany, Kels. Come on."

Grabbing hold of her hand, I lead her through the side

exit door to discover we're in a typical narrow alley in downtown Carmel. There are white lights strung above us, and potted plants and flowers strewn everywhere, along with a quaint wooden bench to the left of us.

There's not an ugly spot in this town, I swear.

"Do we really need to have this conversation now?" she asks, still appearing wary.

"Yeah. We do." I don't let go of her hand. In fact, it's like I can't let go. Her skin is so soft, and her fingers just feel—right in mine.

Fucking stupid. This is the kind of thinking that got me into trouble before. I fell so damn hard for Jessica, and look where that got me. I can't go making the same mistake twice.

Not that I believe Kelsey would ever cheat on me, but we're not even in a serious enough relationship to call us seeing other people cheating.

Shit. I'm being ridiculous right now.

"Aren't your brother and sister waiting for you? And which brother are you with?"

"Camden."

"Oh." Interest flits across her face, faint but there. "I really wanted to meet him."

"You can right now."

"Theo..." Her voice drifts and she closes her eyes for the briefest moment, shaking her head. "I'm freaking out."

"No shit?" I keep my voice light, even though deep down, I'm freaking out too. But one of us has to pretend we've got it together.

"Yeah."

I step closer, until I'm in her personal space, my chest brushing against hers. "What are you freaking out about? The fact that we had sex twice this weekend?"

She tilts her head back with a faint nod. "Don't forget what happened in your parents' guesthouse."

All the memories come flooding back. How beautiful she was. How responsive. I'm not a spontaneous person. I'm not the guy who normally fucks a woman in a public place.

Yet I did with Kelsey. It's like I couldn't control myself. And neither could she. What does that mean?

I don't even know. I'm not sure if I'm prepared to examine it closely yet either.

"As if I could forget." Reaching out, I touch her cheek again, letting my fingers drift across her petal-soft skin. I'm tempted to kiss her, but she'd probably run. "Are you scared that we've taken our relationship to the next level?"

"I'm scared that I'll lose your friendship forever," she whispers, her voice shaky.

Ah, shit. My heart wobbles at her confession. I don't want to lose her friendship either. Not at all. That's been my biggest fear as well. "You won't."

She sighs. "You can't say that so easily, Theo. Sex changes *everything*."

"Sometimes for the better."

"And sometimes for the worst." She rests her free hand on my chest. "I like you. A lot. I consider you my friend."

I steel myself. This feels like I'm about to get dumped.

"What happened over the weekend wasn't *friendly* at all." She curls her fingers into the button placket of my shirt, and I swear she's trying to touch my bare chest. "I don't have friendly thoughts about you anymore, Theo."

I'm frowning. "What do you mean?"

"I mean I can't stop thinking about what happened between us." Her voice is the barest whisper. I tilt my head closer so I can hear better. "And how much I want it to happen again, despite knowing it's probably a mistake."

Her *mistake* comment is like a kick in the dick, but otherwise, I'm on board with everything she's saying. "I can't stop thinking about you either."

Her entire face lights up, but then she tamps it back down. As if she doesn't want me to know she's excited by my revelation. "Really? Then why didn't you text me?"

"I was waiting for you."

"And *I* was waiting for *you*." She shakes her head. "What are we doing, Theo?"

"I'd say we're letting things happen...naturally." I give in to my urges and brush my lips against hers. A gasp escapes her and I nip at her lower lip with my teeth, making her gasp again. "Want to meet up after dinner?"

She runs her hand up and down my chest. "Are you almost finished?"

"Yeah." I kiss her again, and she parts her lips for me so easily. Too easily. I take advantage, sliding my tongue into her mouth, teasing hers. She kisses me back, her hand sliding up my chest to curl around my nape and we kiss for long, unbroken minutes. Until my phone starts buzzing in my pocket.

I break the kiss first to check my phone. A text from Ali.

Quit messing around with your girlfriend and come back to the table!

Grinning, I shove the phone back into my pocket. "My sister is demanding I come finish my dinner."

"I should go back too," Kelsey says with a sigh. Her expression has turned dreamy, and all that tension I could sense radiating throughout her body earlier has dissipated.

"Want to go back to my place once we're done?" I ask, steeling myself yet again for her rejection. She'll probably suggest we meet back out here and she'll offer up a blowjob, then bail on me. I don't mind the idea of a blowjob, but not out here. And I don't want her bailing. I want to take her home. Have sex with her in an actual bed, where I can really take my time with her.

The expression on her face switches from dreamy to worried, just like that. "Do you think it's a good idea?"

"I think it's the best idea I've had in a long time," I say with all the sincerity I can muster, sneaking my arm around her waist. "What's your gut telling you to do?"

"It's telling me I should go home with you," she admits.

My smile is triumphant. "Then do it."

SIXTEEN
KELSEY

I CAN'T BELIEVE I agreed to go home with Theo, but I did, and now I'm headed back to the table where all my friends are waiting for me, feeling a little rumpled and thoroughly kissed and already eager to leave this dinner. Knowing I get to go home with Theo and all the many, many things we can do together is exciting.

And arousing.

"Where have you been?" Caroline asks when she spots me.

I can feel my cheeks get warm, and I wonder what's wrong with me. I never get embarrassed over stuff like this, and lately it's all I seem to do. "I saw Theo," I answer, falling into my chair and reaching for my almost empty wineglass. I polish it off, disappointed there's no more left.

"Ooh, Theo," Stella croons, making my cheeks get even hotter.

"What is going on with you two anyway?" Caroline asks, tilting her head. The curiosity on her face is obvious.

I blink at my friend, then glance around the table, blinking at all of my friends. When I'm casually seeing a man—code for casually hooking up with him—I have no problem telling them all about it. Offering up all the dirty details because it's fun, you know? I wasn't taking the hookups seriously. And when I thought of Theo as just my friend, I talked about him like I'd talk about any of them.

But now that things have changed and I'm scared I actually might have feelings for him, it's like I can't get the words out. I don't know what to say, or what to do. I don't share anything personal with people, and I don't let them get too close. I never really have. When you have a screwed up family who eventually abandons you and you feel like you can't count on anyone, you clam up.

It's what I've always done.

As I glance around the table at the warm, open faces of my friends, I realize that maybe I should change that habit. I care about these women, and they care about me. They've always supported me, even when I do stupid things. They don't judge. They don't talk about me behind my back. They're actual, real friends.

"Theo and I—we had sex this weekend," I blurt, then immediately cover up my face with my hands in embarrassment.

Stella slips her arm around my shoulders and gives me a light squeeze. "I am so proud of you for saying that."

"*Finally* you admit what's really going on," Sarah practically crows. I drop my hands from my face just in time to see her high-five Caroline.

Seriously?

"It only just happened," I say weakly, feeling silly.

"Yeah, but it's been building between you two since you first became friends," Caroline says.

I shake my head. "No, it hasn't. We started out

genuinely as friends. That's it. I had no feelings like that toward him."

I really didn't. Not at first.

The last month or two? Yeah, fine. I started seeing him in a different way. Thinking about him differently. Reacting when he touched me, or when he laughed. Or when he made a personal reference like we were the only two people in the world who would get it.

Yes. That last part especially. I really like it when he does that. As if it's us versus the world. We're a team, Theo and I.

I'm a team with these women as well. I belong. We're almost like...

Family. And that's a feeling I'm not familiar or one hundred percent comfortable with. Yet.

"I thought it became apparent pretty quick that you two are compatible," Sarah says.

She has a point. Theo and I are definitely compatible. He makes me smile. He makes me laugh. We have interesting conversations that I genuinely enjoy. We can argue with each other, and sometimes it turns heated, but we're always quick to forgive and forget. And the sex?

It's amazing.

"I suppose," I finally say, glancing around at everyone in a sort of daze. I don't know what to do. Or what to say next.

"Kelsey." Sarah reaches across the table to rest her hand over mine. "It's okay to fall for a guy you're friends with. It happens all the time."

"Really?"

"Sure." Sarah glances around the table, her brows drawing together. "Well, maybe it doesn't happen that way for everyone."

"Charlie couldn't stand me, and look at us now,"

Candice says with a cheeky grin, waving her hand and showing off her gorgeous wedding ring. Those two are sickeningly in love. Seeing them together makes my jaded heart happy. "I won him over."

Amelia smiles demurely. "I was set up on a blind date." She's with a new guy after finally breaking up with her long-term boyfriend who treated her like absolute crap.

"It didn't happen to you." Stella aims her statement at Sarah.

"No, but Jared and I were a little different." Sarah sends a pointed look at Stella. "Like you and Carter."

Now Stella is giggling. "I hated him so much. Even when we were kids, I thought he was a pain in the ass. And then we had sex, he ditched me the next morning, and I hated him even more."

"Only because you secretly liked him," Sarah points out.

"Yeah, though I didn't realize it at the time. Plus, the sex between us was so ama—"

"Ugh. You really need to quit talking about having sex with my brother, Stella," Caroline interrupts, making the entire table start laughing. Including me.

"You're going to be okay," Sarah tells me once the laughter dies. "You and Theo? It'll all work out."

I smile and nod. "Sure we will."

Not sure how much I believe what I just said, but I have to. We're going to work out. Either as just friends or as—gulp—an actual couple.

I can't think about the alternative.

I just...

I can't.

I EXIT the restaurant to find Theo waiting for me, leaning against a light post and checking his phone. I come to a stop just outside the entrance, not making a sound as I watch him. He doesn't notice me at first, which gives me a little time to look my fill. His head is bent, his dark hair tumbling across his forehead. Stubble lines his firm jaw, as it's wont to do this late in the day, and it gives him a rakish, cold-hearted duke air. He's wearing a suit, as usual, and it fits him perfectly. He spends a lot of money on those suits.

He also looks damn good in them.

It takes him a moment, but eventually he slowly lifts his head. His dark gaze meets mine, and the smile that spreads across his handsome face is devastating. Pushing away from the lamppost, he heads for me and I start toward him, both of us meeting in the middle of the sidewalk.

"Where are you parked?" he asks, resting his hand lightly on my waist. My entire body shivers at first contact. The touch is so casual, yet also possessive. I like it.

I love it.

"Right there," I say, tilting my head to the right.

He glances over to find my car sitting practically in front of the restaurant. He turns to face me once more. "How'd you get so lucky?"

"I've been here a while," I say with a little shrug.

"Night out with the girls?" He raises a brow.

"Yes, it was a good night. I love my friends." I lean into him with a smile. "And they love me."

"Someone had a little too much wine." His fingers tighten around my waist.

"Maybe." I wonder if I should tell him that my friends know about us.

Probably not.

They choose that exact moment to exit the restaurant.

Every single one of them calls out a goodbye to us, and every single one of them wears a knowing smile on their face. But it's like Theo doesn't notice at all. He's either completely clueless, or blind.

Thank goodness. I don't feel like answering those types of questions from him tonight.

"Can you drive home?" he asks once my friends are gone.

"Ummm...I don't think so." I slowly shake my head.

"I can give you a ride back to my place." He hesitates only for a moment, and I can feel his insecurities coming back. And those insecurities are my fault, unfortunately. "You still want to come over?"

"Definitely," I say without any hesitation at all. I need to be honest about how I feel about him. I want this night together.

"You sure?" His tone is serious, as is his expression. He wants to make sure I know what I'm doing, and I appreciate that more than he could ever know.

"Yes, I'm sure." I hesitate for only a second. "Think you could bring me back here tomorrow morning before work?"

"Sure." He's smiling. He looks very pleased with himself, and also extremely handsome. The suit, the hair, the sparkle in his dark eyes, the knowledge behind them. They say, *I've made you come and I can't wait to make you come again.*

My core throbs. Right here, on the sidewalk in front of Tuscany. Maybe it's the wine, but I doubt it. It's the man, and how I feel about him.

"Then let's go." I pull out of his hold and he takes my hand instead, which is almost just as good. And is definitely a public declaration, though no one else is really around. "Where did you park?"

"Kind of far," he admits as he leads me up the hill and away from the restaurant. "Might be a bit of a hike."

"Traffic is always so bad here after five." I gently swing our connected hands to and fro, like we're little kids. It's kind of fun. "Where's your brother and sister?"

"They left a while ago. Cam had a call he needed to take. Ali decided to leave too." Theo frowns. "My sister isn't in the best place right now."

"Why? What's wrong?"

He launches into a story about her dropping out of college and disappointing their parents, which I already knew about. How she has no real drive to do much of anything since, and their mom and dad are worried.

Poor girl. I feel her pain. She should hang out with me and my friends one night. We can give her loads of advice. We all come from such a variety of backgrounds—surely she could learn something from us.

"Cam bought a farm," he says out of nowhere, and I come to a stop, forcing him to do the same.

"What do you mean?" I'm frowning. Who just goes out and buys a farm? Sounds a little crazy. And impulsive.

"The old Carmel Valley Farm? Remember that place?" Theo asks. He knows I grew up here.

"Of course I remember it. I used to beg to go there when I was little." Did my mom ever take me? No. I went one time a few days before Halloween with a friend and her family, and they were kind enough to buy me a pumpkin. I went back to their house and carved it that night. We had so much fun, despite how messy and gross pumpkin guts are. That was the only time I've ever carved pumpkins in my life.

Sad.

"Cam bought it," Theo says, like it's no big deal. But

that place has to cost a fortune, even though it's stood abandoned for a few years and has depreciated in value. Still. That's a huge purchase.

"Why would he do that?" I ask. We start walking once more.

"He wants to renovate it. Bring it back to its original glory he says, and make it even better." Theo shakes his head.

"You don't think he can do it?"

"I think it's a huge undertaking that will take years and lots of money and hard work," he says.

"Sounds like a big project."

"My brother loves nothing more than to tackle a big project." His expression is grim. "It's like he purposely seeks out difficult situations. He's a fixer."

"And what are you?" When Theo sends me a questioning glance, I continue, "Are you a fixer?"

"No. I'm loyal to a fault. I'll stick by someone for too long, even if they treat me like shit." He clamps his lips shut after the words leave him, like maybe he shouldn't have admitted that.

I can't stop thinking about his confession, even after when we climb into his car and he takes me back to his place. We make light conversation throughout the drive, but I'm preoccupied by thoughts of his faulty loyalty.

Is that what happened with Jessica? Did he stick too long by her side, even though their relationship was already falling apart? Would he have married her anyway?

What a scary thought.

One I can't help but let worry me.

SEVENTEEN
THEO

"I HAD no idea you lived this close to the ocean," Kelsey says as she climbs out of my car, the wind whipping her long hair across her face. She bats it away and tilts her nose up, inhaling. "I can smell it."

"You can smell it pretty much anywhere you are on the peninsula," I remind her, slamming the car door and hitting the keyless remote to lock it.

"Not at my apartment, you can't," she says wryly, letting me take her arm and lead her toward my building.

"Where exactly do you live anyway?" I ask, sending her a curious glance.

She seems to struggle with an internal war, as if it takes a lot for her to admit all of this. "In Marina."

That's a surprise. We might've talked about her financials in the past, and she had to tell me her address when she filled out an informational form for me, but that was in the early days, when we weren't quite friends yet. I definitely wasn't as curious about her every move as I am now. "Not too far then."

"It's a really small apartment. Old. Dark. Small." She winces, wrinkling her nose. "Awful, really."

"You should move somewhere nicer," I suggested as we approach my building. "You can probably afford it. I know Wilder pays you well."

"Yes, as a matter of fact—" She stops talking and exhales loudly instead, never finishing her sentence.

"As a matter of fact, what?" We stop at the base of the stairs that leads up to my place. I've rented this little one-bedroom apartment for almost two years, and I fucking love it. Jessica thought it was the biggest waste of money ever, but I didn't care. I wanted the convenience it afforded me by being close to my office. Plus there are the views, and the ocean nearby. The apartment was renovated right before I moved in, and I couldn't resist it.

"Nothing." She shakes her head and moves into me, her hand resting lightly on my suit jacket lapel. "You going to take me inside?"

Her voice lowers to a husky whisper and my dick reacts, just like that. Taking her hand again, I bound up the stairs and she follows, both of us a little out of breath once we pause in front of the door. I unlock it and lead her inside, going over to the lamp that sits on the end table and flicking it on, flooding the room with gentle light.

"Oh." She stops in the middle of my living room and glances around, her expression surprised. "Theo. This is so nice."

"You like it?" I'm proud of this apartment. It may be small, but I had an interior designer friend help me pick out the furniture and some of the art that hangs on the walls. The vinyl plank flooring is a rustic grayish-blond wood and the walls are painted a stark white. It accentuates the uncovered windows that flank the sliding glass door, which leads out onto my balcony and showcases that amazing ocean view.

I feel a catch in my chest every time I look at it. Seriously, who would've thought little old me would make enough money to live right on the ocean? When the timing's right, I'm going to buy a home with an ocean view as well. I've been saving for years, and I've been searching. Waiting for the right moment to make my move. Getting dumped by my fiancée put a glitch in my plans temporarily, but I'm over it. Over her.

Besides, I have a new woman to focus on now.

"Oh my God, I can kind of see the ocean out there, even though it's dark," Kelsey says as she leaves her purse on the couch and makes her way to the sliding glass door.

She's right. The moon is currently full, its bright silvery light shining upon the water outside, and without hesitation Kelsey unlocks and opens the slider, stepping out onto the balcony. "This is so gorgeous, Theo!"

I follow her out there, the wind smacking against my face, the windchimes that hang off the roof's edge jangling. "You like it?"

"I love it." She glances over her shoulder and flashes me a quick smile before she returns her attention to the water. "I've always loved the ocean."

"Me too." I move so I'm standing directly behind her, bracing my hands on the balcony's ledge, boxing her in, my face close to her hair.

"When I was little, that's all I wanted to do. Go to the beach." Her voice is wistful. "I would beg my mom to take me, and she never did. It was torture, living so close yet never seeing it."

"Why wouldn't she take you? It's free to go."

"I don't know." She shrugs. "She said she didn't like it."

There is so much to this woman I don't know, that I want to discover. She keeps herself closed off most of the time. She's sweet and she's funny and supportive. Warm and sexy and she tastes delicious.

But she's also...sad. Maybe a little lonely? I don't think she trusts many people.

That she's here with me, showing her trust in me, is mind blowing. I don't want to disappoint her. And I definitely don't want to hurt her.

We're quiet for too long, and I don't want to continue talking about her mother if it's going to make her feel melancholy. Instead, I nuzzle my face in her fragrant hair, breathing deep. I can feel her body start to relax, and she slowly leans into me, showing that right now, in this moment, she trusts me.

"I'm glad we ran into each other at the restaurant," she finally says, her voice soft.

"Me too." I lean in and drop a kiss on the side of her neck. "It turned into my lucky night."

"I agree." She's smiling. I can feel the curve of her mouth when I kiss her cheek, and then she's angling her face closer to mine, so that our lips brush once. Again. And again.

She turns completely around to face me, her arms going around my neck, and mine going around her waist. I press her into the balcony, kissing her deeply, stroking my tongue against hers. It's cold outside, I can feel her start to shiver, but I don't think it's because of the weather.

I think it's because of me. Us. The way this woman reacts to my touch—it's empowering. She lets me be bold. I say and do whatever the hell I want when I'm with her, and she seems to enjoy it.

That's powerful too.

"Let's go inside," I tell her after a few minutes of kissing. Knowing this woman, if we stay out here any longer, she'll try to get me to fuck her outside, and I don't want that.

Not tonight.

She nods in agreement and I take her hand, leading her back into my apartment and straight to my bedroom. Without hesitation I reach for her, pulling her back into my arms and she comes willingly, a little moan escaping her when I ignore her mouth and kiss her neck instead. Her skin is warm and fragrant and I press my lips against her throbbing pulse, licking the spot. A shiver streaks through her and I reach for the front of her shirt, slowly undoing the buttons.

"Wait." She steps away from me and I blink open my eyes, staring at her curiously. Worry hits me right in the chest.

Kelsey's not going to stop this moment...is she?

Of course not. I shouldn't have worried. Instead, she undoes the buttons on her blouse herself, shrugging out of it and letting the shirt fall to the floor. She stands before me in just her black bra and pants, a siren calling to me, making me hard. Making me want more.

And by the little smirk curving her luscious lips, she knows it.

Her hands rest at the front of her pants for barely a second before she undoes the button. Slides down the zipper. Slips out of her shoes before she lets her pants fall at her feet, stepping out of them and kicking them aside.

Her panties are black and miniscule. They leave nothing to the imagination. My dick strains against my trousers and her gaze drops to that exact spot, her eyes flaring with heat.

"Do you want me to continue?" she asks, her voice husky soft.

"I thought I would get the pleasure of undressing you." My own voice is rough. Gravelly. I don't sound like myself.

Right now, I don't necessarily feel like myself either. I curl my hands into fists at my sides, suddenly desperate to touch her. Suck on those pretty nipples that are poking against the thin fabric of her bra. Stroke her beneath the panties. Watch her eyes dilate when I brush my fingers against her clit. Hear that catch in her breath when I slip my fingers deep inside her.

I don't do any of that, though. Instead, I wait to hear what she'll say next.

She's smiling, letting her hand drift across her flat stomach. Her fingers wander up to trace the valley of her cleavage. "I wanted the pleasure of undressing myself tonight."

I don't stop her, and she takes my silence as permission to continue. She reaches behind her back and undoes her bra, letting the straps fall down her arms slowly, until she's shrugging out of it and the whisp of fabric falls away. She cups her full breasts in her hands, her thumbs streaking across her erect nipples, teasing them.

Without thought I start to shrug out of my suit jacket, eager to be as naked as she is.

"No!" Her voice rings out, sharp and firm, and I pause in my actions, my jacket hanging halfway off my arms. "Please. It's just—"

She goes quiet.

"It's just what?" I ask, shrugging the jacket back on.

"I thought it would be really hot if I was totally naked while you remain completely clothed." She smiles, and it's sweet. Which is a complete contradiction considering she's standing before me like my every sexual fantasy come to life.

"You want me to keep my clothes on?" I ask.

Kelsey nods.

"Eventually I'm going to take them off." I say it as a warning.

"I know. I want you to. It's just, for now, keep everything on." Her smile turns wicked. "I have a plan."

"What's your plan?"

"I can't tell you. It's a surprise. Just—watch me."

I do as she requests, watching as she walks around to the side of the bed and turns on the lamp there, bathing the room in a gentle glow. She reaches for the waistband of her panties and shucks them off in one smooth movement, tossing them aside, and now she's naked.

Beautiful.

Breathtaking.

"Maybe you should sit over there." She points at a nearby chair that rests beneath the window, and I go to it, settling in. It's the perfect spot for me to observe her as she climbs onto the bed, lying on her back, her head propped up on the pillows. She bends her legs at the knees, her feet flat on the mattress, and she slowly spreads her thighs.

Giving me the perfect view of her pretty pink pussy.

"Do you like watching me, Theo?" she asks, her hand wandering once again. She slides those elegant fingers across her stomach. Lower. Settles them over the light patch of dark pubic hair, before her pinky dips down and she barely touches herself.

"I like just about everything you do," I tell her truthfully, my gaze locked on her hand.

"I've never done this for a man before," she confesses,

her fingers sliding down even farther, until she's completely cupping herself.

"Touch yourself?" I arch a brow.

She nods, curling her fingers into a semi-fist, until it's only her index finger that's extended. She slides that finger through her folds, searching. Teasing. "It's very—" She brushes her fingertip against her clit and sucks in a sharp breath. "Arousing."

She's wet. I can see her glistening flesh, and when that index finger disappears inside her body, I groan. She's fucking torturing me.

And I think she's enjoying it.

"This feels good," she admits, her teeth sinking into her lower lip for a moment. "But not as good as your cock would."

I grip the armrests, my fingers curled so tight my knuckles are white. "You should let me touch you."

"Not yet." She inserts another finger and starts to fuck herself. In and out those fingers move, and now they're glistening from her juices. She lifts her hips and leans back, her eyes sliding closed.

My body grows taut. My muscles are fucking trembling from restraint. I want her so damn bad, but I remain where I'm at, eager to see what she'll do next.

And she doesn't disappoint.

Kelsey withdraws her fingers from her body and starts drawing circles on her clit. Tighter and tighter. Faster and faster. She's trying to get herself off, and quick—and I realize I don't want this to end so fast.

"I love knowing you're watching me do this," she admits, her voice low. "I love knowing that you want to touch me so badly, you're squeezing the armrests on the chair extra hard." A pause. "I bet your cock is extra hard too."

"Come over here and find out," I demand.

"Hold on." She bucks her hips. Her fingers are frantic now, as are her breaths. Those busy fingers slip over her flesh and she's panting, reaching for her peak as her toes curl into the mattress in preparation.

The shaking comes out of nowhere when the orgasm hits her. I watch in mute fascination as she writhes about on my bed, her fingers still working her clit, the juicy sounds along with our ragged breaths the only noise in the otherwise quiet room. She lies there for a moment, her gaze on the ceiling, her chest rising and falling rapidly before she sits up, pushing her hair out of her eyes when she swings her legs over the side of the bed.

"Come here," I say to her, and she flashes me a look, rising to her feet. She does exactly as I demand, making her way toward me, her hips swinging. Her breasts swaying.

Without hesitation, she climbs right on top of me, straddling my hips, her knees bent, her wet pussy pressed against my groin. She rests her arms on my shoulders, her face in mine, and I drink her in, mesmerized by her glowing-with-sweat skin. Intoxicated by the musky smell of her.

"I want to mess your suit up." She grinds herself against me, dampening the fabric. "I want you to see the stains on your clothes tomorrow and know I'm the one who marked you."

"Territorial?" I rest my hands lightly on her flaring hips, and she dodges away from my touch.

"Just don't want you to forget about me," she says with a smile.

As if I could.

I grip the back of her neck and pull her down for a

hungry kiss. She returns it, her tongue sliding against mine in time with her grinding body. She keeps dragging her pussy across my erection. Back and forth, again and again. Like she's trying to get me off.

Trying to get herself off.

I slide my other hand across the smooth skin of her ass, reaching between her legs to stroke her. She moans into my mouth when I insert my fingers inside all that wet, tight heat.

"Feels so good," she whispers against my lips as she starts to ride my hand in earnest. "I love the way you touch me."

I stroke her. Tease her. Gather up all that moisture and rub her clit. Fast. Slow. I pull away so I can see her face to find she's already watching me. Our gazes lock, and I remove my hand from between her thighs, circling my wet finger around one nipple. Then the other.

She tears her gaze from mine and tilts her head down, her teeth catching her lower lip. I lean in and dart my tongue out, licking her left nipple. Then her right. Her thigh muscles draw tight and her fingers curl around my shoulders, gripping me when I pull her nipple into my mouth and suck it deep.

We continue the tease for long minutes. Me still full dressed and sweating like a motherfucker while I lick and suck her nipples. Tease her pussy with my fingers. I want to taste her. She's so wet, she's practically dripping, and I'm about ready to bust through my pants, I'm so fucking hard.

I just want to sink inside her and lose myself, but she's determined to put me through this exquisite torture first. So I play her game and do my damnedest to drive her out of her mind.

"Put your knees on the chair arms," I tell her at one point, and she frowns, looking around. "Do it."

It's a demand, not a question, and she rises up, pressing her left knee on one armrest, her right knee on the other, which spreads her wide open and directly in front of me.

Cupping her ass cheeks, I slide down a little, my neck protesting, but fuck it. I want her.

And this is the perfect angle for me to do this.

EIGHTEEN
KELSEY

I WATCH in quiet fascination as Theo slides down the chair, wincing with the movement but otherwise, not saying a word. His large hands cup my backside, his fingers sliding along my crack in a wicked tease, and he lifts me up and lowers his head simultaneously, his mouth making contact with my pussy for the very first time.

And oh God, it feels so incredibly good. And dirty. Even a little—wrong. But in the absolute best way. His gaze never leaves mine as he licks me. Sucks my clit between his lips. My legs are trembling with exertion considering the position I'm currently locked in, but I don't care. All I can concentrate on is the sensation of Theo's mouth eagerly working me over. Those big hands squeezing my ass. His tongue lapping at my clit.

A moan leaves me and I close my eyes.

He stops. Completely. My eyes fly open and only then does he continue, and I realize he *wants* me to watch him. I can't lose myself in the sensations, absorb the way his tongue and mouth work me over. I must observe. Drink in all that intensity and never look away. This is such a vulnerable moment for me. I've never watched a man do this so closely before. It's overwhelming. Intimate.

Exciting.

"You like this?" he asks when he pulls away, his lips shiny from my juices.

I nod, unable to find my voice.

"Do you want me to stop?"

I shake my head. Hell no, I don't want him to stop.

"I'm going to make you come," he murmurs against me. I feel his finger slide around, teasing my entrance, and a whimper escapes. "You're close. You know how I can tell?"

No. I don't know. Enlighten me please, sir.

I shake my head in answer since he can't read my mind.

"Your clit starts to swell." He licks it. Sucks it between his lips noisily before he releases it. "And I can feel you clenching. As if you want something inside you." He teases my entry again, just before he plunges two fingers deep within me, turning his hand so he can curl them upwards, bumping against something that has me immediately seeing stars.

"Don't close your eyes," he commands, and I struggle to keep them open. My entire lower body feels like it's on fire. Tense and preparing for the orgasm that's ready to rip through me. My breaths become shallow as he thrusts those talented fingers inside me, his mouth on my flesh once more, my gaze captured by his. He pulls away to murmur, "Touch yourself. Your tits."

I grab hold of one and squeeze it. Pinch my nipple. Oh my God, that feels good. His fingers withdraw from my body, lightly tracing the skin between my pussy and my ass. Forbidden territory—no one's ever touched me on purpose there before, and holy shit, it feels amazing.

"Someday, if you'll let me..." His voice drifts, and I

know what he's asking. Yes, I've had other men ask me that before, but I've never wanted it. Always changed the subject or knew deep down I'd never be with the guy long enough that we'd eventually get around to that.

Plus, I don't trust anyone enough to try anal with them.

I trust Theo, though.

"Yes," I whisper, and that pleases him, I can tell. He attacks my pussy with gusto, his fingers inside me once more, his mouth basically gobbling me alive. I lift my hips, my thighs numb from being in the same position for so long, my lower body straining against Theo's seeking mouth when the orgasm slams into me.

He grips me close, his chin smashed against my flesh, his tongue flicking rapidly against my clit throughout the entirety of my orgasm. Until I'm begging him to stop and trying to shift my hips away from his devilish mouth.

God, that was so intense. I can't catch my breath.

As if Theo realizes I'm completely overcome, he tugs me down and sits up at the same time, so I'm cradled in his lap, in his arms. I cling to him, my face buried against his chest, breathing in the faint scent of his cologne. He's warm and solid and he holds me tight, his mouth against my forehead, one hand trailing up and down my back. He calms me, sets me back to rights, and once I'm breathing normally and not shivering as much, he leans back so we can look at each other.

"You okay?" he asks.

I nod, grateful he asked. "That was just..."

"Intense?"

Another nod from me. "But good."

So, so good. The best I've ever had.

I can't tell him that, though. My admission would let him know how much power he has over me, and for once I want to tell someone. I want to be open and honest, and confess my feelings.

He contemplates me, his face so close, giving me ample opportunity to ogle him. This calm, composed man knows exactly how to make me fall completely apart, and it's staggering to realize. He breaks down my barriers like no other. I don't understand the hold he has on me, but...

For once, I don't mind. This sort of thing normally scares me to death. Not with Theo, though.

Reaching out, he brushes strands of wild hair out of my eyes, his gaze roving over my face as if he too is taking the opportunity to blatantly study me in amazement. The air becomes thick between us, and I worry the moment could turn too heavy.

I decide to switch it up.

"We have a problem," I tell him solemnly.

He frowns, his dark brows pinching together. "What is it?"

"I'm naked." I gesture toward him. "And you're still fully clothed."

The slow grin that appears on his face makes everything inside of me clench up tight. It immediately disappears, and he touches me, his knuckles feather-light as they brush against my nipple. "We need to rectify that."

"I know." I settle my hand on his lap, curling my fingers around his erection. "It's an issue that needs to be taken care of immediately."

Theo chuckles, and it makes me happy. Worse, my heart soars, like maybe I'm in love with him or something crazy like that.

Nope, no falling in love for me. This will end badly if I do. He's my friend who's turned into my fuck buddy. Nothing more, nothing less.

Right?

"Come on." He drops a kiss on my lips, and I can taste myself. He deepens the kiss, his hand cupping my cheek, his other hand wrapped around my waist, locking me in place. I keep my hand on his erection, wishing he were naked right now, so I could climb on top of him and we could have sex right here in this chair.

Instead, he grabs hold of me and takes me with him when he stands. I can't stop the shriek that leaves me, I'm so startled, and when he carries me over to the bed and deposits me on the mattress, I tell him, "I didn't realize you were that strong."

"I'm full of surprises," he says with a smirk as he shrugs out of his jacket.

I'll say is how I want to answer, but I remain quiet, enjoying him stripping off all of his clothes, item by item. The jacket is gone. Then the tie. He removes his shirt, and that takes a while, which makes him frustrated, and makes me giggle.

Next is the belt, which falls onto the floor with a clank. He takes off his shoes, and slips out of his pants, his cock tenting the front of his boxers and tempting me to reach for it.

But I don't.

Finally, the boxers are gone, and he stands before me completely naked. My gaze lingers on his body, admiring how comfortable he is without a stitch of clothing on, in front of me. Most men don't have hang ups about nudity like a lot of us women do.

Theo runs his hand down the flat plane of his stomach and touches himself, his fingers gripping the base of his cock, and he starts to stroke.

Oh dear Lord, there is nothing sexier than this man

standing before me, sliding his hand up and down his thick cock, his hot gaze on me and nothing else. I part my lips, my heart starting to go wild in my chest, my core throbbing. I want him inside me so badly.

"I could jack off right now," he tells me, his voice deep yet deceptively calm. "Come all over your tits and call it a night."

That would be terribly unfair. That's what I should tell him. "I suppose you could," is what I say instead.

"Or I could slide deep inside you and fuck you until we're both coming." His speed increases and there's a hitch in his breath. "Your choice."

"I want you inside me," I say without hesitation.

"Come here first," he practically growls. "I want to see your lips on my cock."

He's so demanding. He takes complete control in the bedroom—or wherever else we mess around—and it's surprising. When you meet him, you'd never guess he behaves this way.

It's hot.

I sit up and he steps closer. I'm at the perfect level to do exactly what he wants, so I do. Ever so slowly, I rest my mouth on the very tip of his erection, pursing my lips around it, my gaze still on his. His lids fall to half-mast and his lips part. He's still got his fingers wrapped around the shaft, but he doesn't try to push deeper into my mouth.

My tongue darts out and I lick the slit, tasting the faintly sour precome there. He curses under his breath but still doesn't thrust forward, which I appreciate.

"Lick it again," he whispers, and I do. I lick the head. Swirl my tongue around like it's a melting ice cream cone and I'm trying to lap up every last bit. I shift away, only to come back and wrap my mouth around the entire head, my tongue searching, my lips tightening.

"Fuck." The word is a whisper. Shaky and reverent. My gaze lifts to his once more and I withdraw him from my mouth, run my tongue down the length of his shaft until I encounter his fingers, and I lick those too.

"You are the sexiest fucking woman I've ever been with," he says, his gaze glowing as he stares at me with wonder. "I could come just from watching you."

"I bet you'd like that," I tell him. "Coming all over my face?"

He closes his eyes and shakes his head, as if he's trying to get the image out of his mind. Men. They're such simple creatures. They love a good visual.

"I can't take it," he tells me, and the next thing I know, he's on top of me, his cock entering my body, and he starts to move his hips. Slow at first. He drags his cock almost all the way out of my pussy before he plunges back inside. Again and again he does this, and I close my eyes, allowing myself to finally get lost in the sensation of him being inside of me. Driving me wild.

His fingers brush against my clit, and I gasp, my eyes flying open to find him hovering above me, blocking everything else out so all I can see is him. He starts to move faster, and I don't protest. I let him take me, because that's what he wants. Theo is a giver. He gives his time, his energy, his money, his love and care. Everyone seems to take from him.

Even me.

But right now, I'm giving him whatever he wants. His movements are brutal. Hard. Our sweaty skin slaps with his every thrust, and I cry out when he hits me deep. Over and over.

Again and again.

"You close?" he asks me at one point, but he doesn't even wait for my answer. He grabs hold of my waist and pounds into me with smooth, stabbing strokes. Faster and faster, his groans growing louder until he thrusts his hips one last time, straining against me and calling out my name as the orgasm sweeps over him.

I reach between us, touching my clit, and within seconds I'm coming too. Not as intense as the first time, and not as long as Theo's, but it's still good.

So good.

He collapses on top of me, his body still shuddering, and I wrap my arms around him, holding him close. It's only then I realize I can feel the flood of his semen inside my body.

We didn't use a condom.

Shit.

NINETEEN
THEO

I FEEL GOOD. On top of the world, actually. It's been a long time since I've felt this confident, on my game. I come to work every day whistling wearing a smile on my face. Not that I've ever hated my job; I love it *too* much most of the time.

Lately, I've been leaving work at a normal hour, which I know shocks everyone, but screw it. I'm eager to get out of there.

And see Kelsey.

It's been almost three weeks since that night we ran into each other at Tuscany and I brought her back to my apartment, and we've been pretty much inseparable ever since. We spend almost all of our free time together. She came to another family dinner last Saturday. I brought her along with me a couple of weeks ago, when I met up with Cam for drinks and we discussed the new farm. She had good input to offer, which I appreciated, and I could tell my brother did too. Not only is Kelsey beautiful, but she's smart. When she speaks, all I want to do is listen to her voice.

And stare at her pretty face, I can admit it.

The sex between us is just—unbelievable. I think it keeps getting better, which I didn't know was possible. We can't keep our hands off of each other. It was never like this with any of the other women I've dated.

Not even Jessica.

Speaking of Jessica...

It's the week of her wedding to my cousin, and I agreed to be one of Craig's groomsmen a while ago, which is still just—wild.

Life is strange sometimes.

I'm currently going to Monterey for our final tuxedo fitting, and I'm not looking forward to it. We take home the tuxedos tonight as well. Tomorrow is the rehearsal dinner. Saturday is the wedding. Kelsey will be attending both with me.

Thank God. Don't think I could get through it all without her by my side.

I can't wait to walk into that rehearsal dinner with Kelsey on my arm. Jessica's going to be shocked. Craig will probably say something crude, yet secretly be jealous that I bagged such a babe.

Yeah. It feels wrong, referring to Kelsey that way. She's not some babe I bagged. She's a woman I respect and, dare I say, care about. She's smart and funny and strong. She gives as good as she gets. The fact that she's absolutely stunning is icing on the delicious cake that is Kelsey.

Now I'm calling her cake. What the hell is wrong with me?

I pull into the mall parking lot and park not too far from the store. Make my way slowly toward the building, dread making my footsteps heavy. I do not want to hang out with Craig and all his bros this afternoon, trying on tuxes while I have to pretend to be happy he's marrying the very woman he stole from me. The more I think about it, the angrier I get, so by the time I'm walking through the doors of the store, I'm fuming.

Not a great way to make an entrance.

"Theodore! There you are!" Craig approaches me like he's the host of the party, his arms outstretched and wearing a giant grin on his stupid face. "You're late."

I'm not. I'm never late. I glance at my watch. "I'm five minutes early."

The smile falls from Craig's face and he shakes his head. "Right. Shit. I forgot to tell you. The fitting was rescheduled to two-thirty, not three-thirty. We changed it."

I glance around the place, realizing that I don't see anyone else around. No familiar faces. Not even Craig's brother, Rick. I get along with Rick. Much easier than I do with Craig, that's for damn sure.

"Everyone left," Craig tells me. "I was just about to go myself, but Jessica's meeting me here, so..."

Unease slips down my spine. That is the very last person I want to see right now. "Why didn't you text me and let me know about the schedule change?" I ask.

"Figured you were just running late as usual," he says.

I part my lips, ready to blast him for being incorrect. I'm never late. That isn't my style and it never has been. But what's the point in arguing with him? He won't listen. He never has. He won't give a shit either. Craig only cares about himself.

"I should probably try on my suit, right?" I tell him, and Craig leaps into action.

"Yeah, yeah. You're right. Let me get the salesgirl." He turns and starts yelling. "Yo, Lindy! Can you help us out?"

I wince, hating how loud he just was. And how rude. Craig has zero manners.

"She's a looker, this one," he says, nudging me in the ribs with a leer. "Wait until you see her."

Lindy makes her appearance, and fine. Craig's right. Lindy is very attractive. Long blond hair. Pretty smile. Nice figure. "Oh, did your last groomsman show up?"

"Yeah, sorry about that." I step forward and offer my hand for her to shake. "I'm Theo. I still need to try on my suit."

"I'm Lindy." She shakes my hand, then turns to point toward the dressing rooms. "Your tuxedo is waiting for you in the last dressing room. Go ahead and slip it on. I'll come check on you in a bit, make sure it fits."

"I bet you will," Craig says with a cheesy grin.

Lindy shoots him a withering glare before she stomps off.

"Don't be such a jerk, Craig," I tell him the moment she's gone.

"She wants me," he says with all the confidence of an oblivious idiot who believes he has the power to attract any woman in the world. "She's been flirting with me the entire time I've been here."

I don't bother responding to that. Instead, I go to the dressing room and lock myself away, shedding my clothes and trying on the tuxedo. Once I've got myself somewhat assembled, I exit the stall to find Lindy waiting for me with a polite smile on her face.

"How does it fit?" she asks, stepping forward to examine me. "It looks good on you."

I can only imagine the remarks Craig made when she told him something similar. "Thanks. It feels good."

I turn to face the mirror, contemplating myself. I wonder what Jessica will think when she sees me like this.

I've lost weight. Built up muscle. I feel good. And hell, I don't look half bad either.

Wonder what Kelsey will think too. Look at me, hoping to impress her.

Shit, I think I've got it bad.

"Looks like the hem length on the trousers works," Lindy says, tilting her head to examine my feet. "Once you take the suit off, I'll bag it up for you along with the shoes and the other accessories, and then you'll be good to go."

"Thanks," I tell her, flashing her a quick smile before I return my attention to the mirror. "Looking forward to my girlfriend seeing me in this get up."

Well, shit. I can't believe I said that. I sound like a corny motherfucker.

Lindy smiles, looking pleased. "That's so sweet. I'm sure she'll think you look very handsome."

"You do look very handsome," says a familiar voice from behind me.

I glance over my shoulder to see Jessica standing there, basically gaping at me. I turn so I'm fully facing her, trying to fight the annoyance I feel upon first seeing her. Isn't that a good sign? That I don't feel lovesick when I first spot her, but annoyed?

Yeah, definitely.

"Hey Jess," I greet her, praying she doesn't want a hug.

Of course, shit never goes my way where this woman is concerned. She comes right up to me and throws her arms around my waist, pressing her face against my chest, just like she used to. I awkwardly hug her back, neither of us saying a word, and Lindy gets the hell out of there.

Not that I can blame her.

Finally Jessica steps back, and I spot that familiar affection in her gaze. The same way she would look at me when we were together.

I hate seeing it. Worse, I hate that I recognize it. But it also reiterates what I knew as fact.

I don't want to be with her anymore. I don't miss her anymore either. My feelings for Jessica are gone. Looking at her now, I feel...

Nothing.

"I can't believe you agreed to be a groomsman in my wedding," she finally says with a nervous laugh.

"I can't believe I agreed either," I say, because it's the damn truth. "But my girlfriend suggested I should do it, so I why not?"

The laughter fades and she watches me with a solemn expression. "Craig mentioned you were seeing someone."

I nod. "I am." And I'm tossing that *girlfriend* word around much too loosely, but isn't that what Kelsey is? My girlfriend? We've moved beyond the friends pretending to be together thing long ago. We are actually together-together.

Okay, now I sound like I'm in middle school.

"Anyone I know?" Jessica asks.

"No, you don't know her. I met her on a blind date." I don't bother explaining she wasn't my date the night we met.

"Must be true love then." Jessica arches a brow.

I need to change the subject. "Ready for the big day?"

"I suppose," she says with a sigh. "Craig isn't much help. He's always working, so I'm supervising everything." Jessica did always like to take charge. "What's your girlfriend's name?" she asks me, and I can hear the curiosity in her voice. She's dying for more details, but I'm only going to give her a few.

"Kelsey."

"Is she pretty?" Jess covers her mouth with her hand, at least having the decency to appear embarrassed. "I shouldn't ask that."

"Too late. You did. And yes. She's gorgeous."

"She's a lucky woman, dating you." Her voice is wistful. Her gaze full of longing.

Irritation rips through me and I start undoing the bowtie. "Don't say that kind of shit, Jess. Don't waste your breath."

Look at me, not holding back with Jess for once in my life.

Her mouth pops open. "I'm just trying to be nice."

"To the guy you dumped for a supposed better prospect. I hope you and my cousin are happy," I tell her, though I'm lying. I hope she's miserable with stupid, annoying Craig.

"It was a mistake," Jess blurts, right before she slaps her hand over her mouth once more.

Now I'm the one who's gaping at her, and she just watches me in return, her hand slowly lowering from her mouth. I can't come up with anything to say, but it doesn't matter because she keeps talking. "I mean it, Theo. I miss you so much. I should've never broke up with you."

I shake my head, wishing I could shake her confession right out of my brain. "It's too late, Jess. You can't tell me that kind of shit *two days* before your wedding."

"I guess it's just how I operate, you know? I get cold feet." She steps forward, reaching for my hand and lacing her fingers with mine. I feel nothing. My skin doesn't tighten, no tingling, no shivers, nothing. My heart rate and breathing are normal. "I think about you all the time, Theo. And I still wish you were mine."

"Hey, yo, get your hands off my girl, cuz!" Craig appears out of nowhere, yanking Jessica away from me and wrapping her up in a big bear hug.

I tear my gaze from hers to smile coolly at my cousin. "Where'd you go, Craig?"

"Had to talk to Lindy, handle a few last-minute things." He kisses Jess noisily on the forehead. "Glad you didn't see me in my tux, babe. Wouldn't want to put bad luck on the marriage."

"Isn't it the groom who can't see the bride in her gown on the wedding day?" I ask.

"Whatever." Craig rolls his eyes, then chucks his chin at me. "You're looking good in the suit, bro."

"Thanks." I tip my head toward the dressing room. "I'm going to get dressed and get out of here. See you two tomorrow night?"

"Yeah, and don't be late!" Craig guffaws.

"Tomorrow at six, Theo," Jessica reminds me.

"Right. Six. At the Wilder Hotel," I say, thinking of Kelsey.

When am I not thinking of her? She invades my thoughts twenty-four seven, and I definitely don't mind.

I lock myself in the dressing room, glad to be away from obnoxious Craig and ridiculous Jessica. She doesn't mean what she says. No way does she miss me or actually want me back. I think she just has pre-wedding jitters. And no way am I going to be the reason they don't get married after all. That would be fucked up.

If anyone should know how that feels, it would be me.

TWENTY
KELSEY

"KELSEY." My boss appears before me, a neutral, downright bland expression on his face, as usual. "A moment?"

I rise from my desk and follow Alex into his office, knowing exactly what he wants to talk about when he closes the door. I settle into the chair, watching as he rounds his desk and sits down, resting his forearms on the desk's edge.

"I have good news for you, and bad news for me." He smiles.

My heart feels like it just jumped into my throat. The past couple of weeks have been exciting yet excruciating. I've done Zoom interviews with both the Las Vegas Wilder Hotel and the London Trafalgar location. Then I went on to the second set of interviews. Even had to answer a few quick question requests from both of them. It's been nerve wracking and intense, and what makes everything worse?

I haven't mentioned my job opportunities to Theo. Not once. And we've spent a lot of time together. Like every waking moment when we're not working or with family (him) or friends (me). We were so swept up in each other that night after I was offered the interview opportunities, I never got a chance to mention it to him. As time has gone on, it just gets harder and harder to bring it up.

So I don't.

I've been lucky enough to spend more time with his family, and I adore them. Ali is so sweet, and I'm bringing her to our next friend brunch get together, which is this Sunday, the day after the infamous Jessica's wedding. I will be full of juicy gossip and all my friends will want the details.

Huh. Maybe I shouldn't bring Ali with me.

Theo's brother Camden is a complete hottie, and very smart. I love his idea of reopening the Carmel Valley Farm and making it bigger. Better. He said he wants to take it to the next level by offering farm-fresh food, from garden to table. I gave him a few ideas—both Camden and I got excited and came up with a business plan on his laptop right there at the restaurant with Theo looking on proudly. Theo was so impressed, he took me back to his place that night and fucked me senseless on his couch.

I shouldn't say *fuck* anymore, because that's not what Theo and I are doing. It's morphed into something else these last few weeks. Something thoughtful and caring and —loving. Oh God, I can't even believe I thought that word. I think I'm going to be sick.

Resting my hand atop on my stomach, I say to Alex, "What's the news?"

"Vegas wants you. Badly." He pauses. His lips form into a barely there smile. "And so does London."

My mouth drops open. "They're *both* offering me the position?"

Alex nods. "You have until Monday to make your decision."

"That's only four days," I say, my brain scrambling and

short-circuiting. Four days to make the most important decision of my life.

"Plenty of time to consider, don't you think?" His smile stays fixed in place. I give this man a lot of credit for never showing much emotion. Though from what Caroline says, he's the sweetest man alive, and I believe her. "We have to get moving with training. Getting you over there soon—whichever hotel you should choose—is important."

I blink at him, at a loss for words. I can't believe they both want me. "Which one do you think I should take?"

"I don't want to influence your decision—" he starts, but I interrupt him.

"I value your opinion, Alex. Please." I smile. "I need some advice."

He's quiet for a moment as he contemplates me. "Vegas is the busier hotel, no doubt. It has a higher profile as well. Plus, your friend lives there, and I know how close you two are. Her boyfriend is sending people to our resort, and we appreciate that. He's recently become one of our influencers."

That's hilarious. Mitch Anderson, the hotel peddler.

"But London is in another country. A completely different experience, one you might not get the chance to take advantage of again," he continues. "It's a beautiful city. That would tempt me."

"It does," I tell him. "They both tempt me. I don't know what to do."

"That's why you need to take the weekend and try to figure it out," he says, his voice gentle. "Though you're busy with a wedding, right?"

I nod. "Theo's ex is getting married."

Alex chuckles. "That ought to be interesting."

"I'm sure."

"Caroline handled their invitations," he says. His wife and my friend works at and is partial owner of Noteworthy, a specialty stationery shop in downtown Carmel. "She mentioned the future groom as being an...unusual type."

"I haven't met him," I say, though I will be meeting him in a few hours.

"Me either, but I've heard stories. We may live in a bustling area, but it's really just a small town when you break it down." Alex rises to his feet and I do the same. "Think about it, all right? And let me know your choice Monday morning."

"I will. Thank you so much," I say as he walks me to the door.

"You earned it. Thank you for interviewing so well. You make me look good." He grins and opens the door for me. "I have a call in ten minutes. Put them through right away?"

"Yes, sir," I tell him as I make my way to my desk on suddenly wobbly legs.

I collapse in my chair, staring at my computer screen, though I really don't see anything. I'm too much in shock over what just happened. I didn't just get offered one new job, I was offered *two*. And one is in London, which is just—amazing. I applied for a passport right after I learned of the opportunity. I'll have to apply for a work visa as well, and I don't know how long that will take, but they explained during the interview process that I shouldn't worry about it. They'd make it work.

It's an assistant desk manager position at the Trafalgar Square location. Not as high in position as I'd hoped for, but they pay a lot. I did some research, and the cost of living in London is extremely high too. But...it's London. I never would've dreamed in a million years I'd have such an opportunity!

The call Alex is expecting comes in exactly ten minutes after I left his office, and I put the call through to his phone. He'll be talking for at least an hour. Maybe more. Deciding I deserve a little extra break, I grab my phone and text Eleanor.

What are you doing?

Luckily enough, she responds within seconds.

Waiting in between clients. What are YOU doing?

I decide to FaceTime her. I need to see her when I give her the news, because I think I know what I'm going to decide, but I need to hear her opinion first.

"Oh my gosh, look at you!" Eleanor says when she first sees me. "You're...glowing."

I blush, which is silly. Maybe it's all the great sex I'm having with Theo. I don't know. "It's just another Friday in Pebble Beach," I tell her.

"Please. Girl, I hear the rumors." She waves a dismissive hand, a giant smile on her face. Eleanor is blond and bubbly and cute as a button. She's also madly in love with her pro football player. Those two will probably get married eventually.

For once, I'm the teeniest bit jealous. Marriage normally doesn't appeal to me, but since I've been spending so much time with Theo lately...

I've started thinking about it. And realizing that maybe I do want the fairytale. The happily ever after.

"What rumors?" I ask her.

"About you and Theo. My former date." She bursts out laughing, and I can't help but giggle too. "Our financial advisor! Tell me, does he count his money when you two have sex?"

"He's too preoccupied to worry about money when

we're together," I say coyly, making her laugh harder. "Look, I have something serious to tell you."

She sobers up immediately. "What is it?"

"I got offered a promotion—at Wilder." I can barely contain the smile that spreads across my face.

"Oh my God, that's amazing! Congrats! I'm so happy for you!" This is why I called Eleanor. Not only is she one of my closest friends, but she's also probably the most enthusiastic person I know. I was craving her exuberance and she's delivering, just like I hoped.

"Here's the thing." I take a deep breath. "I was offered my choice of jobs. One at the Vegas location—"

"Get the hell out!" she interrupts, making me laugh.

"And one at a Wilder Hotel in...London."

She screams and shouts for a while, and I turn down the volume on my phone, hoping I don't disturb Alex's phone call. Luckily enough, no one else is around in our small office, so I'm not bothering anyone.

I let Eleanor get it all out before I finally say to her, "Help me make a decision."

"Oh, I can't make that choice for you," she says, sobering.

"I don't want you to make the choice, but I need advice."

"What does Theo think you should do?" she asks.

I press my lips together and drop my gaze, feeling like an asshole.

"Kelsey." Her voice is stern. "You *have* told Theo about this, right?"

I lift my head and hiss out a breath. "No?"

"Oh my God." Eleanor sounds completely exasperated with me. "Why haven't you told him? You've been *with* him for a month. You've been friends for longer than that!"

I've given a few details to Eleanor about me and Theo, but not too many. Looks like other people have been talking. Which is fine. It's my friend group, and I know they all mean well, but what Theo and I have isn't that serious—

Wait a minute. I need to stop. I'm lying to myself. What we have is fairly serious. I don't know what falling in love feels like, but I think it's pretty close to what I've been experiencing with Theo these last few weeks.

Holy. Shit.

"I legitimately forgot to tell him about the interviews when I first found out, and then after a while, so much time had passed, I didn't know how to tell him without worrying he'd get upset," I explain.

"Right, so you're going to tell him once you're packed up and ready to leave? That's not cool, Kelsey." Eleanor shakes her head.

I hate that she's disappointed in me. Worse, I'm disappointed in myself. I don't want to hurt Theo. He means too much to me. And I don't want to be another Jessica, breaking his heart and leaving him.

That would be awful.

"I'd tell him before I leave, I swear. I just—I don't know how." My stomach roils again, and I swallow hard, hating how nauseous I feel. My mouth tastes awful too. Quickly I open the top desk drawer and pull out a piece of gum, popping it into my mouth. I hope the minty taste will ease the nausea quickly.

"He deserves to know what's going on in your life. You need to come clean," she says firmly. "Tonight."

"The rehearsal dinner is tonight." I make a face. If I looked out at the lawn that leads to the ocean right now, I'd see them setting up for the grand wedding tomorrow. The rehearsal will be outside tonight, where the ceremony will take place. Afterward, Jessica and Craig have reserved one of the rooms at our restaurant, and it'll be a lovely, intimate dinner for fifty of their closest friends and relatives. Including me and Theo.

I can't wait.

My stomach gurgles at the thought.

"I feel terrible," I tell Eleanor, resting my head in my hands. "He's going to be so mad at me."

"You definitely need to tell him," Eleanor says, pausing when I lift my head and meet her gaze through the camera. She frowns. "Honey, are you okay? You don't look so well."

I frown. "What do you mean?"

"You're looking a little green around the edges," she explains. "You eat something bad at lunch earlier?"

I think of the turkey sandwich I brought from home and immediately want to throw up. As in, the urgency is there, right at the back of my throat. "Oh God. Eleanor, I gotta go."

I don't give her a chance to say goodbye. I end the call and bolt from my desk, making my way down the hall in record time and busting through the door of the employee bathrooms. I don't even bother locking the stall behind me before I'm kneeling before the toilet and puking my guts out.

God, it's disgusting. There's nothing worse than having your lunch come back up on you unexpectedly. I collapse on the floor and press my forehead against the stall wall, appreciative of the cool metal hitting my skin. And I still have to go to this stupid rehearsal dinner tonight.

By the time I'm back in the office, Alex is off his call early, a concerned expression on his face when he spots me. "What's wrong with you?"

I love how he doesn't ask if I'm okay. He just automatically assumes something's wrong. "How was your call?" I ask him.

"An annoyance, but it's over so there's that. How are you?" He tilts his head. "You don't look so well, Kelsey."

"I'm sorry. I don't feel good. I don't know what happened." I try to explain myself but eventually he doesn't want to hear it. And not because he doesn't believe me either. Sometimes my boss is a very impatient person.

"Find an empty room in the hotel and take a nap," he suggests.

"I can't do that."

"Oh yes you can. And I'm telling you that you should. I'll call over to the front desk and make the arrangements."

"I was just going to hang out here until I could change in the employee bathroom and meet Theo outside at six," I explain feebly.

"No. I won't hear of it. I don't want you sick while you're also trying to make a major life decision this weekend. Gather your things. You're off for the rest of the afternoon," Alex says as he comes to my desk and opens the bottom drawer, pulling my purse out and handing it to me. "Did you bring something to change into?"

I nod, taking my purse from him. "I left everything in my car."

"Give me the keys. I'll have someone from concierge take care of it and bring everything to your room."

I hand him my keys and he calls the front desk, finding me a room within minutes. "Someone will meet you at Room 426. You want me to accompany you there?"

"No, I can walk over on my own." My boss also has this way of taking command over everything and handling it with ruthless efficiency.

Reminds me of Theo. He's the same way.

Alex smiles, his gaze gentle. "Go on, Kelsey. Get some rest. Have fun at your wedding this weekend. I'll see you Monday."

"Alex, thank you so much for—everything."

He nods, and then goes back into his office.

I have the best boss in the world.

So why would I want to leave this place?

TWENTY-ONE
THEO

IT'S six-fifteen and Kelsey still hasn't shown up at the rehearsal. I send her a text, but she hasn't answered that either. Craig won't stop asking where my date is and I claim she's running late, but that sounds stupid when she works at the very place where this is being held. Not that he knows, but I do.

I'm worried. Where is she? Is she okay? Is she somehow...upset over something? With me?

There is absolutely no reason for her to be upset with me, so I'm worrying over something that is pointless. Dealing with Jessica and her saying that she misses me and she's making a mistake is fucking with my head. Not that I miss her and want to be with her...

Seeing her dredges up old memories. None of them fond either. I remember the hard times. Finding her with Craig. The way her betrayal cut at my heart, leaving it in shreds.

Well, that shit is pieced back together now, and it seems to only beat for a certain dark-haired woman who's not here yet.

Finally the rehearsal ceremony starts, and I do my thing. I escort my eighty-nine-year-old grandmother down the aisle and guide her to her seat in the front row on the groom's side before I get into position at the altar. My parents are here tonight as well, accompanying my grandmother, and I'm grateful to see them sitting in the chairs watching the run through unfold. Especially since Kelsey hasn't shown up.

I need someone here on my side.

Craig makes his way down the aisle with his parents, making cracks as he passes by familiar faces and acting like this moment is one big joke. Swear to God, his mother just looks relieved. I bet she thought her son would never find a woman to tolerate him.

Or maybe that's just me being mean.

The music changes, and everyone stands up straighter. It's time for the bride to make her way down the aisle. I know it's just the rehearsal and it's not even my wedding, but my stomach twists like I'm a nervous groom, and that is some ridiculous shit.

Just as Jessica is making her way to the start of the aisle with her father, I spot Kelsey emerging from the building in front of us, off in the distance. She's headed toward the ceremony, wearing a short floral dress that looks nothing like the sedate floral dress my grandmother is currently wearing.

The skirt is short and—sassy. That is the only word I can think of to describe it. It swishes and swirls around her slender thighs, accentuating her long, smooth legs. The long sleeves are billowy, covering her up, but the neckline is a deep, sexy V, exposing her chest and a hint of cleavage. Her strides are effortless on strappy nude stilettos, and her long dark hair falls in luxurious waves past her shoulders. The entire look is effortless. As if she rolled out of bed and just showed up.

I can't stop staring.

Our gazes connect and she offers me a little wave, a look of apology on her pretty face. She came into the area at an angle, so she doesn't disrupt the bride-to-be coming down the aisle, and my parents greet Kelsey enthusiastically as she settles in beside them.

I smile at Kelsey. She smiles back, those dark eyes capturing mine once more as she mouths *sorry*.

God, this woman. She has stolen my heart and she doesn't even realize it.

A new song starts up, something romantic and cheesy, and I tear my gaze away from Kelsey to spot Jessica standing with her arm wound around her father's as they slowly walk down the aisle. And she's not watching Craig as she heads toward him. She's watching...

Me.

Her expression is sour. As if she caught me making googly eyes at Kelsey, which she probably did. But so what? I'm not with Jessica any longer. She has no say in who I'm with.

Fuck her.

Damn, those are harsh words, but they describe exactly how I feel. Fuck her. She's the one who cheated on me. She's the one who snuck around behind my back for months and had sex with my idiot cousin, all while pretending to still be in love with me.

That's messed up.

So yeah. Fuck her.

I get bored after a few minutes of standing around and doing nothing as everyone frets over the flower girl and ring bearer, or the speed Jessica is supposed to walk when coming down the aisle. Nearly groan out loud when Craig's mother demands we do one more run through. We go through the ceremony again, and all I can think about is wanting to be with Kelsey. Wishing I was sitting with her and my parents instead of standing up here pretending I care about and support the bride and groom.

Let's be real. I don't.

Finally, the show is over and we're all walking to the restaurant in the hotel where the dinner will be held. I wait for Kelsey to approach, trying my best to avoid seeing Jessica, but she comes to me before anyone else does, and I have no choice but to speak to her.

"I'm so glad you're here. You'll have to introduce me to your girlfriend." Her smile is fake as hell, and I don't know why she bothers.

"At the dinner I'll make sure to," I say, offering a fake smile as well. "Don't you think you should go find Craig?"

The phony smile falls from her face and she takes a step closer to me. "I want to talk to you."

"No."

An exasperated sound escapes her. "Later. Come on, Theo. We need to talk."

"I have nothing to say to you," I bite out.

"But there are things I need to tell you," she practically whines. I don't miss that tone in her voice. Not at all.

"And I don't want to hear whatever it is you have to say," I tell her, my voice low. My anger obvious. "We're through, Jess. I'm not interested in your feelings or your misgivings about marrying Craig. That's on you. You made your choice. I have nothing to do with this anymore."

I leave her where she's standing, making my way toward Kelsey, pleased to see her engaged in an animated conversation with my mother. I love that they get along. She gets along with all of my family. Jess did as well, but I think they like Kelsey better. I know I sure as hell do.

"There you are," I tell my girlfriend, slipping my arm around her slender waist and pulling her in close. She goes with me easily, pressing her cheek against my shoulder before I lean down and drop a light kiss on her lips. "You okay?"

"I wasn't feeling well earlier, but I'm okay now." She smiles weakly. "I'll tell you about it later."

Concern fills me and I press a light kiss to her forehead. "You sure you're all right?"

"I'm fine. Really." Her gaze slides toward my parents, who are now both walking with my grandmother. "Your grandma is so sweet."

"She's pretty feisty," I say, enjoying the easy way we all walk together toward the restaurant. "I'm sure you two will get along great."

Kelsey laughs. "I get along with your entire family. They're all so easy to talk to."

I chance a glance at her, not wanting her to know what I'm thinking. But what I'm thinking is this: she's come a long way from the woman I first met. The one who was very skeptical, a little distrusting, and full of attitude. That woman had her defenses up—they were constructed of impossibly tall, steel walls. These last few weeks, she's become open and warm. All that earlier tension and mistrust is gone. I think I had something to do with that.

I actually know I had something to do with that.

"You look gorgeous," I whisper close to her ear. "That dress should be outlawed."

"I'm completely covered up," she says, her brows shooting up.

"Your legs aren't." My gaze dips to her chest. "Neither is that."

She laughs. "I thought it was just sexy enough to cause a stir, but not too big of a stir."

"You would be correct in that assessment," I tell her.

"Wait until you see what I have planned tomorrow." Her smile is devious.

Mine turns wicked. "Can't wait to peel you out of this later tonight."

"If you're lucky," she teases.

Fuck yes, I'm going to get lucky.

So is she.

We eventually make it to the restaurant, where the manager greets Kelsey personally. This impresses my parents and grandmother, and I explain that Kelsey works at the hotel and she's the personal assistant of the owner of the entire corporation.

Now they're even more impressed.

The party is escorted to a private room in the back of the restaurant, and when we walk inside, there are three long tables set up for everyone to sit at. I head straight for the last table, knowing the bride and groom won't want to sit there. They'll want the spotlight on them the entire weekend, which is their right. It's their wedding, after all.

I settle in with Kelsey by my side, my parents across from us and my grandma sitting next to my mom. There are menus resting on each plate, and I pick it up to give it a cursory glance.

"It's a limited menu tonight," Kelsey explains to everyone. "This is what we usually do for events like these. Makes it a lot easier on our kitchen."

"So smart," Mom says, her generous smile aimed right at Kelsey. "You enjoy working here, Kelsey?"

"I love it. Wilder Corp is a wonderful employer." Worry seems to flicker in her gaze, making me frown, and then I remind myself I'm being ridiculous. Kelsey has nothing to be worried about.

And neither do I.

"Tell me what happened earlier," I murmur close to her ear when the servers enter the room and cause a commotion. My parents start freaking out, panicked over what they should order, which stresses my grandmother out too. Weird.

Kelsey turns to look at me, our faces so close I could easily dip my head and kiss her. But I don't. Not yet. "What do you mean?"

"Why you were late to the rehearsal?"

"Oh, right." She frowns, her forehead wrinkling. "It was the strangest thing. I suddenly felt nauseous. So nauseous I ran into the bathroom and vomited." She looks vaguely embarrassed.

"Are you sure you're okay?" Concern touches my voice, and she sends me a weird look, like she's surprised I care. "Are you still feeling nauseous?"

"Oh. No, it passed." Her smile is one of relief. "Alex made me leave work early and let me stay in one of the rooms. I took a nap. That's why I was late. I overslept and had to get ready in a hurry."

"And this is the result?" I whistle low, my gaze appreciative as I obviously scan her. "Imagine if you'd had more time. You probably would've killed me dead."

She rests her hand on my knee, her touch searing me through the fabric. "I bet you want to slip your fingers under my skirt."

"I definitely want to slip my fingers somewhere," I tell

her, reaching for her thigh when I hear someone call my name.

Glancing over my shoulder, I spot Jessica standing at the head of the table, a hopeful expression on her face and with Craig by her side.

Fucking great.

"Be nice," Kelsey whispers, and I wonder if she saw the disappointment on my face when I spotted them. Or maybe she just...knew.

She's intuitive like that.

"Hey, Jessica, Craig." I rise to my feet, and Craig pulls me into a hug, slapping my shoulder extra hard. I then hug Jessica, but I keep my distance, considering her earlier words made me angry.

Kelsey stands as well, flanking my side, and I wrap my arm around her shoulders, holding her close. "This is my girlfriend, Kelsey," I announce proudly.

Craig stares at her, bug-eyed. He doesn't even try to hide his obvious surprise. "Holy shit, cuz. You found yourself a knockout."

I laugh, but I sound annoyed so I stop. "Kelsey, meet my outspoken cousin, Craig."

"Nice to meet you," Kelsey says, holding out her hand.

He takes it, pumping it up and down, staring at her in wonderment. "Great meeting you too. Glad you could make it to our wedding."

"Hello. I'm Jessica," my ex says, thrusting her hand toward Kelsey, who takes it gingerly. Almost as if she doesn't want to touch her.

That's my girl. With my...ex-girl. This is awkward.

"I'm Kelsey. Hi. How are you?" She sounds breathless. Carefree. She releases Jessica's hand and immediately slides her fingers through mine. Forming a united front. I relax a little once she does.

"Tired," Jess answers honestly. "Nervous. Tomorrow is a big day."

"I'm sure," Kelsey says, arching her brow. "Planning a wedding is a stressful thing."

"I'll say." Jess's nervous laughter makes me uncomfortable.

I don't know what she's trying to get at, but I don't like it.

"Well, I'm sure everything will turn out wonderfully tomorrow. You can't go wrong, having your wedding here at Wilder," Kelsey says, almost sounding like a commercial.

"That's right. Theo mentioned you worked here at the hotel," Jess says.

I never said one word to her about Kelsey or where she works. Someone's been doing some digging.

"Yes, I'm assistant to the owner, Alexander Wilder," Kelsey says proudly.

"Oh, really? We ordered our save the date cards and invitations from Noteworthy. His wife works there," Jess says.

"I know," Kelsey says. "Caroline is my friend."

"Oh really?" Jessica appears surprised.

"Kelsey is very close to a rather large group of women who all work in downtown Carmel," I say.

"Mostly," Kelsey adds. "We lost one of our friends when she moved to Las Vegas to live with her boyfriend, who plays for the Raiders."

"No shit?" Craig asks, sounding interested. "Which player?"

"Mitchell Anderson," Kelsey tells him.

"Well I'll be damned. I think he's from around here

too." He sends Jess a questioning look. "Too bad you're not friends with her, babe. You could get us season passes or something." Craig turns his attention to me. "Does your girlfriend get you into games at the new stadium?"

"No, we haven't made it over there yet." That's not a bad idea, though I'm more of a Niner fan.

"That's a damn shame. They gotta be good for something, right?" Craig guffaws and Jess sends him an irritated glare. He doesn't even notice. "I'd be taking advantage of that perk like, all the time."

Of course he would. Because Craig likes nothing more than to take advantage of people on a constant basis. The asshole.

Yeah, I really need to let go of my bitterness over what they did to me once and for all. I've moved on. I've found someone better. Craig can have Jessica. They're a perfect couple.

I've got all I need right here.

With Kelsey.

TWENTY-TWO
KELSEY

I DON'T REALLY like Theo's ex, and I believe the feeling is mutual. She's giving me uneasy vibes, and while I want to be decent toward her, it's proving a little difficult. At first I wanted to rub it in her face that Theo moved on with me, but that was...before. Before I started to really care about Theo. Before I realized that we were never pretending to be in a relationship at all.

We're actually *in* one, and I'm pretty sure...

I'm falling in love with him.

So how can I leave him now for a new job somewhere else, when I have such strong feelings for him? When I saw him earlier standing at the altar with the rest of the groomsmen, he immediately stood out. So tall and handsome. His gaze locked with mine, I could see all the emotion there. How happy he was to see me.

All I could think was *that man is mine. He belongs to me.*

And yes, that sounds cheesy and ridiculous, but it's true. I was overwhelmed. Theo is mine. And I am his. I can't leave now, no matter how great the opportunity is. Or how exciting it would be, to live in a foreign country and make new friends, learn new things. Live new experiences.

I have everything I could ever want, right here. Right now.

With Theo.

When the realization hits you that everything you could ever want is standing right next to you, you kind of hang on to him for dear life, as if you've lost all sense.

And that's sort of what I'm doing now. I loop my arm around Theo's and lean into him, and he smiles down at me, his gaze dark and even a little naughty. I love naughty Theo. I love sweet Theo too. And smart Theo. When he starts talking about finance and math and numbers, I don't get bored. Not at all. Because I just—love him that much.

Oh holy shit, yes. I'm not just falling in love with him. I am *so* in love with this man.

Conversation is being made, but I'm not really saying anything. I'm tired of us talking to Jessica. She can go speak with her other forty-eight guests. She's currently studying my outfit with unabashed judgement firing her eyes. Clearly she has a problem with me. And I suppose it has everything to do with the fact that I'm with Theo, and she's not.

Well too damn bad. She had her chance and she cheated on him for months. That's on her. The best thing she could've ever done, too.

Because now he's with me.

Someone calls Craig's name, diverting their attention, and they leave us to go talk to them, which fills me with instant relief. We settle back into our chairs, both of us quiet, Theo's parents watching us from across the table. They don't say anything either, and all that silence starts to build up, until I feel like I'm about to burst but then...

"I never did like her," Theo's grandmother says, her shrewd gaze landing on me. "I think you're a major upgrade."

We all burst out laughing, even Theo's parents. His grandmother appears quiet pleased with herself, though Jim admonishes his mother for saying that.

"Jessica is in love with Craig, who's still your grandson," Jim reminds her.

"Oh, that boy is a buffoon. I wish her luck, having to deal with him on a daily basis. And if they have children? Goodness, she'll be raising him *and* the kids." She shakes her head.

They change the subject and start chatting about other family members. Theo whispers in my ear, "Thank you."

I turn to realize his face is directly in mine. And it's a beloved face. His warm dark eyes. His deceptively wicked mouth. The stubble that's always lining his jaw at about this time each day. "Thank you for what?"

"For coming with me tonight. For tolerating my family. For tolerating Jessica." A weary sound leaves him, and his smile is tired. "This is a lot. On me. On you. You've been a good friend to me, Kelsey."

"A good *friend*?" I raise my brows. "Is that all?"

My heart starts racing wildly, and I worry he might give me a disappointing answer.

"No. You know that's not all. I've been telling everyone you're my girlfriend." He suddenly looks just as worried as I feel.

"Good to know. Because I've started telling everyone you're my boyfriend," I say lightly. Well, it's not one hundred percent true. I told Eleanor he is, and that's it. But I swear I'm going to tell everyone we're together.

"Really?" His expression is very, very pleased. So

pleased, he looks pretty damn arrogant, and I can't resist leaning in and pressing my mouth to his. "That makes me happy," he says when I pull away slightly

"It makes me happy too," I murmur against his lips right before he kisses me again.

We are completely disgusting lovebirds throughout dinner. We feed each other bites since we ordered different entrees for dinner. We shoot each other longing glances every once in a while, like we're dying to get out of here (newsflash—we so are). His parents notice and send each other questioning glances, though I can tell they're happy about it. Even his grandma has something to say.

"You two are going to set the room on fire if you keep looking at each other like that," she says right after our dinner plates were taken away, making me flush. Making Theo laugh.

Speeches are made and I tune them out, too preoccupied with how I'm going to tell Alex that I'm not leaving after all. He'll completely understand, though I'm sure the managers at the other locations will be disappointed. Alex told me they interviewed other people, so they have options, but they were both pleased with me the most. They'll find someone else to fill their positions.

It just won't be me.

Craig's father is in the middle of giving a long, droning speech when I lean over and whisper in Theo's ear, "I need to go to the restroom."

"Hurry," he says, his voice urgent. "I think we can bail out of here once the speeches are over."

Laughing quietly, I rise to my feet and scoot around the edges of the crowded room, finally making my way to the restroom.

It's when I'm leaving the stall and about to wash my hands that I stop short.

Jessica is at the sink, staring at her reflection in the mirror as she applies a fresh coat of lipstick.

Offering her a quick smile, I go to the only other sink, which is next to hers, and hurriedly wash my hands, ready to buzz out of there when her words stop me.

"He's still in love with me, you know."

I slowly turn around to find she's still staring at the mirror, her gaze meeting mine.

"You're delusional," I tell her, because I know it's true. He doesn't love Jessica. He hasn't for a long time. Yes, old residual feelings might be churned up tonight thanks to seeing each other in a wedding atmosphere, and the same could be happening to her, but he's not in love with her. I know he's not.

"It's true." Jessica puts the cap back on her lipstick and opens her tiny purse, dropping it inside before she turns to fully face me. "We were together for five years. You can't fall out of love with someone that quickly."

"You certainly did, considering you're now marrying his cousin," I say snidely.

"Who says I don't still love Theo?" She crosses her arms. "I do. I can't help it. Sometimes I have major regret over what I did to him. Like today. If everything would've gone as we originally planned, I'd be married to him right now. I might even be pregnant with his baby."

Realization hits, but it has nothing to do with Jessica and everything to do with Theo. And a baby.

Maybe I'm...

Oh God. I haven't had my period yet. And with everything that's been going on the last couple of weeks, I sort of forgot about it. I need to check my app that keeps track of it. I think I'm late. No, I *know* I'm late. Holy shit.

I could be pregnant.

Normally, this would scare the absolute crap out of me, but right now, I feel nothing but happiness.

"But you're not," I remind her with a faint smile. "And that's your loss." I head for the door and pull on the handle, pausing for only a moment. "See you around," I call to her as I exit the bathroom.

A heady combination of pure joy and satisfaction races through my veins, and it's like I'm floating. I make my way to our table and settle into my chair, surprised to see dessert already waiting for me.

"Cheesecake," Theo says, and I notice he's already eaten half of his. "My favorite."

"Think she planned that?" I ask him.

"If she did, I sort of don't care. Like I said, it's my favorite." He shoves another forkful in his mouth.

I laugh and try it, already knowing it's going to be dense yet fluffy, and absolutely delicious. "It's amazing," I tell him.

"You're amazing," he says, his eyes positively glowing as he takes me in.

That look is all for me, and my stomach flutters.

"No, you are." I tease him.

"You're both amazing, okay? Jeez," his grandmother grumbles, and we start laughing all over again.

I don't think I've ever felt so complete.

Later, when we're back at Theo's place and we're lying in his bed, both of us completely naked and sweaty after a vigorous tangle in the sheets, I turn to him, ready to confess I've been interviewing for two jobs out of state when he says something first.

"Jessica told me she regrets breaking off our engagement."

All thoughts of my plans to confess all are gone and instead, I gape at him, my mouth opening and closing like a fish. "When did she tell you that?"

"Yesterday, when I picked up my tux."

"You saw her there?"

"Yeah. She just showed up. We talked."

"And you never mentioned it to me?" Worry clutches at my heart, and I tell myself to relax.

"I didn't think it was a big deal that she talked to me, but now I realize...you should know. What she said to me. She also said she wanted to talk to me tonight too, but I avoided her. It's the night before her wedding, for God's sake. Besides, I don't care what she has to say. I'm not interested." He grabs hold of my hand and drops a light kiss to my knuckles. "I only care about you."

The tension slowly eases from my muscles, and I loosen the sheet around me so I can go to him, pressing my naked body to his. "Theo..."

"It might be too soon to say this, but fuck it. I'm in love with you, Kels. I think I have been for a while. I just didn't realize it until I saw Jess."

I part my lips to speak, but he presses his index finger against my mouth, silencing me. "I know that might sound a little messed up, but I had to see my past in order to really visualize my future, and when I do, all I see is you in it."

My chest tightens. I feel like I could cry, and I never cry over this sort of thing.

Of course, I've never had a man tell me he loves me before either, so how would I know how I might react?

"Oh—"

He cuts me off. "And you don't have to tell me you love me yet if you're not ready. I know you haven't had the best experiences with men. Or with life in general. And yeah, sometimes I can act like a jealous asshole because you're so damn beautiful and I don't want anyone to try and make a play at you. I realized a while ago you have no interest in anyone else."

"You're right. I don't," I say softly. I've shared a few tidbits about my past with him. Given him a few stories about my relationship with my mother. But not much. I need to share more. I can trust him.

He won't hurt me.

"I'm in love with you," he says almost vehemently. "My family loves you too. I can tell. And whenever you're ready—"

I silence him with my lips, kissing him thoroughly, pushing my hands against his chest so he rolls over on his back and I climb on top of him. I pull away from his delicious mouth and sit up, straddling him, his suddenly erect cock brushing against my backside. "I love you too."

His brows lower as he reaches for me, resting his hands on my hips. "What did you just say?"

"I said I love you too." The words fall from my lips slowly, and he grins. Like he can't help himself, and it is the cutest thing. "You kept interrupting me when I tried to answer, so I did the same to you."

"You love me."

I nod. "And you love me."

His hands squeeze my hips before they curve around to stroke my ass. Everything inside me goes liquid at his sensual touch, and I lean down, my breasts brushing against his chest when our lips meet. The kiss is pure fire, our tongues tangling, soft sounds coming from both of us. I feel his fingers dip into me from behind and I wiggle my butt, wanting more.

So he gives it to me.

His grips the base of his cock and I lift up, taking him deep inside, our mouths never parting. His tongue strokes my mouth in the same rhythm as his cock stroking my body. Slow and purposeful. I clench around him, my fingers gripping his shoulders, my hips working up and down, trying to increase the speed.

But he won't have it. He keeps the pace nice and slow, his hands at my waist, guiding me. Driving me out of my mind with lust.

And love.

Lots of love.

I moan his name as I slip closer and closer to the edge. My entire body tingles, as if I'm one giant live wire, ready to spark and explode. He continues to drive into me, his thrusts coming faster, his movements growing out of control.

"Fuck, I can't hold back," he mutters against my lips before he pumps inside me quickly, pushing me right over that edge, sending the sparks flying. Until I'm coming. Clutching him tight, knowing he's the only one who can make me feel like this.

The only one.

TWENTY-THREE
THEO

FROM THE MOMENT I arrive at the hotel, the ceremony preparations have been a complete shit show. The biggest problem?

We don't know where the groom is.

All the men participating in the ceremony are in a suite, so we can prepare for the wedding together, and when I first arrive, Craig is a no show. Despite the texts and calls from his father and friends, he doesn't respond. Not knowing what else to do, we continue getting ready, figuring he'll show up eventually.

The suite is at least fully stocked. There's an industrial-sized steam iron that any of us can use if we need to get out the extra wrinkles from our suits. There's even a stylist on hand to trim our hair if need be, and a temporary bar was brought in featuring just about every bottle of hard liquor you can imagine, plus a variety of beer, including my favorite IPA. Since I'm staying at one of the rooms reserved for all of us in the bridal party tonight, I decide I can go ahead and have a beer, though I pace myself. Don't need to go stumbling down the aisle with my grandmother and cause her to break a hip.

Finally, Craig shows up. Completely hungover.

"Stayed out too late last night," he announces when he enters the room, bleary eyed and unshaven. "Had to celebrate my last hours of freedom, you know?"

Not the sort of thing he should be thinking of his impending marriage, but I wisely keep my mouth shut.

"Craig, we spent a lot of money on this," his father tells him, waving his hand around to indicate the suite and everything inside of it. "Get your ass ready. The ceremony is in less than two hours."

The still-drunk groom forgot his bow tie and cummerbund, so his brother Rick leaves to go fetch it from his apartment. Craig's father quietly fumes when Craig asks one of his friends to make him a Bloody Mary.

"It'll sober me up," he explains when his father glares.

Again I remain quiet. Instead I send texts to Kelsey, offering her a play by play on everything as it unfolds.

Kelsey: **Sounds like a complete fiasco.**

Me: **It is. Get me out of here.**

Kelsey: **Only 90 minutes until the ceremony!**

I can't stop the grin that forms from her sassy response. She's just reminding me of the torture I still have to endure, and I'm sure she's doing it on purpose.

Me: **Only 90 minutes until I get to see you.**

Kelsey: **Wait until you see my dress.**

Me: **Can't wait to tear it off you later. Hope it wasn't expensive.**

Kelsey: **It was, but I got it on sale. You'll have to be careful with it, though. I love it and don't want it ruined.**

Me: Don't be so damn tempting, and then I won't want to rip it off your body.

"Who you texting? Jess?"

I glance up to find Craig standing there, sneering at me, a little wobbly on his feet. Jesus. "What the hell, Craig? Why would I be texting *your* future bride?"

"Because I hear you're still in love with her," he says fiercely.

Craig's father groans. "Jesus Christ."

I rise to my feet, finding myself in Craig's face. I'm a hair taller, but I don't feel like it's an advantage. Craig is the unpredictable one in this situation. God knows what he might do. "I'm in love with someone else."

"But she told me that you're in love with her," he says, baring his teeth like he wants to take a bite out of me. "That you said so at the tuxedo fitting when you showed up late."

If I weren't so pissed, I'd laugh. This is some straight up bullshit right now. Confessions at the Men's Wearhouse? More like Jess was the one confessing, not me. I won't tell him that thought. What's the point?

"I'm with Kelsey," I tell him. "You saw her last night, right? I couldn't keep my eyes or hands off of her. I'm in love with her. Not your bride."

Craig just stares, and this close, I can see his eyes are bloodshot, and he appears—worried. I almost feel sorry for him.

Almost.

"I don't know about this, man," he mutters with a shake of his head.

"Know about what? Would you like to *see* who I'm texting?" I'm about to thrust my phone in his face when my phone dings. Another text from Kelsey.

Kelsey: **Let's compromise. You can rip my panties off.**

Kelsey: **With your teeth.**

Followed by a bunch of winking emojis.

Nope. Can't share that with Craig. I shove my phone back into my pocket.

"Nah. I believe you. I'd hang on to her too. That new girlfriend of yours is a total smoke show." Craig collapses on the very loveseat I was sitting on, and I have no choice but to join him. Clearly he wants to keep talking.

"Uh, thanks," I tell him when he doesn't say anything. Just keeps sipping on that Bloody Mary he's clutching.

"I just don't know if I should marry Jess."

His announcement strikes fear in my heart. Only because I don't want to witness the aftermath of his declaration if he follows through.

"What are you talking about?" I lower my voice so no one else can hear us, and I wish like hell Rick were here. Craig listens to his brother, who can reason with him. A talent I've never been able to master.

"This entire wedding has been a pain in my ass since we started planning it. It's cost us and our families a fortune. All for what—so I can prove to everyone I nabbed her? We haven't been that happy lately either. We fight a lot. The sex has gotten totally boring." Craig shakes his head. "I think I'm over her."

"Come on. You can't be over her. You're *marrying* her. You want to put a ring on it," I remind him, trying to talk in his language, though I'm pretty sure I sound like a complete moron.

"I guess I do, but I don't know. It sucks. She nags my ass all the time. Always bossing me around and telling me what to do. I hate it," he says morosely.

"The stress of the wedding has to be getting to her too." I can't believe I'm defending Jessica, when she's the one who's saying I came on to her instead of the truth. *She* came on to *me*. But I can't tell Craig that. Not when we're only minutes away from his wedding ceremony.

"You think so?" There's a hopeful twinkle in Craig's eyes, and I decide to continue that route.

"Definitely," I say with a firm nod. "This kind of thing is stressful. This is the biggest day of your lives, and a lot goes into planning an event like this. More so on the brides most of the time." I'm pretty positive Craig hasn't done dick to help her.

"She says that all the time, how I never help her and she has so much to do. You're probably right. God, I can't wait for this shit to be over." He takes a gulp from his drink, leaving a red rim along his top lip. He looks like a little kid. I can't believe Jess is marrying this guy. "Where the hell is Rick anyway?"

"He went to pick up the stuff you left behind, remember?" I don't know how he forgot it. Everything was bagged up together when Lindy the Men's Wearhouse employee handed it over to me.

"Right. Right. I hope he gets back soon. Damn, I need to chill." A ragged exhale leaves him, and he bounces his knee nervously. "Thanks, man."

"Thanks for what?"

"For giving me a pep talk and standing up for me, even though I stole your girl. Looks like you found someone else, though. Good for you." Craig reaches out and socks me on the arm, and of course he does it hard enough to hurt. The fucker. "She's gorgeous."

The heat that spreads across my chest when I think of Kelsey reminds me that everything happens for a reason. At the time, I was so damn heartbroken over Jessica's betrayal, I thought I would never survive it. Figured I'd be a lonely man for the rest of my life. I firmly believed that.

And now look at me.

There's a knock at the partially open door of the suite and then a man enters the room with a pleasant smile pasted on his face. It's Alexander Wilder. Owner of the entire damn hotel and Kelsey's boss.

"Where's the groom?" he asks as he glances around.

Craig rises unsteadily to his feet and holds up his hand. "Right here."

Alex makes his way over to us and I stand as well, nodding at him when he spots me. "Just wanted to stop by and check on everything. Is the suite to your liking?"

"It's fucking fabulous, man. Thank you." Craig reaches out and claps Alex on the shoulder.

Alex winces for only a second before his expression smooths out once more. He turns his attention to me. "Theo. Good to see you. How are you doing?"

"Well, thanks. How about you?" We shake each other's hand.

"A little disappointed to be losing Kelsey, but otherwise I'm fine." He smiles. Tips his head when I just stare at him in complete shock. "She did tell you about her job offers, correct?"

Job offers? No. No, she did not.

"Right. Her job offers." I nod. Chuckle. Trying my best to play it off. "Yes, she's been very nervous about them."

"Which one do you think she'll take?" Alex asks.

I feel like an absolute fool since I didn't even know about Kelsey's job offers in the first place. What the hell is Alex talking about?

"My bet is she'll choose London. It's a magical city," he

continues when I haven't said anything. "Have you ever been there?"

"Once. Right after college," I say, my voice gruff, my thoughts chaotic. What in the fuck is going on? She's taking a job in London? In another fucking country? After she told me she loved me last night?

What sort of sick game is this woman playing?

"If she takes the job, you should definitely go visit her and check it out, which I'm sure you will. The city has changed over the years, but it's still beautiful." Alex shoots me a smile before he turns his attention back to Craig. "Congratulations on your upcoming nuptials. Please don't hesitate to text or call if you're having any problems." Alex presses his business card in Craig's palm before glancing over at me. "Hope to see you soon, Theo."

"Yeah. Same," I tell him distractedly as Alex turns and leaves the suite.

"How do you know that baller?" Craig asks me once he's gone.

"He's Kelsey's boss," I tell him, my mind awhirl with too many questions.

When did she interview for this position? Or positions? And when was she going to tell me?

Was she *ever* going to tell me?

And why did she keep this a secret? Why did she keep me in the dark? Does she not trust me still?

I've been betrayed before, in the worst way possible, and I thought that was the most painful experience I've ever gone through in my life.

But this? Discovering Kelsey has plans to leave the area for a new job, and she never mentioned one word about it, yet declared her love for me only last night?

This betrayal cuts like a knife.

Sinking right into the middle of my heart.

TWENTY-FOUR
KELSEY

I ARRIVE at the ceremony a few minutes before it starts, running late thanks to having a difficult time getting out of bed this morning, which screwed me up. I just feel so lethargic. And a little sick to my stomach, though once I ate some whole-wheat toast and chugged a bunch of water, I felt much better. I've had to forego my usual cups of coffee the last few mornings, only because the mere thought of drinking it makes me want to throw up.

It's like I know what's going on but don't want to confront it. Not yet. I have other things to worry about first. Like getting through a wedding I don't want to attend. Telling Alex I won't be taking either of those job offers after all. Will he be disappointed? Or grateful I'm staying with him after all?

What I really need to do is buy a pregnancy test, but I can't do that alone. I need the support of a good friend with me before I go down that road. I'm not about to take the test with Theo either. Talk about making me nervous. And what if I *am* pregnant? What will Theo say? Will he be upset?

Will he want to keep it, or will he suggest I have an abortion?

If this had happened with any other man I've had sex with—and thank God it hasn't—I would've gone the abortion route, no question. I probably would've never told the guy either. I can't imagine bringing a baby into this world on my own, or with any of those previous men I've been with.

But Theo...I can imagine us talking about it. And him being excited. I think his entire family would be excited. It would be the first grandchild for Jim and Patti, and they'd probably spoil that baby rotten. So would Theo. He'd offer to marry me too, I just know it. Not that I need marriage. It's just he's old fashioned in that way, and I kind of like that about him...

"Kelsey! Oh my goodness, you're absolutely *stunning* in that dress." Patti makes her way to me as I approach the rows of seats set out for the ceremony and wraps me up in a warm hug. "Look at you, trying to upstage the bride," she murmurs close to my ear before she releases me.

I blush, only because that was never my intent. "Ah, thank you. And I'm sure Jessica will look gorgeous."

"Jessica is a troll." Ali appears by her mother's side and Patti gasps, shaking her head at her youngest. "What? It's true! Look what she did to my brother."

I appreciate this girl's loyalty, I really do. "It worked out in my favor," I tell her. "Because now he's mine."

"And you two are *so* adorable together," Patti gushes. "Jim's mother was saying last night when we drove her home what a lovely couple you two make."

It's important to me, to have his family's approval. I like them a lot. I want them to like me too, and I think it's working.

"I love your dress," Ali tells me, and I glance down at

myself, pleased with my choice. I picked it up at the same place I got the dress I wore last night. The fabric is thin and gauzy, and the palest blue, with little yellow flowers scattered all over. The skirt is long and constructed of layers of lace and cotton, and it clings to my waist and hips in a way that accentuates my butt before it flares down to my ankles. The sleeves are frilly but not too fussy, and the neckline again dips into a deep V like my other dress, revealing just a hint of cleavage.

It's deceptively innocent. I'm hoping Theo likes it as much as I do.

"Thank you," I say to Ali, who smiles at me. She's adorable in a sweet pink dress that shows off her slender waist and legs. She's a beautiful woman. All of the Crawford children are attractive.

Especially my Theo.

We engage in small talk before we make our way to our seats. Theo's brothers soon join us, all three of them handsome in their suits. The sun shines down upon us and there's a gentle, cool breeze coming from the nearby ocean. It's a beautiful day to get married, and while I was feeling resentful about having to celebrate these two's wedding last night, now I'm experiencing a pleasurable hum of joy buzzing through my body.

I'm truly happy, I realize. I'm in love with a man who loves me back. I'm sitting with his family, who have all readily accepted me as one of their own. And—I might be pregnant with his baby, which doesn't scare me at all.

The thought of having Theo's baby actually excites me.

Eventually the music starts, cueing that the ceremony is about to start. After the groom walks to the altar accompanied by his parents, Theo is the next to appear, escorting his grandmother down the aisle. He guides her to his seat, which isn't too far from mine, but he doesn't even glance in my direction.

Odd.

Once his grandmother is seated, he heads for the altar and assumes his position, clutching his hands behind his back as the next groomsman heads toward the aisle with a bridesmaid on his arm. Theo stares straight ahead, his expression so firm, it could be made of stone, and something tells me he's angry.

At what? Did Jess try to speak to him again? Did he have a confrontation with Craig? God, I hope not. He doesn't need this additional stress on today of all days.

I keep my eyes on him, willing him to look at me, but he doesn't. Not once, which I find disappointing. We'd been so flirty over text earlier, I figured he'd send me a smoldering look and offer up a sexy wink. But I get none of that.

Not even a quick smile aimed in my direction.

Once the bride makes her appearance—and yes, she is absolutely stunning in her gown, I can't deny it—they all turn to face the minister, and I stare at Theo's stiff back with longing. And worry. Something is bothering him.

I don't know what it could be.

The ceremony is quick, and neither the bride nor the groom wrote personal vows to each other, which I think is a blessing. It's a very straightforward, typical vow recital, and once it's over and the minister says Craig can kiss his bride, he dips her dramatically and lays one on her that would make any woman blush.

"Good Lord, what a spectacle," Theo's grandmother harumphs in the middle of the kiss, making me giggle.

The music soars and the newly married couple exit the ceremony. Craig wears a satisfied grin and Jessica appears only vaguely mortified by that kiss. Everyone participating leaves the altar, and Theo is last. Again, he doesn't look at me, though I catch him smiling tightly at his mother when she makes eye contact with him.

What in the world is going on? We all head to the reception tent together, everyone chattering about the ceremony and Ali lamenting about how hungry she is, but for the most part, I don't pay attention. I can't focus. All I can think about is Theo and how—angry he seemed.

Angry at me.

But what did I do?

Servers walk around the tent with trays of delicious appetizers, but I turn them away. Champagne is being passed about too, but I refuse to drink any alcohol for fear I might be pregnant. I find a table to sit at and plop down in the chair, watching everyone roam about and chat with each other. I know no one except Theo's family, and we're not that close. Besides, much of their extended family is at the reception, so of course they're going to chat and play catch up with each other.

Theo is stuck taking photos with the wedding party for who knows how long. I just wish I could see him. I hope he tells me what's wrong.

I really hope I have nothing to do with it.

"Are you okay?"

I glance up to find Ali standing in front of me, a worried expression on her face.

"I'm fine." I try to smile, but my lips don't want to cooperate, so I give up.

She settles into the seat next to mine and sips from her glass. I assume it's wine, because there are no fizzy bubbles in it. "You look depressed. Are you like me? Weddings always make me sad."

I turn to look at her with a frown. "Why do weddings make you sad?"

"I don't know." She shrugs. "Don't get me wrong, marriage is a great thing. Look at my parents. They've been together forever."

"Your parents are really sweet," I say, my voice quiet. I adore them. I adore this entire family.

"They are," Ali agrees. "But marriage seems like such a —trap. Is that what those two really want?" She gestures at a giant photo of the happy couple that's sitting on an easel close to the tent entrance. "I think they secretly make each other miserable. My parents are the exception to the rule. A lot of people end up divorced."

"The divorce rate isn't as bad as it used to be." My protest is weak. I was Ali not so long ago. A firm believer in the *love is bullshit* theory. But I also had a terrible example growing up. My dad wasn't around. Ever. My mother hated everyone on sight, only because she was so bitter and resentful. Life handed her nothing but lemons, she said, and she never got any lemonade out of them.

Whatever "lemons" she was handed, she squandered. My mother didn't make the best decisions. She'd lavish all that bitterness and resentment on me. When I was in high school, I was merely going through the motions, desperate to get away from her, and then she up and died on me.

She left me first.

I have abandonment issues. I know I do. This is why I'm always the one to end a so-called relationship first. Can't get in too deep, can't stand too long. That's only asking for trouble.

Now I want to be with Theo. Crap, I think I might be pregnant with his baby. But I also worry he's angry at me.

And I don't know why.

"You just haven't met the right guy yet," I tell Ali, reaching out to set my hand over hers and give it a squeeze. "He's out there. I'm sure he is."

"I sort of have a crush on a guy, but he doesn't even know I exist." She sighs and shakes her head. "Isn't that always the way?"

"He's a fool if he can't see you." I squeeze her hand again. "You're beautiful."

"Oh, he sees me, but I'm sure he thinks I'm an annoyance. He's older." She pouts, looking even younger than she really is. "And completely out of my league."

"Who is it?"

"You don't know him," she says quickly.

"You'd be surprised," I tell her. "This town is smaller than you think."

"He owns Tuscany. The restaurant in downtown Carmel? Well, he owns it with his brother," she explains.

"Get the hell out," I breathe. "I'm good friends with their sister, Stella."

"Oh God." Ali covers her cheeks with her hands, her expression made of pure mortification. "This is so embarrassing. *Please* don't say anything to her."

"Of course I won't. This will be our little secret. Though she'll be at the brunch tomorrow, if you still want to come," I explain. "Maybe you can dig her for information. And which brother is it that you're crushing on?"

"Michael," she says dreamily.

He's a solid thirty-five, I believe. And Ali is what... twenty-one? Twenty-two? Hmm.

"No way can I dig her for information. I don't want her to know I have a stupid crush on her brother. God, I sound like I'm thirteen," she practically wails.

When she moans and groans like that, I have to agree.

"You better come with me to the brunch tomorrow. You'll love Stella. She's great. Hopefully you'll love all my friends."

"Thank you so much for including me." Ali smiles, and she looks so grateful, I know she means it. "I've been feeling down for a while now. Ever since I dropped out of school. Most of my friends are away at college, but the few who are here I don't see. I'm afraid they'll be too curious and ask endless questions I don't want to answer."

"If you don't mention dropping out of school to anyone tomorrow, then no one will ask you about it," I remind her. "And that'll solve your problem."

"You're right." She grins. "It totally will. And maybe I could become good friends with Stella, and next thing I know, I've convinced Michael Ricci to fall in love with me."

Sounds farfetched, but hey. You never know...

"Everyone, put your hands together to welcome your bride and groom to their party, Craig and Jessica!" the DJ soundly announces over the loudspeaker, making both Ali and me wince.

Everyone in the reception tent roars their approval. People whistle and cheer their names, and I can see the newly-wedded couple enter the tent hand in hand, Craig raising their arms in triumph and making Jessica laugh as she gazes up at him. He's a little cheesy, but at least he looks pleased to marry her. I hope Jessica feels the same way.

Knowing that the newly married couple is finally at the reception, I can only assume the rest of the wedding party have arrived as well. "I'm going to look for Theo," I tell Ali as I rise to my feet.

"Good idea. I'll wait for you here," she says.

I make my way through the increasingly crowded tent, smiling and nodding at people as I pass them by, my gaze constantly searching for Theo. I spot every single one of his brothers, but not him. I see the bride and groom—Craig shoots me a big smile and yells, "Smoke show!" right at me, which makes Jessica's eyes narrow as she studies me.

Great. Thanks, Craig, for pissing off your wife.

I'm about to give up and go back to the table and join Ali when I spot him standing near the bar with a drink in his hand. He brings the glass to his mouth and tips his head back, downing it in one swallow.

Oh boy.

I go to him, smiling when our gazes catch. He doesn't look pleased to see me.

"Hi," I say breathlessly when I'm close enough that he can hear me.

"Hey." He averts his gaze, staring off into the distance.

My chest hurts. My stomach roils. What in the world went wrong in the past couple of hours that now he barely wants to look at me?

"Are you okay?"

A laugh escapes him, though it completely lacks humor. "No." His stormy gaze returns to mine. "I'm not okay. I'm actually pretty fuckin' pissed off, but I'm trying to remain composed since we're at a goddamn wedding."

I rear back. I've never heard him sound so angry before.

"What's wrong? What happened?" Maybe I had nothing to do with his mood after all. I reach for him, resting my hand on his forearm. He looks so handsome in his tux. It fits him perfectly, and his hair appears freshly trimmed, though it's still a little too long on top, so it flops adorably across his forehead. His eyes are full of angry heat, though, and they practically blast right through me when he stares at me for a second too long.

"Talked to Alex Wilder," he says, his voice tight. "Your boss. He told me something interesting. About you."

Oh. Oh no. I can feel all the color drain from my face and I swear my body sways, like I might faint. "What did he say?" I whisper.

"You know what he said," he growls, setting his empty glass on a nearby table before he grabs my arm and escorts me straight out of the tent. Oh, he's so angry. His body practically vibrates from the force of his emotions, and I have no one to blame for his reaction but myself. I did this to him. I kept something huge from him for a little too long, and now he thinks I did it on purpose. I'm a liar. I'm no better than Jessica, the woman who broke his heart.

My heart wants to break too, but I have to convince him that was never my intent. Will he believe me?

Theo leads me over to the farthest side of the tent, the one closest to the ocean, which I can hear crashing in the distance. No one is around. There are some hotel employees nearby who are currently taking down the chairs from the wedding ceremony, but otherwise we're alone.

"Which job are you going to take?" he asks when he turns to face me.

I stare up into his beloved face, knowing he probably won't believe me, but I say it anyway. "Neither of them."

He scoffs. "Bullshit. I'm sure London is very appealing. That's the one Alex believes you'll accept, by the way."

"If I chose Vegas, that means I can live near Eleanor," I tell him softly. That was probably the wrong thing to say.

"Jesus, Kels." He thrusts both his hands in his hair, glaring at me. "You got two job offers and you never told me! You never mentioned the interviews, none of it. What was your plan? To tell me goodbye once you made your decision?" He drops his arms at his sides, his expression forlorn. Fury mixed with a healthy dose of sadness.

"I was going to tell you. It just—never seemed to be the right time." My words are weak. And there's so much hurt etched into his handsome features, I can barely look at him. "I found out about the open positions, and then other things happened and I never got around to mentioning it to you. At one point, I didn't believe either of them would offer me a position, so I figured I wouldn't say anything unless I heard back."

"When did you find out?" he asks.

"Friday. Alex told me Friday. But then I got sick and..." My voice drifts. I can't tell him how I think I might be pregnant. That is the last thing he'll want to hear right now. It'll probably only make him madder. "I was going to tell you that night, but then you said you loved me and—"

"That would've been the perfect time to tell me, Kelsey," he stresses. "Yet you didn't. Almost like you wanted to keep it to yourself. That's—fucked up."

"I was going to tell you! Tonight!" I reach for him, but he jerks away from my touch. "I swear, Theo. It all happened so fast. Alex told me about the job offers, and that I should take the weekend to think about them. And it hit me at the rehearsal dinner when I was sitting next to you. I didn't want to leave. Everything I could ever want is right here." I hesitate, tears welling in my eyes. "With you. And then you told me you loved me and..."

"I don't know if I can be with you, if you can't be honest with me," he says, his voice hard. Like steel.

I gape at him, my mind swirling, my vision going blurry. Oh my God. He's going to break up with me right here, right now. On the day his ex gets married. How ironic.

"You should've told me. I can't handle it if you're going

to keep secrets from me. That's not the type of relationship I want to have. I need open, honest communication. Especially after everything that happened with—" He waves his hand distractedly toward the tent, indicating Jessica.

I nod, letting the tears fall. They streak down my face, one after the other, falling onto the ground and I keep my head bent so he won't see them.

No way can I mention the possible pregnancy now. He'll really lose it. It's bad enough, what he's just said. My next secret confession will send him right over the edge.

"I need time to think," he finally says.

"It's okay." Sniffing loudly, I lift my head once more, letting him see me. I never cry, and when I do, it's always in private. I don't let anyone see me having a vulnerable moment if I can help it.

But with Theo, I want him to see me. To see my sadness and despair at the thought of losing him.

"Take your time," I tell him once I'm composed enough. "Think it through. I never meant to hurt you, Theo. I love you."

He stares at me for a long quiet moment before he turns on his heel...

And leaves.

TWENTY-FIVE
KELSEY

IT'S SUNDAY MORNING. Almost brunch time. But I'm not going. I already sent a text to the group chat, telling them I'm not feeling well and can't make it. I've been crying in bed since I got home yesterday late afternoon from the wedding. I drowned in my tears, crying so hard I almost threw up.

Juvenile, I know, but I'm broken hearted. Devastated.

I stopped off on my way home at Walgreens to pick up a couple of pregnancy tests, praying no one I know would see me. I got out of there unscathed, but once I arrived home, I couldn't make myself take the test. I was too wound up, too upset. Why add one more thing to my pain?

Lying depressed in bed, not eating, not drinking, only getting up to use the bathroom. That's all I've done for the past, ohhh—sixteen hours or so. I slept fitfully, and when I did, I dreamed. Of Theo telling me it's over and he doesn't want to see me any longer.

I woke up crying.

There's a knock on my door and I sit up, pushing my tangled hair out of my face. No one knocks on my door except for Mrs. Fillmore, the sweet elderly woman next door, but she always calls me first and very rarely does she come to my place. I'm the one who's usually knocking on her door.

So who is it?

Hope lights me up inside when I realize it might be Theo. I stumble out of bed, my feet getting tangled in the sheets and nearly sending me to the ground. I hobble over the mess, stubbing my toe on the nearby chair, and I gasp in pain.

I'm a train wreck, but if it's Theo waiting for me on the other side of the door, I don't care. I want to see him.

I need to.

I run through the tiny apartment and undo all the locks, throwing open the door to find...

Stella, Candice and Caroline standing on my doorstep with matching solemn expressions on their faces.

I frown, pulling the door almost all the way shut behind me so they can't see inside my crappy apartment. "What are you guys doing here?"

"We came to get you," Caroline says gently. "For brunch."

"But I cancelled." I'm confused.

"We know," Sarah says. "But we wanted to check on you."

I don't even know how they found my apartment. I pretty much keep my address a secret.

"Why?" I stand up straighter, going for dignified and failing miserably. "I'm fine. Just—not feeling up to brunch."

"Let me be completely honest with you right now. You look like straight-up hell, Kelsey," Stella says, taking a determined step forward and physically pushing me away from my front door. She grabs hold of the handle and opens the door. My three friends all file inside, me trailing after them, worry twisting me up at what they might think of me after seeing where I live.

They all three face me, Candice wincing when she sees me.

"Stella was a little—cruel just now. We just wanted to check on you and make sure you're okay," she says. "Are you?"

I shrug, feeling helpless. At a loss.

But I also feel relieved. They came to see me. They worried about me, and they want to make sure I'm okay.

That means more than they'll ever know.

"We're still going to brunch." Stella's voice is determined. "So go get ready. Take a shower or whatever you need to do. We bumped back the reservation a half hour so you still have time."

"You guys, I don't think I want to go." I'm whining, but I don't care. This is awful. I don't have the strength to face my friends right now, not after what happened yesterday.

"You're going," Caroline says firmly. "You need us right now. We'll help you."

I try to paste on a smile but it fails. "What are you guys talking about? I'm fine."

"No, you're not," Stella says. "A little birdy stopped by Sweet Dreams today and talked to me."

I'm frowning. "You never work Sundays."

"You're lucky I live close to the café. That little birdy came in asking for me, and told one of my employees she wanted to tell me something about *you*." She sends me a pointed look. "So of course, my curiosity got the better of me and I came straight over."

"Who was it?"

"Alice Crawford."

Oh. Oh shit. I'm guessing Ali told Stella about Theo... but what did she say? I hightailed it out of the reception once Theo ditched me. Ran back into the tent, grabbed my purse and fled. Luckily no one saw me.

Or so I thought.

It makes sense that people would ask about me, though. I'm sure Theo had to deal with it. One moment I was there, the next I wasn't. What did he say? How did he explain what happened? Talk about awkward.

"What did she tell you?" I ask Stella.

"That you and Theo supposedly broke up and that he was a moody jerk for the rest of the wedding reception." I'm about to say something, but Stella cuts me off. "We know you two were pretending to be in a relationship, but come on. You were friends who fell for each other, and that's totally natural. Isn't that the best way to fall in love? You already know you're compatible."

I burst into tears. Only because it hurts too much, realizing that we did fall in love in the best way possible, only for me to ruin everything.

Candice brings me a box of Kleenex. Caroline guides me over to my old, lumpy couch. Stella goes into the kitchen to get me a glass of water and in between sobs, I explain what happened. The job interviews, the job offers, and how I didn't tell Theo about them. His confession that he loves me and I love him, too.

And then...yesterday. Everything was ruined.

"Alex blew it," Caroline says when I'm done explaining. "I can't believe it."

"It's not his fault," I say. "I should've told Theo. Alex didn't know."

"What the hell is this?" Stella asks, picking up the pregnancy test box from my kitchen counter where I left it last night.

They all gape at me for a solid two seconds before all the questions and fretting comes. It's frantic, overwhelming, and Stella yells at the top of her lungs, getting the other two to stop chattering.

"Do you think you're pregnant?" Stella asks.

I nod, my face crumpling before I start crying all over again.

"Okay. This is serious." Stella claps her hands together like she's running her crew at the café and we all need to fall in line. "Kelsey, take a quick shower. While you're at it, take the pregnancy test. Does Theo know about the possibility of this?"

I shake my head.

"Okay. Okay, we've got this. You're going to be fine. Candice, pick out an outfit for Kelsey to wear. We're going to brunch. We need everyone's advice, including Alice's."

"She's barely twenty-one," I say as Candice grabs my hand and hauls me to my feet. "What does she know?"

"She's Theo's sister. She knows a lot," Stella says pointedly. "She's like me, the youngest child, the only girl, raised with a bunch of heathens. We can relate. Plus she has perspective on Theo none of us do. We *need* her."

They're all right. I know they are. And I can't believe they came to my place to rouse me out of here.

"Thank you for coming over," I say in between sniffles while they all walk me to my bathroom.

"Honey, we love you," Caroline says, her voice and gaze soft as she studies me. "We want to help. You just have to open up and let us."

I throw myself at Caroline and hug her tight. Candice and Stella wrap themselves around us too, and we're just one big group hug until Stella pulls away and gets back to business.

She tears into the pregnancy test box she brought with her, hurriedly reading the instructions. "It's time to get real, Kelsey. Here you go. Just take the lid off and pee on the tip. You'll find out in a few minutes whether your life is going to change or not."

I take the pregnancy test from her, my heart bottoming out as I slip into the bathroom and close the door. I've been dealing with that feeling the entire weekend.

It's go time.

WHEN WE SHOW up at the restaurant, we're only five minutes late. Turns out Amelia and Sarah are already there, waiting for us. Along with Ali, who appears relieved when she spots me.

"Oh my God." She jumps up from her chair and comes to me, hugging me. "I was so worried about you."

I withdraw from her embrace, smiling faintly. "I'm okay. I can't believe what you did."

She frowns. "Are you mad I went to Stella?"

"No." I shake my head. "I'm grateful. I'm a very—private person. They didn't even know where I lived." It was Alex who told Caroline my address. She made her confession on the drive over to the restaurant.

"Oh Kelsey." Ali hugs me again, her mouth right at my ear as she murmurs, "Theo is devastated. We need to figure this out."

Once we settle around the table, I introduce Ali to everyone, and then Stella takes over, explaining the situation and what happened between Theo and me.

At least someone takes charge. I don't think I could've gotten through that story without bursting into tears and truly believing my life is over.

But my life isn't over. It turns out...

"Oh, and we just found out Kelsey's pregnant," Stella adds, making my announcement just like I wanted her to.

You would've thought she said I died and came back to life. The shock on their faces is almost humorous, save for Stella, Caroline and Candice. Though they all whip their heads in my direction, every single one of them wide eyed. Especially Ali.

"You're—pregnant?" A wrinkle forms between Ali's eyebrows as she gapes at me.

Unease fills me, making me worry. What if she thinks this is terrible? What if she can't imagine me as a part of their family? She could run off and tell Theo before I even get a chance to, and then let's be real.

Shit will really hit the fan.

"Oh my gosh!" She comes around the table, grabs my hands and pulls me in for another bone-crushing hug. "I can't believe it! I'm going to be an aunt."

I start crying all over again, clinging to her. "Don't tell Theo yet, okay? He doesn't even know."

Ali pulls away to look at me. "Of course I won't. Though he probably deserves to know first."

"Stella found the pregnancy test I bought and it all sort of spiraled out of control from there," I explain. "I need your help." I glance around the table at all of my friends, who are wearing giant smiles on their faces. They're happy for me. This should be the most terrifying moment of my life. My boyfriend broke up with me and I'm pregnant with his baby.

But my friends are lifting me up. Reminding me that

I'm not alone. While I want nothing more than to work it out with Theo, and I'm pretty confident we can get beyond this misunderstanding, I know that in the end, if Theo and I don't end up together? I'll be okay.

Because I have my friends by my side.

"Okay, everyone," Stella says once we're settled in our seats and the server's come by taking our mimosa orders—I only get orange juice, bummer. "We need to help Kelsey out. She's hit a few snags with Theo and she needs our advice."

"Whatever you need, we'll help," Amelia says, her gaze sliding over to me. "Congrats, by the way."

"Thank you," I murmur, overwhelmed with gratitude.

"Oh, I can give you plenty of advice," Ali says with all the knowledge of a little sister. "Trust me. I know what makes Theo tick. I know what makes all of the Crawford men tick."

"Do tell," Stella says, leaning her elbows on the table as she contemplates Ali. "I told Kelsey you would probably have the most beneficial advice out of all of us, since you're related to him."

"Right, well, I know a lot. Um." Ali squirms in her chair. "Maybe you could give *me* some advice."

The curious expression on Stella's face is unmistakable. "I'd love to help you. But with what?"

"I'll—explain it to you later." Ali's cheeks turn bright pink. "In the mean time, let's focus on Kelsey." She glances over to where I'm sitting. "She needs us."

It's true. I need them.

Hopefully whatever we come up with, works. Because I also need Theo.

Desperately.

TWENTY-SIX
THEO

I AM a miserable son of a bitch and no one wants to be around me.

I can't blame them. I don't even want to be around myself. Since what happened at the wedding—hell, before the wedding—I've felt...broken. My heart, my soul, all of it, shattered to pieces. Kelsey's blatant disregard of my feelings when it comes to her leaving the state, or worse, the country, for her job...

We confess we love each other and then it's like oops, forgot to mention this! What the hell? And finding out from someone else was a real mind fuck too.

Once she left the reception, I sulked like a pissed off little baby. Everyone—and I mean everyone—from my immediate family wanted to know where Kelsey went. Ali was thoroughly confused. One minute she's there, the next she's gone, I get it. My parents didn't buy my excuse that an emergency came up. None of them did. Even my grandmother called me on my bullshit.

"Just because you had a little tiff doesn't mean you just

let her go, Theodore. That girl is too good to let slip through your fingers," she scolded me at one point.

Her words rang true, because what she said was true. Kelsey's a good girl. A strong woman. The more I think about it, the more I realize it was pretty damn busy these last few days. When did she ever get a chance to tell me what was going on with her life?

Never, that's when.

Sunday night and I'm staring at my phone, agonizing over texting her or not when my phone flashes with a call. A FaceTime call.

From my sister.

Groaning, I decline it. She immediately calls me again. We play this game a couple of times until I finally answer the damn call.

"What the hell do you want?" I practically snarl.

"So hostile." She doesn't even seem fazed. More like she looks bored.

I slouch against the back of the couch, hoping she doesn't ask any difficult questions. I'm not in the mood to answer them. "What do you want, Ali? It's been a shit weekend."

"Theo, I'm going to ask you a difficult question," Ali starts.

Here we go. How'd I know this was coming? "I probably won't answer."

She ignores me. "Are you still in love with Jessica?"

I sit up straight, nearly dropping my phone on the floor. Luckily, it lands on the couch next to me and I scramble to pick it up, hating how acting frazzled by her question makes it look like I actually am still in love with Jess.

But I'm not. Not even close.

More like I'm surprised Ali would even bring it up.

"No," I say firmly, my gaze locking with my little sister's through the camera. "Absolutely not."

Jessica found me alone at the reception, and confessed to me that she'd had pre-wedding jitters. That's why she said all that stuff to me. I told her it was cool, I understood, even though I thought what she did was a shit move. But I can't hold it against her. Grudges only hurt the ones holding the grudge, so what's the point?

"Okay." Ali nods her approval, sounding pleased. "Good to know."

"Why do you ask?"

"I have another question." She pauses for only a moment before she barrels forward in typical Ali style. "Are you in love with Kelsey?"

A ragged sigh escapes me and I run my hand along my jaw, feel the thick layer of stubble there. "Yeah. But I probably messed that all up."

"You didn't mess it up at all," Ali says hurriedly, her eyes lighting up. As if she were excited. "Trust me. She loves you, Theo. And she feels terrible about the mix up with her job offer and how she didn't tell you about it. You have to know she's not accepting either of them. She doesn't want to leave you."

That's exactly what Kelsey said to me at the reception, but I didn't want to believe her. I was too mad, too hurt. Spinning over finding out what she kept from me. I've been deceived before—in the worst possible way—and I couldn't see or think straight.

So I pushed the one bright and perfect thing in my life away.

"When did you talk to her?" I ask.

Ali's expression turns a little shady, the sneak. "Um, she might've invited me to have brunch with her friends today."

"When did she invite you?" I ask incredulously. And when did they become so close? I love it. Ali has seemed a little lost lately, and I appreciate Kelsey taking her under her wing and introducing her to her friend group, but that moved sort of fast...

Is there anything wrong with moving fast? I suppose not. Look at how we went from zero to friendship to having sex regularly and fooling ourselves into thinking it was something casual.

It was never casual between us. Our friendship was instant. Our respect for each other grew. I enjoyed spending time with her and I think she felt the same about me. The next thing I knew, we were in a full-blown relationship, though we tried to call it something else.

Now here I sit, afraid I might've lost it forever.

"We were talking a few days ago, and she invited me to go to brunch. Of course I said yes. I need new friends, and Kelsey is so great. I really like her. A lot. Her friends are pretty great too." Ali tilts her head, sending me a long look. "You need to talk to her, Theo. She misses you so much, and she hates that you're mad at her. She wants to fix it."

"I'm not mad at her anymore. I'm just—" I exhale loudly and stare up at the ceiling for a moment before I return my gaze to Ali's. "Frustrated by how I acted toward her. I shouldn't have become so angry. I've given it some thought, and she was right. She never got a chance to tell me about her job offers. It's been so hectic with that stupid wedding this weekend." Thank God it's over.

"You should go to her and tell her how you feel," Ali says.

"See, here's the thing." I make a face, embarrassed to admit this. "I don't know where she lives."

"Ha, no one did until today, I hear. It's okay. I have her

address. I'll text it to you right now." Her screen says *paused*, and within seconds, I get a notification with an address in the text. "There you go."

"I can't just go to her on a Sunday night."

"Why not?"

"What if she's already in bed?" Lamest excuse ever.

"She'll get out of bed for you. I promise," Ali says gently. "Go get your girl, big brother. She's waiting for you. She needs you right now."

She's right. My girl needs me right now.

And I need her.

"I'm leaving now," I tell my sister. "Oh, and Ali?"

"Yeah?"

"Thanks. I owe you one."

"Yeah you do," she says breezily. "And don't worry. I'll collect soon."

I PULL up to Kelsey's apartment building forty minutes later, glancing around once I park my car into an open slot. The complex has seen better days. The paint is peeling off the building, and it looks a little rundown. All I can think about is how fast can I get Kelsey out of here, and when I get out of my car and slam the door, a dog starts barking incessantly somewhere in the distance.

Great.

She doesn't live in the best part of town either. Realizing her apartment is on the second floor at least gives me some comfort as I run up the stairs and stop at her door, taking a deep breath for courage before I knock.

No answer. Not even a sound from within.

I knock again, a little louder this time, but still no answer.

Huh.

The door across from Kelsey's creaks open, and I turn around to find a little old lady standing there, leaning heavily on a cane. Her hair is stark white, and her face is lined with wrinkles. Her brown eyes twinkle when they meet mine, though, and she smiles. I can't help but smile back.

"Are you Kelsey's young man?" she asks.

I stand up a little straighter, liking the way that sounds. She reminds me of my own grandmother. "I am. Do you know if she's home?"

If I'm Kelsey's boyfriend, you'd think I'd know this, but the woman doesn't even bat an eyelash.

"I see her car out in the parking lot, so I'd say yes. She avoids people knocking on her door as much as possible." The woman lowers her voice. "She's a very private person."

I glance toward the parking lot and spot Kelsey's car sitting under the carport. Huh. So why won't she answer the door?

"Did you tell her you were coming over?" the woman asks when I still haven't said anything.

"No. I was hoping it would be a surprise." I flash her a weak smile and offer up a little shrug.

"Ah." The woman shakes her head, making a tsking noise. "You should probably pull your fancy phone out of your pocket and send her a message. Let her know you're here. Maybe she's taking a shower."

"Maybe she is," I say as I do exactly as the woman suggests and pull out my phone from the back pocket of my jeans. I send Kelsey a quick text.

I'm at your front door. I need to see you.

Then I wait.

"She answer you yet?" the woman asks.

This woman is giving me a complex with her questions.

"No." I stare at the screen, willing it to receive a reply from Kelsey. "But like you said, maybe she's in the shower."

I hear a lock being undone, and I turn back toward Kelsey's apartment just in time to see her door swing open, and she's standing in the doorway. She's wearing a pair of black cotton shorts and a cropped white T-shirt, and her hair is damp, as if she did just recently take a shower. Her face is scrubbed clean of makeup, and her cheeks are rosy. Her eyes are a little puffy, like maybe she's been crying, and I don't doubt that.

It makes me feel like shit, knowing I'm the reason she shed tears.

"What are you doing here?" she asks me, her gaze going to the older woman standing just behind me. Kelsey smiles gently. "Are you flirting with my boyfriend, Mrs. Fillmore?"

I like that Kelsey still calls me her boyfriend.

"Perhaps," Mrs. Fillmore says, a lilt in her voice. "He's a fine-looking man, Miss K. You better hold onto him tight, or I might snag him up!"

The woman cackles and slowly closes the door, turning the lock with a loud snap.

"You want to come inside?" Kelsey asks, sounding worried.

"Yeah, sure."

I follow her into the apartment, the scent of her fragrance trailing after her and slowly driving me out of my mind. I can't just jump on her, though. I need to talk to her first. We need to work things out, I need to tell her I'm sorry, figure out where we're at, and then maybe...

I can jump her.

"I didn't know you were coming or I would've cleaned up." She waves a hand around the dark apartment. The furniture is old and a little shabby. The carpet is shit brown and the windows are small. It's kind of awful. "Not that cleaning up would improve this place."

"I don't care if you cleaned up or not, Kels. I just wanted to see you." I go to her, taking her hands in mine. They're ice cold and I cover them completely with my own, wanting to warm her up. I decide to cut to the chase. "I'm an asshole."

"No, you're really not." She shakes her head, the faintest smile curling her beautiful mouth. "You're the farthest thing from an asshole, Theo. You are literally the nicest guy I know, and to be honest, I always believed I had a thing for bad boys. I figured nice guys were boring, and that's why I never bothered. Until you. You're not boring. Not at all. You're sweet and kind and smart. You make me laugh. You make me smile, even when I'm just thinking about you. You also give me multiple orgasms in one go, and if that doesn't mean you're a keeper, then I don't know what else does."

Even though I feel like my very future is on the line right now, I can't help but laugh. "You'll keep me because I give you multiple orgasms?"

"It's one of the many reasons I want to keep you as my own," she says, that little smile still on her face, though her eyes are sad. "I just hope you want to be with me after I kept such a big secret from you."

"I overreacted," I tell her, bringing our linked hands up and dropping a quick kiss on her knuckles. "After everything that happened with Jessica, and then finding out from Alex that you had job offers and you interviewed for them and everything, I felt—betrayed."

"It was wrong of me to not to say anything. I'm so sorry I didn't tell you sooner. I should've mentioned it from the start, but when Alex first told me about it, we weren't even that serious. We were really just friends, and honestly, I didn't think I had a chance to even qualify for those positions, you know? Plus..." Her voice drifts and she glances down. "It's hard for me to open up to people sometimes."

I slip my fingers beneath her chin and tilt her face up so her gaze meets mine. "I know you do. I'm glad you open up to me, though. I'm sorry I hurt you. That's the last thing I ever want to do to someone I love."

Her eyes widen the slightest bit, and some of the shadows disappear thanks to my declaration.

"I'm sorry I wasn't open enough." She smiles tremulously. "I'm not going anywhere. I'm telling Alex first thing Monday morning that I'm declining both job offers. I'd rather stay here. With you."

"You're not giving up on those opportunities only because of me, are you?" I never want to be the reason she turns something down. What if she regrets it later on?

"There are—other factors coming into play, but neither job feels right to me right now. I don't want to leave. Not yet. I still have a lot to learn from Alex anyway," she says.

Lowering my head, I hover my mouth just above hers. Her words make me so fucking happy, I can hardly think straight. So I say the first thing that comes to mind. "I'm really sorry I made you leave the reception early. I was being a complete jerk."

"It's okay. I heard your family drove you crazy for the rest of the night, constantly asking about me." She sounds a little smug about that fact.

"I assume Ali told you all about it?" I ask, brushing my mouth against hers.

She exhales sharply. "Yes, she did."

I drop another kiss on her lips. "I love you, Kelsey."

"I love you too, Theo."

I kiss her yet again, loving how responsive she is. How she releases her hold on my hands and winds her arms around my neck, shifting closer. I wrap my arms around her waist, and realize she fits perfectly in my arms.

As if she were made for me.

TWENTY-SEVEN
KELSEY

EVERYTHING'S GOOD AGAIN. Theo's holding me in his arms, we've apologized to each other, we've declared our love for each other. I'm not going anywhere.

But there's one more thing I need to tell him...

"Theo." I rest my hands on his chest, pressing a little, and he withdraws, his eyes blinking open to watch me carefully. "I have something else I need to say."

"What is it?" he asks warily.

Swallowing hard, I curl my fingers into his T-shirt, holding onto it tight. This is huge. Like, the biggest thing I'm ever going to say someone in my life. And I thought confessing I'm in love with him was hard. "I'm..."

How do I tell him this?

"Kelsey." His voice is firm, and I know I've remained quiet for too long. "You're kind of freaking me out."

"I'm pregnant," I blurt.

There. I said it.

He blinks once. Twice. His lips curve upward. Very, very faintly. "Are you *serious* right now?"

His voice is hoarse. His expression is one of complete surprise. But he also looks...

Excited?

"No, I'm lying." I roll my eyes. "Yes, I'm serious. I'm pregnant. I took a pregnancy test. It came up positive." I actually took two, and they were both positive.

Looks like we're having a baby.

"But...but...how?" He's sputtering. He also appears to be in shock.

"It has a little something to do with that orgasm thing we discussed earlier," I tell him solemnly.

"I know that, but..." He gazes into the distance, as if he's thinking, and I wonder if he's trying to put together exactly when it happened. Because I kind of know.

Actually, I do know.

"Was it the first night you came back to my apartment?" he asks.

Ah, he figured it out.

"We didn't use a condom," he continues.

"I know. And yes, I think it was that night."

"Well, holy shit. I guess all that talk about using protection is correct." He chuckles, then immediately sobers up, his gaze searching mine. "Are you—happy about it?"

A few hours ago, I didn't know how to feel about it. Having a baby is a big deal. It's a *huge* deal.

But now...knowing Theo and I are okay and we love each other...

"I'm happy," I tell him, grabbing his hand and resting it on my bare stomach, just beneath my T-shirt. "Hey, guess what? There's a baby somewhere in there."

His big, warm hand caresses my skin, reminding me how much I like it when Theo and I practice making babies. "A baby. *Our* baby."

His voice is full of wonder, and vaguely possessive.

I really like possessive Theo. A lot.

"I know this happened sort of quickly," I say.

His gaze meets mine. "I'm all right with it if you are."

I raise my brows. "So we're going to do this?"

Theo nods slowly. "Oh yeah. We are so going to do this, Kels. First things first, you need to move out of here and into my place."

I wrinkle my nose. "Your place is small."

"Better than this," he retorts, glancing around.

I laugh. "True. But don't forget. We're going to be a... family soon."

"As if I could forget," he practically scoffs. "So in about eight months? You're barely a month along, right?"

"I guess. I don't know. I need to go see a doctor."

"That should be plenty of time for us to find a house," he muses.

My mouth drops open. "You want to buy a house together?"

"Well, yeah. We'll need to get married too." His voice is light, like he didn't just ask me to be his wife.

But he so freakin' did.

"You want to *marry* me?"

He drops down to one knee, and I cover my mouth with my right hand as he takes the other and holds it lightly in his. "Kelsey Phillips, will you do me the honor of becoming my wife?"

I nod, fighting the tears that want to fall. "Oh my God."

"Is that a yes?" He quirks a brow.

"Yes, yes." I yank on his hand and he stands once more, sweeping me into his arms and kissing me so thoroughly my knees are wobbly when he finally breaks away from my lips. "I love you."

He kisses the tip of my nose, his hand returning to my belly. "I love you too. Both of you."

"Oh my God. I'm going to have your baby, Theo." I start blubbering all over again and he holds me close, running his hand up and down my back, offering up soothing words of love.

"We're going to be just fine," he tells me at one point.

And I believe him.

EPILOGUE

SEVEN MONTHS later

"OH MY GOD, this is so cute!" I'm squealing as I hold the frilly white dress up to show everyone. The crowd around me oohs and ahhs, and I beam at all of them before dropping the dress back into the box it came in.

I'm at my baby shower at my brand-new home, surrounded by people I love and who love me, and I've turned into one of those obnoxious mothers-to-be who has to show off every single one of my gifts and carry on like a ridiculous person.

I'm having the time of my life.

"Who got you that?" Eleanor asks. She's sitting beside me, writing down each item and who gave it to me in a little notebook so I can write thank-you notes to them later. She's a good friend. One of my favorite people, besides Theo and the little bun in my oven. That's what we've taken to calling our future baby.

We're having a girl. We started calling her Bun Bun

months ago. It's awful, but it cracks us up and makes us smile and annoys everyone else who hears us say it, so we keep it up. Even though we have her name already picked out and everything. Not that we're telling anyone.

We're keeping it a secret until the day she's born, and it's driving everyone out of their minds guessing what it could be.

"I gave it to her," calls my sister-in-law, Ali, raising her hand. She's sitting next to Stella, no surprise—both of them have become closer over the last few months, though I'm not sure if there's necessarily anything going on between Ali and Michael Ricci. If there is? Her parents probably won't like it. He's much older. But he's definitely charismatic. Charming. Attractive. Successful. I get the appeal.

"You're spoiled rotten," Eleanor mutters a few minutes later as she writes down yet another gift from Stella. All my friends have spoiled our baby completely—including the very woman sitting next to me—and I've never felt so loved.

"No, *my baby* is spoiled rotten," I correct as I carefully set the gift bag on the floor, groaning with the movement. This baby makes my lower back ache, and she's sitting on my sciatica nerve too, which makes my butt cheek and right thigh hurt as well.

It's not much fun. But my aches and pains result in nightly backrubs from my husband, which tends to lead to sex. Once I hit the second trimester, I turned into a total sex monster. As in, I wanted it. All. The. Time. But now that we're getting closer and closer to the due date, I'm becoming more and more miserable.

Our little girl needs to make her way out and soon. Her daddy and I are impatient to meet her.

Eventually the rest of the gifts are opened and then a few of the guests leave, mostly Theo's family, who I'm so glad came. His grandmother attended the shower, as well as Mrs. Fillmore, and they became fast friends. They made arrangements to meet for lunch this next week.

So cute.

My friends and I go outside to enjoy the sunny afternoon, all of us sitting around the giant teak table on my new back patio. We moved into our house a couple of months ago, but this is the first social event we've had here.

"Can I make a confession?" Candice asks at one point.

We all nod encouragingly.

"You were the last person of our friend group I expected to have a baby first," she admits, her cheeks turning the faintest pink. "I thought it would be me."

They all chime in with their agreement of how I was the last person they believed would be pregnant, most of them saying it would be themself.

"Mitch and I practice all the time," Eleanor admits, her cheeks turning flaming bright red. There's more laughter, and Eleanor giggles too. "But yeah. No babies yet. We're not even married."

"That didn't stop us," I say.

Eleanor inclines her head toward me with a grin. "True."

"Jared wants a baby right away. He wants to start trying right after the wedding," Sarah admits. "And I think I want to try too. But I don't know. It's kind of scary."

"It's very scary. I know I'm not ready, and I don't think Carter is either," Stella says. "I feel like I can barely take care of myself."

"Isaac is too young. I can't imagine him as a father yet," Amelia says. Her boyfriend is a few years younger than her. "Which is perfect because I'm not ready either. We haven't even talked marriage, so I don't to get too ahead of myself."

Ha, I know how that is. Sometimes I feel like Theo and I did everything backwards. But that's okay, because it totally worked out in the end.

"I can't even fathom having a baby," Ali says. "That is the last thing I want right now."

She's young too, and busy living in the moment. Good for her.

"This is all perfect because guess what, guys?" Candice hesitates for only a moment before she announces, "I'm pregnant!"

We all cry out in happiness, then take turns hugging her. I'm last, because I move the slowest, and when Candice rests her hand on my giant belly, the baby kicks.

"Was that her?" she asks, her eyes full of wonder.

I nod and grin, resting my hand over hers. "She kicks really hard."

The baby kicks again, and then everyone's got their hands on my belly, all taking turns to feel her move and shift. Candice is crying, she's so overcome with emotion and hormones, and soon we're all crying, because I'm also full of emotions and hormones, and the rest of them are sympathy criers.

"Our lives are totally changing," Stella says at one point. "Soon we'll be forming mom groups and arranging playdates."

"That sounds like so much fun," Candice gushes, making Stella roll her eyes.

Eventually they all leave, and it's only Eleanor who's with me. She helps me pick up around the living room, throwing away the discarded wrapping paper and gathering the paper cups still scattered around. When Theo arrives home a half hour later, he grabs all the gifts and takes them to the baby's room.

"I'm so happy for you two," Eleanor murmurs when I walk her outside to her rental car. She came into town for the weekend with Mitch, and they're staying at some fancy hotel in Big Sur. "I can't believe you're going to be a mom."

"Me either." I smile, suddenly feeling tired. "I need a nap."

Eleanor laughs. "You're going to need a lot of naps to prepare for all those sleepless nights."

"Don't remind me," I say with a groan.

We hug goodbye and I watch her leave, waving frantically when she turns onto the next street. I glance over my shoulder to find my husband standing in the open doorway, watching me with fondness lighting his eyes while he watches me.

We ran off to Vegas a few months ago and got married. Eleanor was my maid of honor. The rest of the gang came with us, and so did Theo's family. Our wedding even made the tabloids, thanks to Mitch accompanying Eleanor. The paps thought they were the ones getting married.

"You have fun?" he asks as I make my way toward the front door.

"I had the best time," I say, wincing when I feel the shooting pain radiate down my leg.

Theo rushes toward me, gently grabbing hold of my arm and guiding me into the house. "Here, sit down," he says as he leads me to the couch.

I settle in, resting my hands on my protruding stomach. "I could balance a dinner plate on this belly."

Baby girl kicks my palm in answer, making me laugh.

Theo settles in beside me, resting his hand on top of one of mine. "You got a lot of nice stuff."

"We did," I tell him. "Your family was so generous."

"Mom and Dad are excited. First grandbaby and all."

"I'm excited too," I admit.

"Not scared anymore?"

I got scared at about the five-month mark. I told Theo I wasn't made out to be a mother, I had a terrible example growing up, so what do I know? But he reassured me as usual that I'll be just fine, I'll be a good mom and he loves me.

That's all I needed to hear. As we draw closer to her due date, I'm so excited to meet her, to hold her. I can't wait.

"No, I'm not scared," I say softly, closing my eyes when he leans in and kisses me. His lips are soft, but I feel the urgency there. Mixed with a little bit of hesitancy.

Like he wants to push, but believes I'll most likely turn him down.

"Are you trying to get me back into the bedroom?" I ask him when we finally end the kiss.

"If you're asking if I'd like to have sex with you, then yes." He runs his hand up and down my belly. "You're sexy when you're pregnant. You're sexy all the time."

"I don't feel sexy," I say.

"Well, you are." His voice is firm and he leaps to his feet, offering both of his hands to me. "Come on, wife. Let's go get it on."

I burst out laughing and let him pull me to my feet. "I won't be feeling up to much sex after she's here, you know. I guess we better do it as much as possible."

"Exactly, so let's do this." He pulls me into his arms once we're standing at the foot of the bed, his fiery gaze meeting mine. "I love you, Mrs. Crawford."

I smile, pure joy threatening to overwhelm me. "I love you too, Mr. Crawford."

ACKNOWLEDGMENTS

The Dating series has come to an end, and I'm feeling nostalgic. Not only did I love creating stories for each of the women in the friend group, I also had a lot of fun building the friendships with these women throughout the series. Their honesty with each other, and how they make time for each other no matter what, is what we all deserve in a friend. I want to be friends with these women, and I hope you do too!

A big thank you to Nina and the rest of the team at Valentine PR for always taking good care of me and my books during release (and year round, truly). A huge thank you to the bloggers, reviewers and readers who read my books, who reached out to me about this series and fell in love with it. Thank you so much for your support.

I do plan on writing a spinoff series involving Theo's family. I have plans. But nothing concrete yet, so watch for more details and preorder links coming soon!

Thank you for reading. It would mean the world to me if you left an honest review for this book.

THE DATING SERIES

If you love WEDDING DATE, make sure you check out the other books in the series!

Out Now:

Save The Date
Fake Date
Holidate
Hate to Date You
Rate A Date
Wedding Date

WANT A FREE BOOK? SIGN UP!

Dear Readers,

I hope you've enjoyed reading **RATE A DATE!** If you haven't already, please sign up for my newsletter so you can stay up to date on my latest book news. Plus, you'll get a **FREE** book by me, just for signing up! Click below:

Monica Murphy's Newsletter

Are you on Facebook? You should join my reader group! Click below to hang out with us:

Monica Murphy's Reader Group

ALSO BY MONICA MURPHY

Dating Series

Save The Date
Fake Date
Holidate
Hate to Date You
Rate A Date
Wedding Date

The Callahans

Close to Me
Falling For Her
Addicted To Him
Meant To Be

Forever Yours Series

You Promised Me Forever
Thinking About You
Nothing Without You

Damaged Hearts Series

Her Defiant Heart
His Wasted Heart
Damaged Hearts

Friends Series

One Night
Just Friends
More Than Friends
Forever

The Never Duet

Never Tear Us Apart
Never Let You Go

The Rules Series

Fair Game
In The Dark
Slow Play
Safe Bet

The Fowler Sisters Series

Owning Violet
Stealing Rose
Taming Lily

Reverie Series

His Reverie
Her Destiny

Billionaire Bachelors Club Series

Crave
Torn
Savor
Intoxicated

One Week Girlfriend Series

One Week Girlfriend
Second Chance Boyfriend
Three Broken Promises
Drew + Fable Forever
Four Years Later
Five Days Until You

A Drew + Fable Christmas

Standalone YA Titles

Daring The Bad Boy
Saving It
Pretty Dead Girls

ABOUT THE AUTHOR

Monica Murphy is a New York Times, USA Today and international bestselling author. Her books have been translated in almost a dozen languages and has sold over two million copies worldwide. Both a traditionally published and independently published author, she writes young adult and new adult romance, as well as contemporary romance and women's fiction. She's also known as USA Today bestselling author Karen Erickson.

facebook.com/MonicaMurphyAuthor
twitter.com/msmonicamurphy
instagram.com/monicamurphyauthor
bookbub.com/profile/monica-murphy
goodreads.com/monicamurphyauthor